FRAGILE

A.K. EVANS

ISBN: 978-1-951441-21-0

Cover Artist
cover artwork © Sarah Hansen, Okay Creations
www.okaycreations.com

Editing & Proofreading
Ellie McLove, My Brother's Editor
www.mybrotherseditor.net

Formatting
Stacey Blake at Champagne Book Design
www.champagnebookdesign.com

DEDICATION

As always, the start of a new series goes to my husband and my two sons. I love the three of you so much.

FRAGILE

PROLOGUE

Demi

"IT'S NEVER GOING TO CHANGE WITH YOU, IS IT, MARTIN?"

"Oh, fuck, Brenda. Won't you ever just shut up?"

The yelling never stopped.

I felt sick to my stomach.

It was Thursday, this was the third time this week, and they were still at it. How had they not lost their voices yet? I was exhausted just listening to them for the few minutes that I did. I didn't even know what they were arguing about anymore. I just knew I couldn't take the yelling much longer.

I closed my bedroom door as quietly as I could. Considering how loudly they were shouting, I don't know why I was being so careful not to make any noise. It wasn't like they'd hear me anyway.

Moving across the room to my desk, I picked up my headphones, put them on, and turned on my music. Anything to drown out the noise and help me focus.

I sat down at my desk, listened to one song, and tried to get lost in the words, hoping they'd erase all the garbage in my mind. When the song ended and another started, I was at least able to concentrate enough on my homework.

I was a freshman in high school, a place I hated almost as much as being at home. School was tough, and it wasn't the work that was the problem, either. I was an average student and did well enough.

My issue was with trying to find a place where I fit. I wasn't one of the jocks. Though I loved music, I didn't play any instruments, so the band was out. I wasn't one of the nerds. I didn't join the drama club. I was just… me. And who I was didn't seem to fit anywhere.

I wasn't a complete loner. I did have a friend from my homeroom that was also in a few of my classes. But beyond school-related stuff, we didn't really hang out ever.

I'd gotten through nearly all of my homework when a hand gently touched my shoulder, and I practically jumped out of my seat.

Spinning around, I saw my mom standing there. She was wearing her scrubs, which meant that she'd be leaving for work. It seemed that it was the only time there was ever any peace in the house. Mom was a nurse who worked the night shift at the hospital. She worked twelve-hour shifts that started at seven in the evening. Given that the hospital was only a ten-minute drive from our house, my mom would get home during the week just as I was leaving for school.

I pulled my headphones off my ears and said, "You scared me."

"I'm sorry. I just wanted to come in and say goodbye to you before I left for work," she started. "Are you getting your stuff done?"

I'm trying to, I thought.

"Yeah, I'm almost finished with it," I told her.

She smiled at me. "Good. Listen, I was thinking that since I'm off this weekend that you and I could do something special together. Maybe some shopping followed by dinner and a movie. What do you think?"

"That sounds great, Mom," I answered. And it did. Not because I was overly interested in shopping but because it meant that we'd be out of the house, and I wouldn't need to listen to them yelling at each other. "I can't wait."

"Okay. I know you didn't eat much at dinner, so I've put some leftovers in the fridge if you get hungry," she said.

She hadn't been making that up. I didn't eat much at dinner because I didn't feel well. Then again, it was rare that I didn't have an upset stomach all the time these days. Most days, I managed to power through and eat. Today, I just couldn't.

"Thanks," I replied.

My mom bent down and kissed my forehead. "I'll see you in the morning before you leave for school," she stated as she brought her body upright. "Bye, Demi."

"Later, Mom."

With that, she turned and walked out of the room. I watched as she walked out. Then I waited and listened to her leaving the house.

Knowing there'd be no more fighting, I turned off the music, set my headphones down, and finished up my work. Thirty minutes later, I had completed it.

I thought I should try to eat something even though my stomach still felt a bit unsettled. I figured that the uneasiness would subside now that my parents wouldn't be fighting for the rest of the night.

Walking into the kitchen, I found my father sitting on a stool at the island drinking a beer.

"Hey, Demi girl," he said. "Hungry?"

I wanted to scream. Both of my parents acted like everything was fine. They'd talk to me like I hadn't just listened to the two of them arguing about everything and nothing.

I shrugged. "I don't feel great, but I thought it might be because I haven't had anything to eat."

"Your mother left food in the fridge if you want to heat that up," he remarked.

My mother. Like she wasn't also his wife.

God, they were both just as bad as each other. Mom barely mentioned my dad to me, and he never referred to her as anything other than my mother.

"Yeah, I think I'll do that," I replied.

As quickly as I could, I pulled the food out and popped it in the microwave to heat it up. Ten minutes later, I wasn't feeling any better.

When I pushed the plate away and sat up, my father's eyes came to me. "What's going on?"

"I think I'm just going to go to bed early tonight," I told him. "Maybe it'll help to sleep it off."

He assessed me a moment, and something moved through his face. "Okay. Good night, Demi."

"Good night, Dad."

At that, I put my plate in the sink and made my way back to my room. It was still a bit earlier than I'd normally go to bed, but I didn't care. I felt horrible.

Minutes after I climbed under the blanket I was asleep.

It felt like I hadn't even been sleeping for five minutes when my eyes shot open.

I glanced at the clock on my nightstand. It was just before ten o'clock at night. I hadn't even been asleep a full two hours. In the thirty seconds my eyes had been open, I realized that my stomach issues weren't related to my parents arguing with each other earlier.

I was going to be sick.

Throwing the blanket back from my body, I hopped out of bed and dashed into the bathroom. I just barely made it in time to empty the contents of my stomach into the toilet.

Ugh.

I was sick.

Legitimately sick.

Once I was sure that I'd finished vomiting, I stood up straight, looked in the mirror, and brushed my teeth.

I wanted to tell my dad that I'd just thrown up, so I walked out of the bathroom and ambled down the hall to my parents' bedroom. With each step I took, I felt worse and worse.

Freezing.

I was freezing.

Putting my hand to the doorknob, I turned it and pushed the door open.

"Dad," I called as I flipped on the light.

"Shit, fuck, Demi," he cursed.

His response hadn't been startled because I woke him from a deep sleep. It came because I'd just caught him with his pants down. Or technically, they were off. He was standing at the side of the bed he shared with my mother, and a woman who was not my mother was naked on her back, her torso propped up on her elbows, and her legs wrapped around him.

Well, they had been wrapped around him. The second I walked in, my father had stepped back from her and unfortunately, he turned toward me.

I couldn't respond.

That was mostly because the moment I opened my mouth, which was several seconds after I took in the scene before me, I vomited all over the floor.

As soon as I could, I turned and ran back down the hall to the bathroom. I locked myself inside, laid down on the floor, and burst into tears.

I didn't open the door again until the following morning when my mom got home.

Suffice it to say that we didn't go shopping or to the movies that weekend.

CHAPTER 1

Demi

Sixteen years later

"Hello. How can I help you?"

"I'm so sorry, but I forgot my key in the room. Is there any way you could make another one for me?"

I looked at the woman who had just walked through the sliding door that led into the lobby of the hotel I was the manager at. She had a tiny baby strapped to her chest in one of those baby swaddling things that were supposed to keep your hands free to do other things. Those things always freaked me out because, one time, I saw a father come in wearing one with his daughter who couldn't have been even a year old in it, and it broke. The carrier had some plastic pieces that snapped, which caused the baby to fall. Luckily, the father caught her before she was hurt, but I'd always been wary of them any time I saw them after that.

Looking at the one this mother was using, I noted there was no plastic on it. It was all fabric, and it seemed to be fastened securely to her, so that put me at a bit more ease. On top of that, despite the carrier making it possible for her to be hands free, the mother was protectively cradling her baby anyway.

"Sure," I answered. "Do you have your ID on you?"

"Oh, yes. Sure," she replied.

Keeping one hand firmly on her baby's body, she set her purse on the counter, dug through it, and pulled out her license. When she handed it to me, she said, "I wasn't paying attention when we checked in. My husband might have put it under his name, which is the same last name, but we used my credit card."

"Okay, no problem at all," I told her. "Just give me one second."

My eyes left the face of the woman who seemed slightly distressed and shifted to the computer. I wanted to ask her if she was okay, but on the occasions that I'd done that whenever I thought something was wrong, I always regretted it. In this situation, she was probably just frazzled, adjusting to life as a new mother. It was clear the baby was very newly born.

"Room 632?" I confirmed with her.

She nodded. "Yes, that's correct."

A moment later, I handed the ID back to her and said, "Here you go. I love your name, by the way. Is it pronounced Chasey?"

"Yep, that's correct," she responded. "And the connotation is correct. I'm always the one doing the chasing."

I wasn't quite sure what she meant by that and decided it was best to ignore it. I made up another key card for her room and held it out to her.

"You're all set," I declared.

Chasey took the key card from me, allowed her eyes to drift to my name tag, and said, "Thank you so much, Demi."

"You're welcome. Enjoy the remainder of your stay."

As she walked off, two hands back on her baby, I watched. That was something I did a lot of in my line of work.

Watching.

Observing.

And in most cases, hating every second of it.

I'd been working at this job for years now. I did it because it paid the bills and put food on the table. I didn't do it because I loved it.

Having said that, I'd lost my drive for becoming anything noteworthy a long time ago. I couldn't even remember a time when I had a dream about what I wanted to be when I grew up. So, naturally, I just took the days as they came and handled what needed to be handled. When this job opened up, I applied and got the position. It came with benefits and had a decent salary, so I couldn't really complain about that.

But deep down, I despised working here. There were just too many things I saw that didn't sit well with me. And as much as I wanted to jump in and say something in those instances, I managed to hold myself back.

Instead, I'd unload my frustrations on my best friend, Samantha and my cousin, Calvin. Sam also worked here, but she was the event sales director for the hotel. She handled all the weddings, corporate events, baby showers, and more. Cal was the owner of Granite, a relatively new bar here in the small town of Finch, New Hampshire. He handled serving drinks and lending a listening ear whenever Sam and I had a bad day.

Lately, I'd been having more and more of those days here.

For that reason, I was just about to head back into Sam's office to see if she wanted to stop for a drink after work when Chasey rushed up to the desk. Her face was red with rage, but her eyes were filled with sadness and horror.

"Are you okay?" I asked.

She shook her head and placed the key card back on the counter. "Thank you for your help," she rasped. "I'm sorry I lied."

I blinked in surprise, trying to figure out what was going on. "Lied?" I repeated.

Nodding, she explained, "I didn't check into the hotel, but I saw my credit card was used here. My husband wasn't home, so it wasn't hard to figure out."

Oh no. No way was this happening.

"Chasey!" someone yelled out.

"Don't you dare come near me, you piece of shit," Chasey shouted in the direction she'd just come from, which was by the elevators.

My eyes followed hers, and they settled on a man who was wearing a pair of baggy underwear, a wifebeater tank top, and a pair of socks that went up to the middle of his shins.

See?

Lots of unsavory things to witness in this line of work.

"Wait," the man begged. "We need to talk about this."

"There's *nothing* to talk about. I *never* want to speak to you again!"

As I stood there watching the scene unfold, unable to move, I realized Sam must have heard the commotion and come out of her office. I knew this because she walked up behind me and asked, "What's going on?"

"This poor woman walked in here and told me she'd forgotten her room key," I started. "She showed me her identification and credit card, so I made her another key for the room. As it turns out, she never checked in. She just realized that her credit card was being used at a hotel. The next thing I know, she's down here yelling at him, and he's not only panicking but also in some serious need of his clothes."

Sam did not respond. Part of that was probably because she was just as riveted to the scene unfolding before us, but the other part was probably because she knew I was feeling very much on edge.

I wanted to scream.

I wanted to cry.

This was beyond horrible.

Chasey was backing away from the man I now knew was her husband as he continued to approach.

Eventually she stopped, and so did he. The moment was tense, and though I knew people had walked into the lobby, I couldn't take my eyes off of what was happening in front of me.

"You son of a bitch," Chasey shouted. "I can't believe you. While I'm at home struggling to take care of our five-week-old daughter on my own, my husband is here screwing some bimbo."

I gasped.

Five weeks old.

This poor woman. Her beautiful little baby.

"He did not," I seethed, unable to stop myself. "Tell me he did not do that."

Chasey stood firmly rooted to the spot, her eyes pinned on her husband as she clutched her baby against her chest and confirmed, "He absolutely did."

"Bastard," I clipped.

"Baby, please," her husband said as he took a step toward her. He had resorted to begging. It was evident, as ever, in the tone of his voice.

Begging or not, Chasey didn't stand for it. She took a step back from him and demanded, "Don't you 'baby' me. I just saw something that no wife, let alone a new mother, needs to see her husband doing. You just lost me, so I hope it was worth it."

My heart was breaking by the second for her.

I could imagine how she must have felt. I never caught a boyfriend or a husband, but I caught my own father. I figured that had to give me some idea of what she was going through.

"I promise it was just sex," he declared. "It didn't mean anything. Please, Chasey, we're a family."

"You've got to be kidding me," she countered. "Just sex? Just sex?! Are you serious right now?"

"Chasey, baby, it's been a long time," he tried to reason with her.

A long time?

His wife just had a baby!

"I'm literally going to lose my mind," I muttered, though I wasn't sure anyone heard me. I mean, in the midst of all that was going on, I was not the one who was at the center of attention.

"A long time?" Chasey repeated. "Oh, I'm so sorry, Aaron. I was put on pelvic rest for the last eight weeks of my pregnancy and then managed to push a baby out of my vagina just five weeks ago. I should be more understanding of everything *you've* been through over the last thirteen weeks. What was I thinking? How insensitive of me, during all of that, not to be concerned about you getting your dick wet."

Fucking asshole.

I thought what I'd witnessed at the ripe age of fourteen was bad. Obviously, it was. I mean, I saw my father completely naked with his dick inside a woman who wasn't my mother. But this? This was just a whole new level of disgusting. His wife couldn't have sex because she was carrying his child and had a medical issue.

What a selfish prick.

"Excuse me, miss?"

I had been so caught up in what I was watching and the rage I felt on behalf of Chasey and her daughter that I hadn't realized all the people who'd walked in the front door.

Beck Emerson, the man who played the keyboard and synthesizer for My Violent Heart, was standing beside Chasey.

My Violent Heart was *the* industrial rock band. Nobody compared to them. And now, not only was Beck in the hotel, but so were the remaining five members of the band: Cash Morris, Walker Rhodes, Holland Oates, Killian Scott, and Roscoe Perry. There were four other individuals with them who I assumed were managers, security, roadies, or a combination of the three.

Chasey's jaw dropped open at the sight of Beck beside her. I couldn't blame her. The man looked incredible. And considering everything she'd just witnessed—though I didn't know exactly how bad it had been—she deserved to have a man that looked like Beck looking at her the way he was.

Beck didn't seem the least bit fazed by her reaction. Instead, with a gentle voice, he asked, "Is there anything I can do to help?"

There was a moment of hesitation, but Chasey eventually shook her head. "No. I just found out my husband is cheating on me. Actually, correction. He's now my soon-to-be ex-husband."

"Do you want me to kick his ass?" Beck offered. There was a devious look in his eyes and a smirk on his face.

"Hey!" Aaron shouted. "You can't do that! I'll have you arrested for assault."

Beck looked in Aaron's direction and ordered, "Shut up, dickwad. I'm talking to your wife."

Chasey leaned toward Beck and reminded him, "Soon-to-be ex-wife."

His lips twitched as he returned his attention to her and said, "Why don't we go for a walk outside? You don't need to be around this douchebag any longer, not when you've got this sweet little baby in your arms."

I hated men. Hated them.

I thought they were nothing but lying, cheating, selfish individuals.

But in that moment, I loved Beck Emerson for what he did for Chasey.

Whether he was doing it for show or something else, I couldn't say. It didn't matter, though. He took that woman out of a horrible situation and gave her something so many women probably wished they'd have happen at a time like this.

The minute they'd exited the hotel through the sliding doors, I shifted my focus back to Aaron. He stood there, much like my father had, and allowed the harsh reality to smack him in the face.

He fucked up.

He fucked up so badly, and he knew he lost his family.

Too bad.

There was no excuse, *none,* for what he'd done. I hoped Chasey would stick to her guns and follow through on the divorce because I had no doubt that if she went back to him, Aaron would only cheat on her again.

As he walked back toward the elevator, I took in a deep breath and let it out.

This was too much drama for me, and I needed a major change.

Unfortunately, I was still here, and I needed to do my job.

I glanced up at the remaining members of the band standing in the lobby, and one caught my eye.

Cash Morris.

Fuck, the man was sex on a stick.

He was gorgeous, and he had a voice on him that could easily set panties ablaze.

That's why he was the lead singer.

And right now, he was staring at me like he wanted to eat me up.

No thanks.

I'd give credit where it was due—he was hot and he could sing—but that's about all he was getting from me.

Right. Time to get back to being professional.

Unfortunately, before I could say anything, Cash approached and shot me his megawatt smile as his eyes went to my nametag. "Hello, Demi Stokes. I'm Cash Morris."

Do not react.

That look, that voice. It was, without a doubt, the reason why there was no shortage of women for him.

In a different life, one where I hadn't been burned by the man I should have trusted the most, I might have fallen victim to that smile. Lucky for me, I got to see the truth of how men really are, and I'd never end up in a situation like my mother did or like Chasey just did.

No way.

Pulling off an almost impossible feat not to react, I ignored Cash's flirtatious demeanor and replied, "Hi. I'm really sorry about what you just witnessed. That's not a common occurrence. Well, the public fighting anyway. The cheating is more rampant than I care to admit. Anyway, how can I help you?"

Cash let out a laugh, and I swear it took everything in me to remain standing. Then he answered, "Aside from giving me your number, we're going to need a couple of rooms."

Cocky, self-assured, and convinced he could snag any woman he wanted.

Yep.

Cash was just the kind of guy I expected him to be.

Of course, there was no chance I'd ever give him what he was asking for even if he'd gone about it in a different way. But the simple fact was that he didn't even try to put any effort into it. He simply assumed that because he was who he was he'd get what he wanted.

Well, not this time.

Deciding to be as pleasant as I could, I smiled at him before I said, "Rooms I can do. The phone number is not going to happen."

The jerk didn't even seem the least bit disappointed. He grinned at me. The asshole thought this was a game.

Then he pulled out his credit card and handed it over.

I took it from him and looked down at the computer in front of me. "How many rooms did you need?"

"Enough for ten of us," he said. "We don't mind sharing rooms if we have to as long as everyone has their own bed, but Holland gets a room to herself."

That was surprising.

Holland was the only female in the band, so I was glad that they respected her enough to make sure she had her own space. I could only imagine what it would have been like for her if she had to share a room with any of the guys. I realize I didn't know them at all, but I saw the way some guys lived, and gross would have been an understatement.

"Sure," I replied.

For the next ten minutes or so, I worked on getting some rooms booked for Cash, his bandmates, and the rest of their crew. I handed out key cards and said, "Enjoy your stay."

There was a round of gratitude tossed my way as they walked off. Once they were out of earshot, Cash said, "I'm definitely planning on enjoying my stay. It was nice to meet you, Demi. I'll see you around."

Smug.

So damn smug.

The man thought he was God's gift to women.

Visually speaking, maybe he was. When it came to music and his voice, there was no doubt he'd been blessed.

But that was as far as it was going to go.

Because when it came to being humble, I wasn't sure Cash even knew what that meant.

Once again, I did my best to remain professional and not react. I simply offered a smile and a nod, nothing to indicate that it was nice to meet him or that I was interested in seeing him around.

He seemed amused by my response and chuckled as he walked away toward the elevator.

The moment he was out of sight, I let out a huge sigh of relief.

If one thing was for certain, I needed a new job because this one was bound to do more damage than I could handle.

On that thought, I left the front desk in the capable hands of my staff and walked back to have a talk with my best friend.

CHAPTER 2

Cash

"IS EVERYTHING ALRIGHT?"

"Yeah, it's fine."

Sitting on the couch in our hotel room—a suite I was sharing with Beck—I watched as one of my closest friends walked over and sat down on the chair off to the left of the sofa. Our suite wasn't the swankiest of accommodations we'd ever had, but the room was clean and spacious, so I had nothing to complain about.

Noting the look on Beck's face, I had no doubt he'd just fed me a line of bullshit.

"You're lying," I declared.

"Yep," he replied, his eyes pinned on the television. I knew he was staring at that in order to avoid looking at me. That wasn't out of embarrassment; he was merely pissed off. Sure enough, he confirmed that a moment later when he clipped, "That guy is a fucking asshole."

He was referring to the half-naked guy in the lobby.

"I can't say I don't agree," I told him.

"Shit. That baby was only five weeks old," Beck muttered.

It sucked.

Anyone who witnessed what happened downstairs would have thought the same thing. But I knew this was hitting Beck harder than it would the rest of us.

Beck was raised by a single mother. His father walked out when Beck and his younger sister, Sadie, were just kids. Beck was six at the time; Sadie was only two. Their mom busted her ass to take care of them. So, while Beck and his sister didn't have a father around, their mom more than made up for the loss.

"Are you planning to do something about this?" I asked. "How was… what was her name, when she left?"

"Chasey," Beck answered. "And I talked with her for a while to make sure she was okay. I mean, how good can a woman who's just recently given birth to a baby feel when she *walks in* on her husband cheating on her? Anyway, before she got back in her car and took off, I gave her my personal number and told her to call if there was anything I could do to help her."

I cocked an eyebrow.

I realized Beck had a soft spot for single moms, but I had to wonder if what he'd just done was a wise idea.

"Do you think that was smart?" I questioned him.

Maybe that wasn't the right thing to say to Beck given his current state of mind, but I wanted him to be careful.

The truth was, we'd seen our fair share of women over the years who were only after one thing. Well, maybe two things. They either wanted money or the score.

Luckily, the majority went after the latter, so in most

cases, it worked out for everyone. These women could say they fucked a rock star, and we got laid in the process. It was a win win in most of those cases.

But over the years, we'd seen our fair share of scandal, and in almost every case, it came down to money.

The last thing I wanted was to see Beck's offer, which was coming from a good place, to wind up being a nightmare for him.

"I don't give a fuck if it was or not," he shot back. "I can always change my number, but she might not have anyone there to have her back. To me, it was worth the risk."

I nodded my understanding. He'd made up his mind already, so it wasn't like anything I said was going to change it.

Then again, that was how it always was with us. Beck and I had been friends for as long as I could remember, having gone to the same school since kindergarten. I'd known him and Killian the longest. Killian and I grew up in the same neighborhood in a small town in Pennsylvania. That very neighborhood was where the three of us would practice our music for hours after school or all day long in the summer in the garage of my parents' home.

We were all thirteen at the time. When we decided to get more serious about it, we realized we needed a drummer. I could play drums, but I preferred to sing. One day, two years later, a new kid moved into the neighborhood. Walker had been walking his dog one summer afternoon and saw us in the garage.

"You need a drummer," he told us.

"Yeah, um, they aren't exactly easy to come by here," I retorted. "We think all the cornfields are keeping them hidden away."

"I play," he declared.

"Are you any good?" Killian asked.

Killian didn't give a shit. He played the guitar, and his solos could rival that of Eddie Van Halen, Randy Rhoads, and Slash. Killian wasn't going to allow us to settle for less than the best.

Walker looked down at his dog and ordered, "Stay."

Then, without an invitation, he strode into the garage and sat down at the drums. Seconds later, Beck, Killian, and I were all exchanging looks. Walker wasn't just good. He was amazing.

Our band grew by one that day.

It started to feel like we were the real deal at that point. We practiced all the time, either coming up with new material or remaking some of our favorites.

As time went on, we started to find our own style, and three years later, Roscoe joined our crew as a bassist. Things only got better from there.

Four years later, after we'd already released two albums with mediocre success, Holland became the final missing piece of My Violent Heart. No sooner did we add her as a vocalist and songwriter when everything exploded for us.

Suddenly, money was pouring in, we were touring, and we had the best of the best to produce our music with. It had been a whirlwind, but it was something I knew we were all so grateful for.

My bandmates were my best friends. They were as much a part of my family as my actual family was.

I'd spent so long thinking about where we started and how far we'd come that Beck stood and declared, "I'm jumping in the shower. Maybe that'll help cool me off. Who would have thought some small town like this could have so much drama?"

I didn't know the answer to that, but I had my own thoughts about this small town. I wasn't sure drama was the word I would have used to describe it, but I didn't tell him that. Instead, I said, "Well, it's only Thursday, and we don't leave until Monday, so there's plenty of time for more to be had if that's what you're looking for."

Beck grunted as frustration washed over him. Then he turned and walked toward the second bedroom in the suite, where he'd find his own bathroom.

As I sat there, I thought about what Beck had just said. Though he had a point about it being drama here in this small town in New Hampshire considering what we witnessed upon entering the hotel, I couldn't look at all of it as a bad thing.

Because for the first time in a very long time, I had a challenge before me.

Her name was Demi, and she was beyond fuckable.

My cock got hard just thinking about her sassy attitude, plump lips, and blue eyes. Plus, the way she wore her hair, most of the brown strands with champagne-colored highlights cascading down over her shoulders and only the very front pieces around her face had been pinned back. It was as though she wanted it to look sexy but not like she'd tried too hard.

Or maybe that was just it.

Maybe she was a woman who was effortlessly sexy.

Or perhaps I had it all wrong.

Perhaps I was so drawn to her because she was so very

different from every other woman who'd come into contact with me.

Being a rock star had its perks. I never really had to work very hard to get laid. It was all part of what I'd been thinking about before when I was talking to Beck. Women just wanted to make that score and be able to say they fucked a rock star.

But not Demi.

She didn't seem the least bit impressed by my rock star status. In fact, though I hadn't had a whole lot of time to gauge exactly how she felt, I was willing to bet I'd learn quickly that she despises the very idea of me because of the fact that I do what I do for a living.

And that was what made her so much more appealing to me.

Demi wasn't going to be easy to land.

But I had a feeling that if I took the time to make that happen, she was going to make it worth it. Even if for no other reason than to see that beautiful mouth wrapped around my cock.

Damn, her pretty pink lips were perfect.

What I liked even more was that she didn't hold back from saying exactly how she felt with that mouth either.

Seeing her all fired up about that asshole in the lobby was a huge turn-on.

God, I wanted her in my bed and talking back to me more than I wanted to have a successful show tomorrow night. Considering how important our shows were to me, that was saying something.

Groaning in frustration, I stood and moved to my bedroom. Maybe I needed a cold shower, too.

We had a show tomorrow night, the night off on

Saturday, another show on Sunday, and then we were back on the road on Monday.

Just as I told Beck, we had a few days here. I could use a bit of excitement and didn't mind if we shook up the town a little bit.

Or, more specifically, I didn't mind stirring up Demi just a tad to have some fun. Coming into this part of the tour, I didn't think New Hampshire was a place I'd really remember. Now, I wasn't so sure.

Because with eyes, lips, and an attitude like that, I had a feeling Demi wouldn't let me forget it.

Demi

My head snapped up as I heard something get slapped down onto the counter at the front desk.

Cash Morris.

Ugh, did this guy ever give up?

It was Saturday night, and I was at work. Things were particularly busy for me because there was a wedding being held in our grand ballroom tonight. Of course, as the person in charge of the wedding, Sam had everything under control. But it was par for the course that there was always just a bit of a heavier workload for me on nights when there was a wedding. Many guests booked rooms at the hotel so they could enjoy the open bar at the wedding without the worry of having to drive home intoxicated.

I didn't mind the busier nights. In fact, unless something

crazy happened, I enjoyed the faster pace. It made the time pass quickly.

But right now, it seemed there was a lull in the typical demands for a night like tonight. Maybe that was because Sam was on top of her shit and had a wedding party with guests who weren't completely crazy, or maybe it was just my luck.

"Can I help you?" I asked Cash.

He shook his head. "These are for you," he declared, sliding his hand forward on the counter.

When he removed his hand from the reception desk, I looked down to see what he was giving me.

No way.

"What is this?" I asked, even though I was certain I already knew precisely what I was staring at.

"Two tickets for you and a friend to tomorrow night's show," he answered.

"I didn't ask for tickets," I told him.

He grinned. "I know that. But I'd love to see you there, so I'm giving them to you," he explained.

Damn.

In any other situation, I would have loved to go to see My Violent Heart play a live show. This situation was anything but ordinary. I mean, the front man for the band was interested in getting in my pants.

I knew I wasn't making that up in my head either. Cash made it clear what he was after, what with his wicked smile and flirtatious persona.

Sadly for him, I had no intentions of giving in to what he wanted. He could play this game without me.

When I spent too long thinking about all of this, Cash asked, "Do you not like our music?"

"What? No, I never said that," I replied. I might not have liked his demeanor, but that didn't mean I'd lie about his band and their talent.

"So, you do like us?" he pressed.

"I enjoy the music," I corrected him. Then, because I wanted to really stick it to him, I decided to add some fuel to the fire. "Holland seems cool, though. And I don't know... Killian can play a guitar like I've never seen before. I can only imagine the things that man can do with his fingers."

Cash narrowed his eyes on me. He looked about ready to murder me if given the chance.

Serves him right for not backing off.

But no sooner had the murderous expression formed on his face when it was gone. It was replaced by a smirk.

"What's that look for?" I asked, feeling less than amused.

"You like me," he declared.

"What, in all that I just said, gave you that impression?" I retorted.

"The fact that you're trying to make me jealous tells me you like me, and you're now doing everything you can to avoid dealing with how I make you feel," he explained.

Damn it.

I needed to get away from this guy before I went against everything I'd been doing all my life to protect myself. How much torture could a woman take?

Not that I'd ever tell him this, but Cash was beyond sexy. He had the whole rock star vibe going for him with his jeans, leather jackets, and silver rings. His body was phenomenal, something I knew from seeing pictures of him online. He also had a voice that was meant for making music.

I could only imagine how it would sound to hear him in bed.

Shit.

What was I thinking?

Get your head screwed on straight, Demi.

"Don't you have somewhere to be tonight?" I asked.

"Nope."

"What? You're telling me that there wasn't a single groupie from your show last night that wanted you to rock her world?" I questioned him.

Cash tipped his head to the side. "Would that have made you jealous?" he wondered. "Do you wish it was you whose world I was rocking?"

"Fuck no."

The asshole smiled at me.

He didn't believe a word that was coming out of my mouth. And even though there was some small, stupid part of me that was wishing I could have one night with Cash, there was the much larger and smarter part of me that knew I'd never give him a one-night stand.

That would surely ruin me, even if I went into it expecting it to only be one night.

There was no doubt in my mind, especially with his level of experience and his confidence, that Cash would be a great lay. The problem was that a woman like me would want far more than just one night. And men like Cash didn't know how to commit and remain faithful.

He was hot.

He was tempting.

But he was a man I planned to stay very far away from.

"That's a lot of anger for someone who claims to not have any feelings for me," Cash pointed out.

Narrowing my eyes on him, I lowered my voice and seethed, "Oh, I've got plenty of feelings *about* you, Cash. Unfortunately for you, none of my feelings lead me to wanting to be your fuck toy for a night before you move on to the next town and the next groupie."

"Maybe you'll rock my world and I won't want another groupie," he reasoned.

I wanted to burst out laughing. He didn't honestly believe that, but man, was he smooth.

"Do you think I'm stupid?" I asked.

He shook his head and leaned closer. His voice dropped a couple octaves, and he said, "Quite the opposite, Demi. I think you're probably the smartest woman I've encountered on this tour. And you're definitely the sexiest."

I cocked an eyebrow.

"You should go," I suggested.

"You know what room I'm staying in," he offered before giving me a wink and moving toward the elevator.

"Hey!" I called out.

He stopped, turned around, and came back. "Change your mind already?" he asked.

I stared him straight in the eye and deadpanned, "Nope. You forgot your tickets." Then I pushed them back across the counter.

He put his hand on top of mine without losing eye contact and slid my hand backward. "They're yours," he stated.

"I don't want them."

"Do you have a boyfriend?"

Yeah, right. Like that was *ever* going to happen.

I shook my head.

Cash assessed me a moment and said, "Keep them. Maybe you'll change your mind."

"I won't," I promised.

Without another word, he simply smiled and walked away. Before he even made it to the elevator, he was stopped by two women. I couldn't hear what they were saying, but it was clear to see they were beyond thrilled that they'd just run into Cash.

One of the women ran up to me and asked, "Can I borrow a pen please?"

I wanted to roll my eyes. Handing the pen over, I could see the other woman was already taking a selfie with Cash.

No thanks.

After signing autographs for the women, they giggled their way out of the hotel doors.

Cash looked at me and shouted, "Good night, Demi. I'll be in my room all night."

I wanted to tell him to go fuck himself, but I didn't think it was a good look for the hotel. Instead, I ignored him and got back to work.

Luckily, things picked up after Cash walked away, and I only spent half of the remaining time I was at work thinking about him.

CHAPTER 3

Cash

BECK PUSHED THE BUTTON FOR THE MAIN LOBBY, AND I watched as the bulbs lit up indicating our descent.

This weekend hadn't gone anything like I thought it would.

Actually, that's not entirely true.

I had suspected we'd have two great shows here in New Hampshire. We had. The crowds were incredible, and the vibe both nights were killer. But not long after I'd arrived here last Thursday, I had expected that not only would we have incredible shows, but that I'd also have a great time with the woman I saw the moment we entered this hotel.

Demi.

I didn't know what it was about her, but I'd never, *never,* been so distracted by a woman before her. In the beginning, part of me liked this challenge with her. She was gorgeous, but she was feisty. She talked back. She didn't take anybody's shit. The woman could make my dick hard with just one look or wise-ass comment.

Unfortunately, it was now Monday morning, the shows were over, and we were checking out to head to our next location.

To say I was disappointed would have been an understatement. And that was something I never expected I'd say when it was time to leave this small town.

The elevator came to a stop and the doors opened. Beck and I stepped out.

As we started walking toward the lobby, he asked, "You want me to handle the check-out?"

My eyes shifted toward the reception desk. Demi was there. I should have told Beck to take the lead. It was obvious she wasn't interested, but I wanted to take one last shot.

Shaking my head as I returned my attention to Beck, I replied, "No, that's alright. I'll take care of it."

He jerked his chin up and said, "Good luck, man."

"Yeah. Thanks."

Beck knew I'd had a bit of a thing for Demi. He had been just as shocked as I was that Demi didn't seem interested.

Walking up to the front desk as Beck moved toward the exit to meet the rest of the crew outside, my eyes remained focused on Demi.

"Checking out?" she asked.

I nodded and placed the room keys on the desk. "Yes."

Demi took the key cards, but something strange washed over her face. I didn't know what it was, and before I could really take the opportunity to dissect it, it was gone.

I hated the fact that I had to leave the first woman who made me feel this way without so much as a phone number. Figuring this was my last chance, I decided to try one last time.

"I missed seeing you at the show last night," I told her, doing my best to remain nonchalant.

"That's because I didn't go," she replied. "I told you I wasn't going to come."

"I thought maybe you were bluffing. I can't believe you didn't use those tickets I gave you," I said.

"Well, they didn't go to waste," she reasoned.

Confusion washed over me. What was that supposed to mean?

"What?" I asked.

"Your tickets were used, Cash," Demi assured me. Then a devilish grin formed on her face. It nearly knocked me on my ass. "I gave them to your selfie-taking, autograph-requesting groupies from earlier in the evening. They were ecstatic."

I wanted to laugh. How this woman managed to infuriate me while also making me want to strip her naked was a complete mystery to me.

She had no issue denying me in any way that she could. And damn if that didn't make her seem that much more appealing.

As she worked at the computer in front of her, I asked, "So, I've got to make one last-ditch effort here. What are the chances of me walking out of here with your number?"

There wasn't an ounce of hesitation in her voice when she responded, "Zero."

"Ouch."

"What would be the point in doing that anyway?" she questioned me.

I'd take that. Demi did her very best to indicate she wasn't even remotely interested in me, but if that were truly the case, she wouldn't have asked me this follow-up question.

"What do you mean? The point of exchanging phone numbers is so that two people can communicate with one another when they aren't around each other," I explained even though I had a feeling that wasn't the answer she was looking for.

Demi rolled her eyes at me. "I know what a phone is used for, Cash," she insisted. Fuck, I loved hearing her say my name. "What I'm saying is that I don't understand what the point is in me giving you my number when you're leaving and never coming back here."

"I didn't say I was never coming back. Plus, I can promise you that if I had something waiting for me to come back to, I'd definitely make the trip. There's no doubt I'd come back for you."

Shooting me a look of disbelief, Demi insisted, "I'm sure that's what you tell all the women who work at the hotels you stay at."

"I don't."

Her expression didn't change. If anything, Demi only seemed to grow more leery of me. "Why do I have a hard time believing that?" she asked.

I shrugged. "I don't know. It's the truth, though."

I waited for her to respond, but she didn't say anything.

"So that's it then?" I asked.

"That's it."

Not wanting to walk away from her, but knowing I had to, I took one last long look at her before I said, "Well, take care of yourself, Demi."

She gave me a simple nod and returned, "You, too. Good luck with the rest of your tour."

"Yeah. Thanks."

With that, I turned and walked to the front door. Normally, having someone wish me luck with our tour would have left me feeling good. This time it didn't. Because while I stepped out into the morning sun, trying to come to terms with the fact that Demi wasn't interested, I silently wondered how the remainder of the tour would be for me.

Sure, I knew I'd be able to move on to the next location and pick up a woman with a simple snap of my fingers if I wanted to. The problem was, I had a feeling I wasn't so easily going to forget the one who stood behind that reception desk in this hotel and didn't take an ounce of my shit.

Demi

"Enjoy the remainder of your stay."

That came from one of my staff members, Izzy. She just finished checking in a hotel guest, and I had just gotten back to the front desk after a meeting with my kitchen staff.

The moment the guest had taken off, Izzy looked in my direction and said, "Hey, Demi. Everything okay?"

Nodding, I confirmed, "Yes, it's all good. I just finished my meeting with the kitchen staff. I wanted to let you know that I'll be heading into the back to work on some budget stuff. I know you can handle just about anything out here, but if you need me, that's where I'll be."

"Sure. I've got it covered."

"Thanks."

With that, I made my way back to my office and sat down at my desk.

I wanted to laugh. It wasn't going to be my desk for much longer.

It was now Wednesday, and I'd just officially done it. I submitted my two-week notice. I was *finally* leaving this job.

The truth was, I couldn't take it much longer. The day Chasey had come in and the whole staff got to witness her heartbreak, I sort of lost it. Sam and I had gone to Cal's bar, Granite, that night. I begged him for a job.

After spending entirely too long now working at a place that was bringing me such heartache, I decided it was time to do something about it. I couldn't simply quit because I still had bills to pay, but I knew I couldn't continue to work in an environment where I felt partly responsible for breaking up marriages.

Deep down, I knew people like Chasey's husband had made their own choices. If it wasn't my hotel, it would have been another. But the bottom line was that seeing something like that was the last straw. I had had enough.

Thankfully, Cal was willing to hire me. And after a long talk with him and Sam, we decided that I could be in charge of handling the entertainment at the bar for him. Cal had recently started having bands play live performances at his bar. While the outcome had been great, he couldn't deny that it had been a lot of work and preparation.

So, now I was going to be in charge of that. Having spent all these years as a hotel manager, I knew I could easily manage all of the responsibilities and headaches that would come with hiring live talent.

Of course, Sam and I told Cal all about what happened

that day that brought me to that place. Sam, however, didn't seem interested in holding back the news that My Violent Heart had come into the hotel that day. She also felt compelled to tell Cal that Cash Morris was 'seriously interested' in me.

Yes, those were her words.

Seriously interested.

I had wanted to tell her that he was only seriously interested in finding an easy score, but I refrained. At least for the time being. I was too heartbroken at what I'd witnessed that day to really think too much about anything other than how horrible I felt for that woman and her brand-new baby.

Only two more weeks.

I'd suck it up for the next two weeks, and then I'd be out of here.

On that thought, I got started working on budgets and other financial reports. But I hadn't even gotten two or three minutes into my work when Izzy walked in and called, "Demi?"

"Yeah?"

"There's a call waiting on hold for you," she said.

I glanced down at the phone on my desk. Only one of the lines was lit up.

"I'll get it. Thanks," I told her as I put my hand to the phone.

"This is Demi. How can I help you?"

"Shit, I forgot."

Three words. With just three words, my body went on alert because I knew precisely who was on the other line.

"Cash?" I called.

There was a momentary pause before he replied, "Yeah."

Why was he calling? He said he forgot. If he forgot something, he could have easily asked Izzy.

"Did you forget something in your suite?" I asked. "I can talk to housekeeping and see if they found anything."

"No, that's not it," he said. "It been a few days since I left. I realized I didn't give you an option."

"An option?" I repeated.

"Well, I started thinking about you, and I realized it was totally possible for you to change your mind about wanting to give me your number. The problem is that you have no way to contact me. And while I do think that you're a very determined woman who would find a way to get what she wants, I didn't want you to have to go to the trouble."

What was he talking about?

"I'm sorry. I'm not following you," I told him. "You think I've been sitting here pining over the fact that I didn't give you my number and now I'm devastated that I may never get the chance to talk to you again?"

He let out a soft laugh. God, the sound was magical in my ear. "I don't know, Demi. Are you pining over me?"

"Not at all."

"I don't know why, but I have such a hard time believing that," he said.

"It's probably because your ego can't handle the devastating blow that not everybody wants to see you naked," I remarked.

"Are you thinking about me naked, firecracker?"

Damn.

I hadn't been. At least, not at that moment. But I was now. And I would have been lying if I said that I hadn't thought about him naked at least a thousand times since he had walked into my hotel.

"You're so full of yourself. Do you know that?" I countered.

"You didn't answer the question," he pointed out. "I think that says a lot more about you than it does about me. I don't have to pretend to be somebody I'm not."

Okay, time for a new tactic. I considered just slamming the phone down and hanging up on him, but I had a feeling that wouldn't dissuade Cash. This guy was far too determined to simply give up. I mean, if he was still hung up on the fact that I hadn't given him my number days after he'd moved on to the next stop on his band's tour, I needed a serious answer as to why.

Or, better yet, I needed to make sure I shut it down.

"Why are you being so persistent?" I asked. "You've already left New Hampshire."

"Maybe I want to come back," he replied.

This guy.

"Well, it's not me that's stopping you," I said.

I didn't mind putting that out there because I knew My Violent Heart was still on tour for a few more weeks. Even if Cash thought this was my way of giving in, by the time he came back, I wouldn't be here.

"Do you want me to come back?" he asked.

For a brief moment, I allowed what felt like genuine curiosity in his tone affect me. He sounded like he actually cared to know the answer to that question and that he desperately wanted the answer to be yes.

Pushing beyond that unwelcome feeling the sound of his

voice gave me, I remembered how men like him were and answered, "What I want doesn't matter, and you know that."

"What is that supposed to mean?"

"Exactly what it means. Guys like you don't actually care about the feelings of the women you get involved with, which is precisely the reason why I won't ever get involved with you," I explained.

"That's quite the assessment you've made," he noted.

"It's accurate, though," I said.

Cash didn't respond, and I found that strange. Someone like him, with the cocky attitude and inability to accept being denied, didn't just shut down. There was always a reply, a witty comeback. Something, anything, to make the person they were speaking with feel worse about the situation.

When too much time passed without a reply, I declared, "You never answered my question."

"What question?"

"I'm not a fool. I know you can easily find another woman at your next destination. Why are you being so persistent with me?"

There was another lengthy pause before his voice dropped an octave, and he said, "Because you aren't like the other women. You don't fall all over yourself for me."

Now it made sense.

"I see. So, this is just a game for you then," I announced. "You've never had to actually work to get a woman in your bed, so maybe that's made life a little monotonous for you, even if you spend every night with a different girl."

"You've got it all figured out, don't you?" he asked.

"Yep. I'm going to be nice and do you a favor, though. I understand your need to conquer this and come out on top.

I'll save you the work and the struggle and tell you that I promise it's not going to happen. I have absolutely zero interest in playing this game with you just so you can get your rocks off and move on."

The silence stretched between us.

"Demi?" he eventually called.

"Yeah?"

"You're wrong," he said.

No, I wasn't, but I could see why he wouldn't want to admit that to me. "Oh?" I scoffed. "How's that?"

"Actually, you're mostly right," he corrected himself. "This is definitely a challenge. One that I'm up for. But where you're wrong is in your assumption about what happens in this game."

"How so?"

Another lengthy pause ensued before his voice dropped to a level so low it was a wonder my whole body didn't burst into flames.

"*When* I win this game, I intend to keep the prize."

My lips parted, and I stopped breathing.

"I..." I trailed off, unsure of what to say.

"I'll be back for you, Demi."

The next thing I knew, the line went dead.

CHAPTER 4

Cash

"It's definitely broken."

Panic gripped me as the words spilled out of my mouth. I didn't know how I'd be able to perform tonight now that I'd come to this realization.

"I'm sure it's not broken," Beck said.

"Well, it doesn't work anymore, Beck," I noted. "That's the very definition of being broken."

It was Monday evening, two weeks after we'd left New Hampshire to continue with our tour. This show was the first of two we had this week before a week-long hiatus began. Then we had another fifteen weeks of shows to play before the tour was over.

It had been a particularly long tour for us, so the end approaching was a good thing. While I loved what I did, I had a feeling I was going to need a nice long break. Ever since I'd met Demi, so much had changed for me.

Some of those things were not so good, as I had just found out.

"What's broken?" Roscoe asked as he and Killian walked up. Killian sat on the opposite end of the couch as me while Roscoe made himself comfortable in a chair off to the side of the sofa. Beck and Walker were sitting on another couch directly across from the one Killian and I were sitting on.

We were in our dressing room at a venue in upstate New York. For now, it was just the guys and me. Holland was currently in her own dressing room; however, she always joined us for a bit before we went out on stage.

"Cash thinks his dick is broken," Walker informed them.

This wasn't a matter of debate. There was no thinking that needed to be done. I was certain it was broken.

Roscoe and Killian started laughing. "What the hell would make you think that?" Killian asked.

I sat back on the couch, pressed the bottoms of my feet into the edge of the coffee table, and said, "I don't think this. I know it."

"You're serious?" Roscoe pressed.

I nodded.

The worry that consumed me was beyond anything I'd ever felt before. Was this it for me? Was I done? Had I used it so much that I'd never have sex again?

I was only thirty-two years old. Surely I hadn't reached the point of no return yet.

"Maybe it's just a phase," Walker suggested.

"I don't think it's that," Beck declared with a knowing smirk on his face.

"Guys, this isn't funny," I began. "I may never have sex again."

God, I felt sick at the thought.

"What happened?" Killian asked.

It was her.

Demi.

She broke my dick.

Ever since I was in New Hampshire, it seemed to have one interest and one interest alone. Her. Nothing else mattered.

At the time, I kind of liked it. I was so focused on trying to get her that I didn't necessarily take notice to the fact that no other woman was doing it for me. Demi had kept me so excited and engaged that every other woman ceased to exist.

And now I was paying the price.

I hated the way this felt. Terror unlike anything I'd ever experienced before was pulsing through every part of my body.

Maybe that was the problem. My cock was living in fear. The thing was, I couldn't understand why.

Before I could answer Killian's question, a knock came at the door before it opened a crack.

"Is it safe?" Holland asked.

"All clear, Holls," Walker told her.

Holland opened the door and came inside. She'd made a point to knock before entering every time now because one time, years ago, she walked in and found that Roscoe and Killian had both brought some women back to the dressing room. She'd gotten an eyeful that night and refused to repeat it.

After closing the door, Holland walked over and sat down between Killian and me. I always thought the middle seat of the couch was awkward. If any of the guys had sat down in that seat between Killian and me, I had no doubt we'd have kicked his ass. But Holland was different. She was the only one who could do that and get away with it.

"Okay, fill me in," she demanded. "What did I miss?"

My eyes moved through the group. Beck shared, "Cash's dick is broken."

Holland snapped her head in my direction. "Are you serious?" she gasped.

"Jesus, Beck, can you stop fucking saying it like that?" I begged. This was already difficult enough. Every time he said it like that, it was as though I could feel the pain of my new reality all centered in the spot that was causing all this stress.

Beck ignored my request and just laughed it off.

"Cash?" Holland called.

I turned my attention to her, and in that moment, I couldn't have been more grateful she was part of our group. Where the guys would be quick to turn it into a joke—something I probably would have done as well if the roles were reversed and it was one of them—Holland showed genuine concern.

"Yeah?" I responded.

"What's going on?" she asked.

I decided it was time to tell the rest of them the truth. I had a feeling Beck already knew what was going on with me.

"I've been having this problem ever since we left New Hampshire," I told her.

"What exactly is the problem?"

"It doesn't work anymore," I admitted. Fuck, it hurt to even admit that to Holland. The thing was, I was just as close with her as I was with the rest of the guys. We all were. Holland being a woman didn't affect our friendship. Obviously, we were a bit more protective of her and gave her the respect of her own dressing room or hotel room. But deep down, she was just as much a part of us as any of the guys were.

Narrowing her eyes on me, she cautiously pressed, "How do you know this? Did you have an… incident with someone?"

I shook my head. "Not exactly. At least, not like I'm sure you're thinking," I answered. "It's just that over the last two weeks, things have happened that indicate there's a problem."

"Like what?"

I swallowed hard. "Twice already I've been flashed by women, and I feel nothing," I confessed. "And even though I hadn't exactly asked for it, the other night when we all went out to that bar in Delaware, do you remember when that group of girls came up to us?"

Holland nodded.

"Well, one of them walked up to me, grabbed my cock, and pressed her tits in my face," I shared. "I felt nothing. Nothing at all."

Holland seemed shocked. "Is that really all it would take for you?"

"I'm a guy, Holls. It doesn't take much for us," I shared. She cocked an eyebrow at me before I added, "Or, at least, it didn't."

Sympathy washed over her.

Roscoe chimed in and asked, "So, how long has this been a problem?"

"Since we left New Hampshire," I replied.

"Did something happen there?" Walker questioned me.

"Yes, but no."

"What?"

Just share it, Cash, I thought.

My eyes slid to Beck's, and I was convinced he already knew where my problem started.

"Remember the woman who worked at the hotel we stayed at there?" I asked the group.

"Which woman?" Roscoe countered.

"The one with the blue eyes, gorgeous mouth, and sassy attitude," I clarified. "She was the one who checked us in the day we arrived."

"Oh, the one who was just as pissed as Beck was at that douchebag in the underwear who cheated on his wife?" Killian guessed.

I nodded. "Yes, that's her."

"Okay, so what happened with her?" Holland wondered.

Shaking my head, feeling nothing but disappointment, I answered honestly, "Nothing. Well, I mean, not anything that I wanted to have happen. I asked her for her number, talked with her, teased her about coming up to my suite, and gave her tickets to our show. Shit, I even called the hotel to talk to her a couple days after we got back on the road."

"I didn't know you called her," Beck said.

"I did."

I'd left them all shocked. With the exception of Beck's declaration, nobody spoke. The tension mounted in my body. Tonight was going to be a disaster of a show. There was no way I could perform on stage when I was terrified I'd never be able to perform in a bed again. Hell, it didn't even need to be a bed. I'd settle for just about anywhere.

Finally, Holland bubbled, "Aw, Cash, this is great news."

I shot her a look of disbelief. "Excuse me?"

"I think you're ready to settle down," she explained.

No, I wasn't. I just wanted a night with Demi. Maybe two. Okay, depending on how it all went down, I could probably see myself being very happy having her sassy mouth around for much longer than that.

That didn't mean I was ready to settle down in the way Holland was indicating.

"I don't think that's it," I told her.

"That's exactly it," Beck stated.

"Let's go back for her," Holland declared.

"What?"

"After we play our last show before the break on Wednesday night, we'll go back to New Hampshire," she said.

"We were supposed to be getting to our next location early so everyone could have some time to relax," I reminded her.

Before Holland could answer, Killian said, "Yeah, but we can't spend the next however many weeks listening to you talk about your cock, Cash. Time off is time off. We can do it anywhere."

"Agreed," Walker chimed in. "I'm down to go back."

"Me too," Roscoe said. "Moral support and all."

My eyes slid to Beck, and he gave me a nod.

I had a feeling I knew what was going on in the back of his mind. He would have zero problem returning to the place where he knew a single mom was waiting and struggling. Heading back might give him the opportunity to check in on her, assuming he could locate her. I wasn't sure she'd ever followed up and reached out to him after he'd given her his number.

"So, it's settled then," Holland declared. "I'm so excited for you, Cash. You'll be the first man down."

Shaking my head, I told her, "It's not going to be as easy as you think. It's not as simple as just showing up there."

"What do you mean?"

"She's not interested in me," I shared. "Or, I should say, she claims she's not interested in me."

"But you got her number and talked to her on the phone," Killian reasoned. "Isn't that enough to indicate she has at least some interest."

When I explained this, they were going to think I was crazy. Any chance I had to go back and see her was going to go right down the tubes. The last thing they'd want is for us to get caught up in some situation where I was chasing after a girl who didn't want me.

But I needed to do this. I needed to see her. If nothing else, I'd resort to begging. Okay, I wouldn't do that.

But fuck, what was happening to me?

"I asked for her number, but I never got it," I admitted. When their eyes went wide, I added, "She's the most beautiful woman I've ever laid my eyes on, and she's got an attitude that I love, but she wants absolutely nothing to do with me. I called the hotel's number just so I could hear her voice."

"Maybe you should move on then," Roscoe suggested.

"I would if I could," I assured him. "But Demi broke my dick."

Holland put her hand on my arm and gave it a squeeze. "Your penis isn't broken, Cash," she insisted. "It's just tired of random, meaningless hookups. Give it the one woman it wants, even if that means the rest of you has to work to make that happen. It wouldn't kill you to put in a little bit of effort."

The voice of reason. She made everything sound so simple, but she didn't know what I knew. She hadn't heard Demi's words on the phone.

Maybe that was the problem.

I'd already made my mind up when I talked to her on the phone. Hearing some of the things she said had me thinking twice about the direction I was heading with my life.

It wasn't as though I was on a bad path filled with drugs and booze. Sure, we occasionally had a fun night out as a group, but we didn't touch anything more than a couple of drinks.

But it wasn't a secret that I'd spent the better part of my career taking advantage of the perks. Beyond that, it was just as Demi said. I hadn't really cared if the women I'd been with wanted more than just a one-night stand. The reason for that was that I never wanted more than that with them.

She was different, though.

Nobody but her had ever made me want more. I had hoped she'd tell me that she wanted me to come back, that she wanted to see me again.

And when she didn't give me that, suffice it to say, I didn't like how it felt.

Maybe I was getting a taste of my own medicine.

What hit me the most about our entire conversation was not that she'd figured me all out, but it was the disappointed tone I could hear in her voice that had me second-guessing a lot of the choices I'd made.

People changed, though.

I could put in effort.

I already told the woman I was coming back for her. Of course, I hadn't intended for it to be so soon, but this was even better. It would show her I was determined, that I was going to follow through on what I said I was going to do.

That or she was going to call the police on me for being a crazy stalker.

I wanted to laugh.

This usually worked the other way around. Typically, we were the ones who had to worry about someone stalking us. Now I was here, desperate to figure out a way to convince Demi to give me a shot.

"Alright, we'll go back," I told them.

"Good. Now we need to get out there and put on a show," Walker advised. "Do you think you'll be able to handle yourself?"

Grinning, I said, "At least I won't have to worry about the groupies."

"More for me," Roscoe declared, standing up.

"I'm with you on that one," Killian chimed in.

That was me. That was how I'd always been, too. It blew my mind that I didn't even feel the slightest hint of jealousy that they'd have that and I wouldn't.

I didn't want it because I wanted her.

With that, the rest of us got up and started moving to exit the dressing room. As I made my way there, I couldn't help but recall the conversation I had with Demi. It made me think about how I was going to approach her when I returned. I didn't think I'd be able to completely pull back from being the guy I'd always been.

I was confident; that wasn't going to change.

And truthfully, I didn't think that was a problem for Demi. Even if she thought I was being cocky, she didn't seem to have an issue handing it right back to me. That's what I liked so much about her.

She kept me on my toes and constantly surprised me.

I just hoped I'd find a way to get her to open up a little bit more when I returned. She stunned me a bit by opening up just a touch when we were on the phone. The things she'd said to me that indicated she didn't approve of my behavior with women made me think that perhaps she'd been burned by an ex.

Maybe I needed to be myself while also trying to be mindful of whatever it was that made her shroud herself in a protective bubble.

There was no boyfriend, and there was a definite attraction between us.

This was going to be new for me. This was going to require effort. But just as I told her on the phone, I was up for the challenge. I needed something different in my life.

And once I got her, I didn't think that feeling was going to fade.

I'll be back for you, Demi, I thought as I smiled to myself just moments before we walked out on stage.

Then I envisioned those perfect lips of hers and felt my cock stiffen.

Well, there I had it.

It still worked.

Feeling relieved about that, I joined the rest of the band on stage as the crowd went wild.

CHAPTER 5

Demi

"Oh, my God. It's totally true."

That came from me and was directed at my best friend, Sam, and my cousin, Cal.

It was Thursday, and Sam and Cal had decided to have a mini-celebration with me tonight. I'd finished my last day of work at the hotel yesterday—something I very desperately needed—and my best friends thought it was worth celebrating.

I had just arrived and walked up to the bar, and for the first time, I saw them with their lips locked. For years, I watched as the two of them danced around their feelings for one another, holding back from giving in to what they both wanted. They were perfect for each other, so I was happy to see they'd finally found a way to express those feelings.

Of course, they'd only officially gotten together over the weekend, so I was just now seeing them like this for the first time. I always had a feeling it would happen for them but it still caught me off guard to see, so I needed to make the declaration.

At the sound of my voice, I watched as they both broke out into a smile while not pulling away from one another. In fact, Cal gave Sam another peck on the lips before they separated.

"Why do you look so surprised?" Sam asked.

Feeling the shock wash over me, I shook my head and answered, "I know you told me you and Cal were finally together, but I guess I just didn't prepare myself for seeing it in the flesh. And you're both now going to do this flaunting thing."

"Flaunting?" Cal repeated.

Nodding, I clarified, "Yeah. You know, where the two of you have to let the entire world know how much you love each other and are unable to keep your hands off one another."

They both laughed.

"It's not like that," Sam insisted.

I didn't believe that at all. That's when Cal chimed in and proved me right. "It is for me."

Sam rolled her eyes at him, but she also smiled. It was like that for her, too. And the truth was, I might have been pretending to give them a hard time, but I was really happy for them.

"We'll be on our best behavior tonight since this is your party. How was your first full day no longer working as a hotel manager?" Sam asked.

I settled my ass in the stool beside her just as Cal placed a drink in front of me. Then I answered, "It was glorious. Honestly, I didn't know it would feel this wonderful. Now,

I'm going to fully enjoy these next few days because I've got to get down to business on Monday. I'm making it my mission to take Granite to the next level, and with a live band playing next week, it'll be a great way to start."

"Just a heads-up on that," Cal interrupted. Sam and I turned our attention to him. Cal smiled at her before he focused his gaze on me. "Sam and I were talking before you got here. I told her to get some business cards made up and to get a few shirts here. We can display them, have the staff wear them, and maybe drive some eyes to her website."

Cal was one of the few amazing men in the world. Sam was so lucky to have him. For years, she'd had a side business, dipping her toe into the world of designing and selling T-shirts. She was incredibly talented, but it had been hard to really get things moving for her. That's why she still worked at the hotel as the event sales director. To know that Cal was now doing something to help spread the word about her shirts made me happy.

"That's a great idea, Cal," I declared.

Standing up from his hunched-over position, Cal held his hands out to his sides and said, "What can I say? We can't all be this brilliant."

"Yeah, yeah," I mumbled. I turned my attention to Sam and asked, "So, how was your day?"

For the next few minutes, Sam filled both Cal and me in on her day at work. It wasn't so much that she filled us in on what happened at work, rather she filled us in on a phone call she'd received from her ex. He'd realized what a mistake he made in the way he treated her during their relationship, and now he wanted to talk about reconciling.

Thankfully, not only was Sam happy with Cal now, but

she was also a smart woman. She didn't listen to any of the garbage her ex tried to spew and hung the phone up on him.

"What a clueless jerk," I declared when she finished.

Nodding her agreement, Sam said, "Yeah. Anyway, it's done and over, and tonight is not about him. We're celebrating Demi."

Yes, we were. But in the back of my mind, we were also celebrating Sam and Cal. I just didn't need to tell them that. I tossed back the remainder of my drink and ordered, "You're coming with me."

"Where are we going?" Sam asked.

I beamed at her. "To dance."

"Can I join you?"

At the sound of the voice that made my body want to simultaneously burst into flames and melt into a puddle on the floor, I froze.

Cash.

That was Cash's voice.

I'd spent time earlier in the week telling Sam about how I didn't care that he'd called the hotel because I wasn't going to be there much longer. He would have no way to reach me.

But now he was here.

Just like that.

And damn, did he smell good.

No way was I going to let that steer me off the course I'd been on for a long time. I narrowed my eyes at him and barked, "What are you doing here?"

The change in my mood didn't affect Cash at all. He didn't seem to care that I was showing my rage. I knew this because the corners of his mouth twitched.

What I told Sam earlier in the week was true. The

angrier I was, the more I pushed back, the more turned on he became.

With a voice as smooth as silk, he answered, "I came back for you."

"What is that supposed to mean?" I questioned him, feeling beyond irritated. This was supposed to be a clean break for me. I had made up my mind. I had left the hotel for reasons unrelated to Cash. There had been a few moments of weakness where I daydreamed about what a man like him could do to my body. Everything about those daydreams had been magnificent. But I quickly remembered what a man like Cash could do to my heart and was instantly relieved that I was leaving the hotel without him having any means to contact me. I'd made peace with that decision.

And yet, now he had found me.

"It means exactly what I said," Cash began. "I was on tour with my band, and we have a short break before our next show, so I told them we were coming back here."

"And what exactly are you hoping is going to happen with your big band here in this small town?" I pressed.

"This trip isn't about the band," he shared. "It was about me needing to make a statement. You see, there's this girl I like, and she's… struggling with how she feels right now. I tried contacting her over the phone, but progress has been slow."

He was not serious.

I cocked an eyebrow. "I see. So, you show up here hoping you can strong-arm your way into getting what you want? Are you honestly that hurt by this? I mean, why not just move on to your next conquest? Or, is it just that you can't handle having a woman turn you down?"

"Because you're the one that has me intrigued right now, darling," Cash shared, his voice a low hum. "And when I find something I like, I go after it."

Fuck. Fuck. Fuck.

I did *not* need Cash Morris talking to me in a voice like that while saying things like that. Time to shut it down.

"Well, then I'm sorry," I apologized. "Because you're going to have to figure out how to tell that big ego of yours that he's not getting his way this time."

Before Cash could respond, Cal interrupted.

"Cash?" he called, taking a step to the side so he came in line with him.

"Yeah?" Cash replied, lifting his gaze from mine.

Cal extended his hand to him and introduced himself. "Calvin Gates. I'm the owner of Granite, and Demi is my cousin."

Cash reached for Cal's extended hand, and his arm crossed directly in front of my body. I couldn't help myself. It was the closest I'd ever been to him, and he smelled so incredible. I closed my eyes briefly and inhaled the scent of him. I might have been angry, but I wasn't immune to natural reactions.

"Pleasure to meet you, Calvin," Cash replied.

"Cal."

Cash gave him a nod of understanding. Then his eyes moved around the entire bar. They hesitated momentarily on the stage, and when he finished his survey of the space, he declared, "This is a great place you've got here."

It was a great place. But I had to wonder if he meant that or if he was simply trying to butter Cal up and get on his good side.

"Thanks, man," Cal responded. "I'm definitely honored that you'd stop in and check it out, even if it's only to try and warm up my cousin's cold, dead heart."

I was going to kill Cal.

Cash's eyes immediately came in my direction. "That's not true, is it? Do you need me to warm up your heart?" he asked. He was very clearly enjoying himself.

"What part of the word no don't you understand?" I countered.

Something sparked in his eyes, and they grew intense. "I understand the word just fine," he assured me. His voice was all seduction once again. "The problem is that the rest of you is telling me what your mouth won't."

"You're crazy," I spat.

"And you're lying. To yourself and to me."

My lips parted in shock. How dare he?

Okay, that's what I wanted to say.

But I didn't. Because I couldn't wrap my head around the fact that this infuriatingly handsome man could read me the way he was.

Not only that, but Cash looked away from me and returned his attention to my cousin. "Do you have live performances here?" he asked.

No.

No, no, no!

I knew exactly what he was going to do, and I wanted to scream at the top of my lungs. Once again, I couldn't.

Because this would be a dream come true for Cal, and I'd never take it away from him.

"Yeah, we've been doing them for a while now," Cal answered. "Mostly local cover bands for now, though."

Cash grinned.

Sam grinned.

I did not grin.

"If you don't already have someone booked, I can talk to the rest of the band and convince them to play here on Saturday night," Cash offered.

Cal smiled at Cash and shared, "Well, personally, I'd say yes to that since we don't have anyone booked. The problem is that booking the bands is no longer my job."

Cash's brows shot up. "It's your bar," he countered.

"Yep. And I just hired Demi to handle all of the entertainment and events for me," Cal informed him.

It was official. As soon as I could figure out how to do it without getting into trouble, I was going to kill Cal.

For now, I had to hold back because the cocky musician was looking at me again. "So, what's it going to be, Demi? Are you and I going to be working together to get this nailed down for Saturday, or are you going to deny Cal from having what could possibly be the biggest thing to ever happen here at Granite?"

I scowled at him. "I don't start my new job until Monday," I seethed. "And tonight, I'm here celebrating, so if you want to play here on Saturday and Cal wants that, he can work it out with you. Sam and I are going to dance right now, and we're doing it *alone*."

With that, knowing I needed to get away from his sexy voice, killer body, and masculine scent, I slid off the stool. Cash didn't step back, which meant I ended up even closer to him.

I reached for Sam's arm, yanked on her wrist, and

stepped around the rock star. Then I dragged my best friend toward the dance floor and away from temptation.

This day was turning out way better than I had anticipated when I first arrived in New Hampshire.

Earlier today, I'd arrived at Demi's hotel only to learn that she no longer worked there. Panic had immediately consumed me.

Had I lost my shot?

Despite being unable to get any of the staff at the front desk to help me reach Demi, I still found her.

Because just as I was about to lose my mind, I heard someone call my name.

"Yeah?" I replied, looking in the direction the voice came from.

A woman was moving toward me and asked, "Are you looking for Demi?"

I nodded.

"I can't tell you where she lives, and I'm not going to give you her number, but she's my best friend, so I'm going to give you something," the woman started. "But I swear to God if you hurt her, you'll be answering to me."

In any other situation, I might have laughed that a petite woman like Demi's best friend was threatening me like she was. In this situation, I didn't. While I wanted to blame that on the fact that I'd been slightly panicked only moments before, I knew that wasn't it. I simply didn't like the idea of Demi being hurt. And it hit right then just how deep I was for a woman I barely even knew.

I stared at Demi's friend and said, "Okay."

"Follow me outside, and I'll tell you where you can find her tonight," she said.

I didn't hesitate. I followed her outside.

And now I was here at her cousin's bar struggling to remain unaffected by the discomfort I felt below the belt.

Demi was out dancing with Sam, and she was gorgeous. Her dress fit her perfectly, her legs were long and muscular, and she had curves I itched to touch. I hadn't been able to take my eyes off of her.

"She's fragile."

That came from Cal. I twisted my neck in his direction and said, "Pardon?"

"Demi," he clarified. "I know she shows the world, especially you, this tough side. Don't get me wrong, she's a strong woman. But underneath that tough exterior, Demi holds a lot of hurt in her heart. I'm telling you this partly because I want you to understand that you can't go into this hoping for a score before you just up and move on. She's important to me, and I'd hate for you to use her like that. The bigger reason I'm telling you this is because I don't think that's what you want. I think you see just how special she is and you might be a bit more serious about her. If that's the case, Demi stands to gain a lot. She deserves that."

Fuck.

I was dealing with a woman who, based on the way she'd been with me and now this new information I'd been given by Cal, had experienced some serious emotional trauma.

Some might say I didn't need that in my life. Surprisingly, it didn't bother me.

Well, the fact that she'd been through something horrible bothered me. But knowing that there might be some stuff to work through with her before I could make any real progress didn't bother me.

I told her before that I was up for the challenge. This new information didn't change that.

Because when I glanced back out at her on the dance floor, saw the way her body moved, and felt my cock stiffen, I knew I wasn't walking away.

Focusing my attention on Cal again, I said, "I appreciate the heads-up. You're not wrong about what I want, and I'm glad you can see that."

Cal nodded. "Happy to hear you confirm that."

"Yeah," I responded. Then, because I was desperate to make progress with her, I asked, "Any advice you can give me on how to get in there with her? I can't even manage to get her phone number."

Cal thought a moment. Eventually, he answered, "Keep showing up. Keep proving to her that everything she believes about who you are isn't the truth. She's got the biggest heart in the world, so if you can find a way to soften the hardened edges, I think you'll see a change."

"Got it. So, are we on for a show this weekend or what?" I asked.

I didn't often offer up a show without first checking with the rest of the band. But they had come here with the intention of helping me win Demi over. I was confident they wouldn't mind playing an intimate show at a bar in a small town. We hadn't done that in a while, and sometimes, it was nice to go back to the way things were before we got so big.

"I am not turning this opportunity down," Cal said. "It's last minute, but I think we can pull it off."

At that, Cal and I got down to sorting out the details for a show in two days.

But I did it while making frequent glances to the dance floor and loving what I saw.

CHAPTER 6

Demi

"HEY, WHAT ARE THOSE?"

I turned around at the unfamiliar voice and was stunned to see Holland walking toward me. I was in one of the rooms in the back of the bar, sorting through a couple of boxes in preparation for tonight.

This felt completely surreal. It was as though I were living in a dream right now.

Holland Oates from My Violent Heart was within touching distance, and she was talking to me.

Quite frankly, I was still in shock that My Violent Heart was going to be playing at Granite tonight to begin with.

And to think that Sam and Cal were surprised to see me here.

Earlier this evening, minutes after I arrived at Granite, I was greeted by my two best friends in the strangest way.

"We didn't think you were going to come here tonight," Sam said.

"But I'm so happy you're here," Cal added.

I shot them a look that I hoped indicated I thought they were crazy and asked, "Where did you think I would be?"

Cal and Sam exchanged nervous glances. They seemed to know what the other was thinking while I was stuck there trying to figure out what the awkward looks meant. Luckily, I didn't need to work too hard to figure it out because Sam finally said, "We just thought that with My Violent Heart playing tonight, meaning Cash is going to be here, you wouldn't want to put yourself in the position to be around him."

No sooner did she get that out when Cal chimed in, "And if that's what it was for you, Demi, you know I'd completely understand."

"Cal, this is going to be one of the biggest nights of your life," I started. "I wouldn't miss this for anything. And I'm not the least bit concerned about Cash. He already knows where I stand. If he wants to continue putting himself in the position to be turned down, I'm happy to oblige him."

"Are you sure?" he question me.

Nodding, I insisted, "I'm positive. Besides, I might think Cash is full of himself, but the man can sing. And the rest of the band is awesome. They're one of my favorites, so I'd be a fool to miss out on a live performance in my own backyard because of one guy."

That had been the truth, too. Cash, the lead singer and front man for My Violent Heart, was incredible. Cash, the guy who wanted my number so I could just be another notch on his bedpost, wasn't somebody I was remotely interested in giving my time to.

Sam seemed amazed by me and communicated that when she said, "Gosh, you've got such willpower. I don't know how you'll make it through one song with him singing, let alone a whole set."

"Trust me, he's not all you're both making him out to be," I argued.

"You're right, Demi. He's probably way bigger than what we think," Cal retorted.

He was. I had no doubt he was.

It's just that, well, I couldn't bring myself to admit that out loud.

Instead of arguing the point, I announced, "Well, tonight isn't about him. I mean, I guess it is about his band. But for me, tonight is about being here to support my cousin on what is bound to be one of the biggest nights of his life. And while I'm doing that, I'm going to make sure I tell everyone I know about my best friend's T-shirt business. That's what tonight is about for me."

That was precisely what I was doing right now, and it seemed as though it was what Holland was asking about.

I held up two of Sam's shirts in front of me and asked, "These?"

Holland nodded. "Yeah. Where did you get those?"

I stepped to the side and gestured to the boxes lining the floor. "My best friend, Sam, is dating Cal, who is my cousin and the owner of Granite. Anyway, Sam has been designing T-shirts for years. She has an online store and sells a few shirts every week, but she's not been able to make a full-time gig out of it. Cal and I want to help her get to a point where she could leave her day job and follow her passion. We had been planning to display the shirts next week when a live band came in to play, but now that you and the rest of the band are playing tonight, we figured we'd bump it up a week."

Holland stepped forward, bent down, and pulled out a shirt. She held it up in front of her and allowed her eyes to roam over the design. Her thumbs stroked along the fabric for a few moments. Then she asked, "Would it be alright if I purchased one to wear tonight?"

"Are you serious?"

She nodded.

"That would… that would be amazing," I stammered. Sam was going to lose her mind. "Sam has been working so hard at this, and I just want to see her be successful with it."

"Well, she's obviously very talented because these are awesome," Holland praised the T-shirts.

"Pick out whichever you want."

For the next few minutes, Holland looked through all the shirts, draping a few of them over her arm. Finally, she said, "I'm going to take these four. Just let me know how much they are, and I'll get you money for them before I leave tonight."

I nodded. "Thank you so much, Holland. This is so incredibly kind of you. And wearing it tonight is honestly the icing on the cake."

Before Holland could respond, Cash's voice filled the room and startled me.

"Toss me a shirt, babe," he urged.

I spun around and saw him lifting his shirt over his head.

What was he doing? Why was he getting naked?

It suddenly felt very hot in the room.

I vaguely heard Holland say something about leaving the room to go get her shirt changed, but I couldn't pay much attention let alone respond to her. My eyes were still focused on Cash.

Or, more specifically, Cash's naked torso.

Holy moly.

Why?

This just wasn't fair anymore. How much torture was I supposed to go through?

I'd already turned him down. Did I have to have a constant reminder of what I was giving up?

Though, maybe I didn't need to give it up. Maybe it wouldn't hurt to have a little fun.

What?

"Demi?" Cash called, pulling me out of my ridiculous thoughts.

"Hmm?" I responded, still struggling to pull my eyes from his body.

Just one lick…

A moment later, before I even realized it had happened, Cash was standing inches away from me.

I begrudgingly tore my gaze from his body and tipped my head back. Cash was grinning at me. "Like what you see?" he asked.

That was all I needed to snap me right back to reality.

"Just trying to see what all the fuss is about. Sadly, I can't say I get it," I lied.

I got it. I totally got it.

Damn.

Cash let out a laugh. Seeing that up close was not a good thing for me. He was becoming more… relatable.

I couldn't do this.

"Which shirt did you want?" I asked him.

"Whichever you like best is fine with me," he answered.

That's when I cocked an eyebrow and countered, "Even if I pick out one that's a pale pink color?"

Not the least bit fazed by my attempt to embarrass him, he said, "Even if you pick one out that's pale pink."

Narrowing my eyes on him, I tried to figure out what he was up to. But considering he was standing so close with his shirt off and still smelled so damn good, I couldn't concentrate hard enough on coming up with an answer.

So, I spun around and moved toward the T-shirts.

As much as I might have liked to tell him to take a hike, I wouldn't. This would be huge for Sam, and she deserved every ounce of success with her business.

Sadly, after rummaging through all the pink shirts, I was disappointed there wasn't one available in his size. I decided on another color and said, "Here, you can wear eggplant."

"Eggplant? You mean, purple?"

I shook my head. "No. It's eggplant."

"Right."

"Don't give me an attitude," I ordered. "I could choose the raisin instead."

A strange look washed over Cash's face. "I didn't expect this," he started. "My half-naked body is really doing a number on you. Eggplant. Raisin. We aren't talking about T-shirt colors anymore, are we?"

My eyes widened in disbelief. "What? Yes!"

Of course, now that he'd brought it up, I couldn't think about anything other than one part of his body, which was still covered by his pants, thankfully. I mean, if I was this off balance with Cash's chest and abdomen on display, how would I even function if I saw more of him?

"Are you thinking about me naked again, firecracker?" Cash asked as he pulled the shirt over his head.

"To do it *again* would indicate that I had to do it at least once before. Since that never happened, I'm sorry to say the answer is no," I lied again.

Cash ignored my statement and switched topics. "How do I look?" he asked. "Am I going to do Sam's T-shirt business justice?"

"You look fine," I grumbled.

"Just fine?" he pressed. "Yikes. Maybe I should take the shirt off and try a different one. Perhaps a different color would look better with my skin tone."

He couldn't get naked again. I wouldn't survive.

"No!" I shouted as he started lifting the shirt up and revealing his washboard abs. "No, don't do that. This one looks amazing on you. It really brings out your eyes."

Though I'd just thrown those words out, the minute I said them was the minute I realized they were true. The shirt looked incredible on him, and even though he was already a killer in the looks department, the color of the shirt really did make his eyes stand out.

Cash's lips were twitching as he fought to keep himself from busting out with laughter. He knew precisely what he was doing to me, and he didn't care at all.

"Hey, Demi, I just saw Holland and oh, I didn't realize you were in here Cash."

That came from Cal.

Cash and I both directed our gazes at my cousin, who immediately noticed the shirt Cash was wearing. Cal took it in, shifted his attention to me, and smiled.

"Sam is going to go crazy," he said.

I smiled because it was the truth. "Yeah, she is."

Cal looked Cash in the eye and said, "Thanks, man. I really appreciate what you're doing here tonight. It means a lot."

"You're welcome," Cash replied. "But you should really be thanking Demi. She's the reason I'm doing this."

Cal nodded, gave me one last glance, and walked out of the room.

If I had been thinking clearly, I would have gone after Cal to share the news with Sam. But I wasn't thinking clearly, so I stayed put.

Keeping my eyes focused on the empty space where Cal had just been standing, I asked, "Why are you doing this?"

"Because I like you," Cash answered without a moment of hesitation.

Tearing my gaze away from the empty doorway, I craned my neck to look up at him. "Why?" I pressed.

"For starters, you're beautiful," he began. "Just the thought of your mouth makes me hard. And your body in that dress two nights ago only made thoughts of you more appealing."

"So I'm just nice to look at?" I challenged, trying to ignore the fact that he said my mouth made him hard and he was looking at my mouth at that very moment.

Cash shook his head. "No, but that's the truth about my initial attraction to you," he clarified. "Like I've already told you, you're the first woman who hasn't thrown herself at me. At first, I found it amusing. There aren't a lot of women who can make me laugh, but you do. And now that I've had some time to think on it, I think I want a woman who isn't interested in Cash, the rock star. I want a woman who is interested in Cash, the guy who grew up in a small town and loves his family and friends."

"Are they different?" I asked.

Cash tipped his head to the side as he considered his answer. "The guy on stage is me in the sense that I still have all the same beliefs and morals that I've had all my life. But I am performing." Cash shrugged. "I don't know. I guess over time I've become a version of the two."

For the first time since I met him, Cash seemed more like an everyday guy. In that moment, he wasn't a rock star trying to maintain a persona. He was… real.

I didn't get a chance to respond to him because Beck walked into the room, shifted his attention between the two of us before settling on Cash, and said, "We're up."

"Be right there," Cash replied.

Beck jerked up his chin and returned, "Nice shirt."

"Hey, Beck," Cash called out as he started to walk away.

"Yeah?" he answered, peeking his head back around the doorframe.

Cash looked down at the shirt, over to me, and back to Beck. "You like this shirt, so what do you think about having some T-shirts and swag made up specifically and exclusively for the band that we could sell on tour?"

I could see his mind working a few moments before he said, "I'm cool with it."

"Ask everyone else, and I'll be right there."

Beck dipped his chin. Without another word, he disappeared.

Looking up at him, I asked, "Are you going to ask Sam to make T-shirts for My Violent Heart?"

Cash grinned. "Yep."

Sam was absolutely going to lose her mind. And she'd probably never have to work another day as an event sales director if that was the case.

If I wasn't so stuck on making sure Cash knew that there'd never be anything between us, I might have thrown my arms around him and hugged him. Instead, I urged, "You better get out there."

"Yeah," he agreed. But he didn't move. He just stood there, staring at me, his eyes roaming over my face.

Unable to handle the pressure of his intense stare, I looked away and moved toward the door. When I got there, I stopped, looked back, and said, "Good luck tonight, Cash."

He smiled back at me. "Thanks, Demi."

With that, I walked out and finally managed to get my lungs functioning again.

Before I knew it, I was standing off to the side of the raised platform where My Violent Heart was performing, watching them.

No, that wasn't accurate.

I'd told Sam and Cal earlier that My Violent Heart was one of my favorite bands and that I'd be a fool to miss them just because of Cash. However, now that they were all on stage, I found I could only keep my focus on him.

The sound of his voice moved through me in a way I hadn't ever experienced before. I wanted to blame that on the fact that I was hearing him sing live, but I knew that wasn't it. This was all about him and the sweet, albeit brief, moment we had only minutes ago.

Was this how it started?

Did women become consumed with a man like this and struggle to keep their desires hidden?

When they could no longer resist the temptation, is that when they gave in and risked their hearts?

Deep down, I knew I couldn't take that risk. But as I stood there completely wrapped up in his voice, I wondered how long I'd be able to resist him. Especially if he continued to show me a side to him that I never thought existed.

I never got any answers.

Even following a long set, I hadn't managed to figure out what to do.

I needed to talk to Sam. She'd help me sort myself out.

Unfortunately, when I finally found Sam, she was in the midst of a heated argument with her ex. "You should leave," she said to her ex, Mitch.

Mitch's eyes shifted between Sam and Cal. Eventually, they settled on Cal. "I've got to know, did you at least wait until I was out of the picture before you started fucking my girl, or was she spreading her legs for the both of us at the same time?"

Sam gasped as my mouth dropped open. I shouldn't have been surprised because Mitch was a dick, but for some reason, I hadn't expected that response from him.

The next thing I knew, Cal charged forward and swung his fist at Mitch's jaw. And just as Sam stepped forward, she was stopped.

Cash had come up behind her and held her back. "Let him handle this," he told her.

There was a fight happening right before my eyes, and yet, I could only focus on Cash. Just like that, he stepped up to hold Sam back and prevent her from getting hurt.

It wasn't until Cal spoke again that I returned my attention to the commotion before me.

"She's not your girl anymore, dickface," Cal seethed. "You had her, and you lost her. Now you're realizing the colossal mistake you made because there's nobody like Sam. *Nobody.* Then again, you never appreciated her for everything that she is. So, I'm sorry, man. You need to go. You should have put the effort in while you had her. You're too late now. She's with me, and I'll never let her go."

"Fuck you," Mitch spat. He struggled against Cal's hold and looked at Sam. "Sam, we need to talk."

"I have nothing to say to you."

"Is this what you want?" he asked, a look of disgust on his face. "Some guy that owns a bar that'll never be able to take care of you?"

This guy thought he was something special. He was crazy.

Surprisingly calm about it, Sam declared, "Cal takes care of me better than you ever did. He took better care of me than you did when I was with you. He's *always* taken care of me in all the ways that matter."

My turn. I hated this guy, and I wanted him to know how much of a douchebag he was.

"Money isn't always the way you take care of people, asshole," I started. "Sam's the happiest she's ever been in her life now that she's with Cal. Even if things didn't work out with them, you wouldn't stand a chance with her again. She knows what it's like to be loved by a real man."

Mitch looked at me like I was speaking a foreign language. He didn't respond to me, but he took in my words because he looked at Sam and said, "Love? He loves you so much, and yet, he's okay with you continuing to work your shitty job."

"Sam's actually leaving her job," I shared.

I felt Sam's gaze on me, but I didn't look at her. This wasn't how I wanted her to find out.

Cash loosened his hold on Sam, stepped out from behind her, and explained, "I told Demi we want you to design a bunch of gear for the band for us to sell at our shows on tour."

Sam was in a state of utter disbelief.

Looking down at the T-shirt he was wearing, Cash assessed it. Then he brought his attention back to Sam and said, "This shirt kicks ass."

If things hadn't been so intense between Cash and me from the start, I might have used that moment to launch myself into his arms and kiss him senseless. He'd already made my best friend's whole year by wearing her shirt on stage and asking her to design gear for the band to sell on tour, and it still wasn't enough. He went that extra step and told her that her shirt—the one I'd picked out for him—kicked ass.

Sam let Cash's words sink in before returning her attention to Mitch. She started speaking to him, but I couldn't pay attention to what was happening beyond that. My eyes were still on Cash. He glanced over at me, and for some reason I couldn't say what I wanted to say to him.

Despite my silence, his features softened, and the expression on his face was enough to make me think, even if only for a moment, that perhaps he wasn't nearly as awful as I had originally made him out to be.

He held my gaze a moment longer before redirecting his focus on Sam and Cal. Mitch, it seemed, had left. Once again, I didn't pay attention to what was being discussed because I was too distracted by all the unexpected actions from Cash.

He'd shown me a side of him that I didn't know existed again, and I just didn't know how to react or respond to it.

Eventually, Cash concluded his discussion with my best friends and turned toward me. He held my eyes briefly before he smiled and walked back toward the stage to play another set. My eyes followed him the whole way there.

And I wasn't too proud to admit to myself that I felt a longing unlike I'd ever felt before.

This was a disaster, and I had no idea what I was going to do about it.

CHAPTER 7

Demi

MY HEAD WAS POUNDING.

As much as I wanted to blame it on the loud music from last night's live performance by My Violent Heart, I had to be honest with myself.

I had a headache because I didn't sleep well, and it had nothing to do with the music being too loud.

For the better part of the night, I tossed and turned in my bed, struggling to settle down and get comfortable. The truth was, I hadn't been able to get everything that had happened at Granite out of my mind.

Obviously, My Violent Heart's performance last night had been huge. It was such a big deal for Cal and the bar. Sam made out well, too. Not only that, the bar patrons also had the time of their lives.

It seemed I was the only one who hadn't benefited from the evening.

And that was all Cash's fault.

Okay, that might have been a slight exaggeration. I did

thoroughly enjoy the actual performance. Being able to see one of my favorite bands ever playing live in front of me was beyond my wildest dreams. I had no reason to complain about that. I was up close and personal. And I'd technically met Holland, which totally made my night.

But that's where it stopped for me.

Because not only had there been so much that happened with Cash prior to the band's first set of the night along with what happened when Sam's ex showed up, but there was also more I had encountered with him when the show ended.

Instead of me just being a witness to Cash in a situation that was unrelated to anything pertaining to me directly, I had another face-to-face encounter.

And that chance meeting had been the biggest part of why I couldn't seem to find sleep.

Following My Violent Heart's performance, there was still a large crowd. The band interacted with a lot of the patrons, and I was happy to see that our little corner of the world got the attention it did.

It was nice to know that Cash and his bandmates didn't just walk off. They loved their fans, something that was obvious long before they played at Granite. In fact, when it came to a couple of the guys in the band—namely Cash, Killian, and Roscoe—it might not have been a far stretch to say they loved their fans a little too much.

Of course, that wasn't to say that Holland, Beck, and Walker didn't love their fans. They did. They just didn't have all the same antics that the other three did when it came to the groupies.

As the crowds started to thin out and the rest of the employees at Granite started winding things down for the night, I decided to do my part and chip in. Unfortunately, that meant that I ended up in the same room I'd been in earlier in the evening with Cash. And I hadn't been in there for more than a few minutes when he found me.

"Hey, oh..." he trailed off as he entered the room.

I had been bent over, my ass to him, rummaging through the T-shirt boxes. Apparently, a bunch of Sam's shirts had been sold, so I was trying to condense everything down to fewer boxes.

When I stood and turned around, I watched as Cash's eyes has shifted from my waist up to my face. Clearly, he'd been checking out my ass.

Typical.

"So, what did you think?" he asked.

"About what?"

Cash shot me a look of disbelief. "The performance," he replied.

"Oh, it was great," I told him. "It was my first live My Violent Heart show, and it definitely exceeded my expectations. You guys are amazing."

"Thanks," he returned. His eyes shifted to the empty boxes of T-shirts. "Looks like a lot of shirts sold."

"They did."

"Holland went and found Sam to pay her for them directly, but I told her I'd find you and let you know we weren't just walking off with them," he explained.

I let out a small laugh. "I didn't think either of you were going to do that," I assured him. "Though, even if you had, I get the feeling Sam is still going to sell a lot more of these shirts now. Thank you, by the way."

Cash tipped his head to the side. "For what?"

"For what you did for her," I clarified. "Not only offering her the opportunity to create some stuff for your band, but also for doing it in front of her ex-boyfriend. He's a dick."

"I got that much," he said. "But I think I should be honest with you."

I knit my brows together, feeling confused. "What did you lie to me about?" I asked him.

Shaking his head, Cash answered, "I didn't lie. I just want you to know that the reason I offered Sam that opportunity was for you."

"Me?"

Cash shrugged. "I heard you talking to Holland earlier tonight before the show," he started. "You were so excited for Sam and wanted to see her succeed. I wanted to see you happy and excited like that again."

He wasn't serious. He had to be playing me.

"Why do I get the feeling you're feeding me a bunch of lines?" I asked.

"I don't know. Seems like you're a little wary of me," he suggested. "But I'm telling you the truth. I liked seeing the look on your face when Holland asked if she could wear one of the shirts tonight. Why do you think I took off my shirt and asked you to pick one out for me?"

I cocked an eyebrow. "Because you want me to give you my number, and since I have continued to turn you down, you thought I'd cave if I saw you half naked," I guessed.

Cash chuckled. "Okay, so maybe that was part of it, too. Did it work?" he asked.

"No."

"Damn," he hissed. "I would have thought between that

and my nice gestures to help out your best friend that you'd at least see that I'm not a bad guy."

Whoa. Whoa. Whoa.

"Hold up a minute," I ordered. "I never said that."

"What? You never said what?"

"I never said you were a bad guy," I remarked.

"You could have fooled me," he scoffed.

Obviously, this had gotten to a point where he was mistaking my unwillingness to bow to his whim as me thinking he was an awful person. Just because there were things that I refused to accept didn't mean that I thought all men were bad people.

I felt compelled to clarify my position.

"Cash, you're a phenomenal singer, and I'm sure you're a decent guy," I began. "You showed me that tonight with what you did for Sam and even the way you are with your fans. But I know I'm not wrong when I say that you'd be a horrible lover."

Shock and disbelief washed over him. Cash's look of horror lasted a matter of seconds before he grinned at me. "I can promise you that is *not* the case, firecracker," he said, his tone low and seductive.

What?

It took me a moment to figure out why he was acting like that, and that's when I realized he completely misunderstood what I was trying to say.

"No, no. That's not what I meant," I replied, feeling horrified that I had implied he was bad in bed. "What I meant is that I'm not interested in a one-night stand with you. I did not mean to imply that you were bad at the actual… thing.

I have no doubt that you're just as great at that as you are at singing."

Cash's lips twitched, and I suddenly started thinking I wasn't making this situation any better for myself.

"So, what you're telling me is that you've considered what it'd be like for you and me to do the actual… *thing?*" he asked, taking slow, deliberate steps toward me.

Shit.

This was not what I had intended.

I mean, I had thought about what it would be like to be with Cash. I might not have liked his ways, but I wasn't blind. The man was breathtaking. And his voice alone could do things to me that nobody's voice should ever be able to do to anyone. So, I had considered what it would be like.

But I was not going to tell him that.

"Absolutely not," I lied.

The corners of his mouth tipped up. "I think you're lying."

"I don't care," I retorted as I stepped back away from him.

Unfortunately, in my haste to get away from him, I forgot about the T-shirt boxes behind me. I stumbled backward and started to feel myself fall, but at the last second, Cash caught me and hauled me up against his body.

"Are you okay?" he asked.

Cash's arms were wrapped firmly around my body, the scent of him was invading my nostrils, and his body felt like heaven against mine. My chest was rapidly rising and falling, and it felt like that was the only movement I was capable of at that moment.

Cash held on just a bit longer, and when he confirmed I was steady on my feet, he loosened his hold.

I was grateful for it at the same time I hated it.

"Thank you," I rasped.

"You're welcome, Demi," he returned.

This was too much. I needed to clear my head after that encounter with him.

"I should probably get back to work," I told him, pointing to the boxes behind me.

"I thought you didn't officially start until Monday," he noted.

Shit.

I had said that.

"Yeah, but I couldn't let Sam and Cal do this alone tonight," I said.

I didn't know whether Cash believed me or not, but he never called me out on it. Letting it go, he finally declared, "Well, then I guess if you don't need my help, I'll get out of your hair."

Shaking my head, I insisted, "I'll be fine."

"It was nice to see you again," Cash remarked before moving back toward the door.

Each step he took away from me filled me with such longing. I couldn't begin to understand what was going on with me. One minute I was backing up trying to get away from him, and the next minute I felt myself wishing he would stay.

Maybe that was it.

Deep down, even if I wanted to believe he was a good guy, Cash would never stay.

And that was something I couldn't handle.

Stopping at the door, he looked back at me. "Good night, firecracker."

I don't know why he kept calling me that, but I knew I liked it a lot. I just wondered how many other women he had a nickname for.

"Good night, Cash."

With that, he walked out.

And now I was here at my place with a massive headache because I hadn't been able to sleep. I was up all night thinking about him.

With all the drama of Mitch showing up at Granite last night, I hadn't had a chance to speak with Sam. I decided now would be the best time. Maybe I could find some clarity in a conversation with her.

I picked up my phone, found her name, and tapped on the screen.

Three rings later, Sam answered, "Hey, Demi. How's it going?"

"Miserable," I mumbled.

She let out a laugh. "Why does that not surprise me?" she asked.

"You know me too well."

"Did something happen?" she questioned me. I couldn't miss the tone of her voice. She was oddly curious. It was almost as though she had already anticipated what I was going to say. Even still, she waited for me to respond.

"I didn't sleep well last night," I told her.

"Oh?" she replied. At that, I could hear hope and excitement in her tone. Sam was definitely heading in the wrong direction with this.

I took several seconds to think about how to share what

I was feeling, and I struggled to come up with a way that felt right. So, I blurted, "Cash Morris is making me lose sleep. If I didn't like him before, I definitely don't like him now."

"But is he making you lose sleep in a good way?" she countered.

"There isn't any way that I would consider good," I told her.

"You know what I'm talking about," she said.

I did. I knew all too well exactly what she was referring to. The issue was, I had spent the better part of the night thinking about that, so the last thing I needed was more reminders.

"I've never felt so confused in all my life," I admitted.

Sam hesitated briefly before she replied, "I think that's the best news I could hope to hear from you."

"I'm confused, and you think it's a good thing?"

Soft laughter came through the line. "In this situation, absolutely," she confirmed. "It tells me that perhaps you haven't completely given up on the possibility of allowing yourself to find some happiness."

Even if I wanted to believe that I could one day find some happiness in a romantic relationship, which was already a far stretch, believing that I could find that with Cash was simply naïve.

I'd be such a fool.

He'd chew me up and spit me out.

And I'd be far worse off than I already was.

"I don't understand why I can't do it," I declared.

"Do what?" Sam asked.

"Treat Cash like the rest," I clarified. "I mean, it's not like I've had loads of partners or anything, but I have taken care of business when I have the urge. Why can't I do that with him? Just fuck him out of my system and move on. Isn't that what he does? I could beat him at his own game and get myself a few orgasms in the process."

"I'm pretty sure it's because you told me not that long ago that Cash Morris isn't the kind of man that a woman would only want to have sex with once," Sam answered. "You said that he was the kind of man that a woman hopes she'll be able to change, that she'll be the one he wants to stop and settle down with."

Right.

She was exactly right.

I had said that to her one day when I was still working at the hotel. Hearing it again, I realized it was the truth.

That was the reason why I couldn't bring myself to give him any more of me than my crappy attitude. If I softened even a little bit, I had no doubt I would regret it.

When I took too long to respond, Sam added, "You know, it's okay to want that. And it's okay to want it with him."

"Wanting it and actually believing it could happen are two different things," I reminded her. "I can't take that risk… not with someone like him. He'd be so uninterested so fast once he got what he wanted."

"Maybe he won't," she argued. "Honestly, I think you should just give him your number. In fact, I was so close to doing it myself on Thursday when I was leaving work."

"What?"

Sam gasped. There was a long pause before she whispered, "I have a confession to make."

"What?" I asked, already not liking where this conversation was headed.

"I might have been the one to tell Cash that you'd be at Granite on Thursday night," she shared.

I didn't respond.

Sam did this.

Why would Sam tell him that?

"I'm really sorry, Demi," she apologized. "I just… I just really think that you deserve to be happy. Cash could have gone anywhere for this break his band is on right now, but he chose to come back here for you. I'm sorry, but I think that's got to count for something."

She had a point.

If nothing else, Cash had proven to be persistent. But even if that's what he was being right now, I didn't know if I could trust that it was genuine. To me, he could have just been very determined to win this game. And if that were the case, I stood to lose a whole lot more than he did.

"Maybe it should," I reasoned. "But I don't think I can risk this. I'm so confused, Sam."

"You're confused because you want this," she insisted. "I don't think there'd be any harm in giving him your number."

"He's going to be leaving," I pointed out.

Sam didn't hesitate to respond, "Exactly. That's all the more reason to give it to him. Maybe you can try something different for once. Perhaps it would be good for you to get to know him better. Honestly, it's a way better idea than what you had planned."

"What did I have planned?" I asked, unsure of what she was referring to. When it came to Cash, I didn't have any plans.

"You were considering fucking him out of your system," she reminded me.

If only it were that simple.

"That was an empty threat. I never would have followed through with it."

"Think about it, Demi," Sam begged. "The phone number, that is. I really think you should consider it seriously."

I went on to tell Sam about what happened last night both before and after My Violent Heart's performance. I don't know why, but I was hoping that once she heard about everything that went down between Cash and me, she'd have different advice.

But this was Sam.

The same Sam who apparently decided to tell Cash where he could find me.

So, I shouldn't have been surprised when she urged, "Give him your number, and get to know him better. The worst possible thing that could happen is that you realize you're not romantically compatible. But if you don't give it to him, the worst possible thing that can happen is that you spend the rest of your life wondering if you made a huge mistake. Avoid making that mistake, Demi. You'll never forgive yourself. Trust me."

She paused a moment to let that sink in. When she'd given it enough time, she continued, "You've never experienced this much emotional turmoil over a guy. That should tell you something."

There was that, too.

Maybe I was creating more stress and worry by sticking to my guns.

"Maybe you're right," I murmured.

"I am."

That was that. There was nothing left to discuss regarding Cash, so I decided to switch topics.

"I can't believe Mitch showed his face at Granite last night," I told her.

"Tell me about it," she groaned.

Just like that, Sam and I had moved on from our discussion of Cash. If there was one thing we both saw eye to eye on, it was how much we despised Mitch.

Quite frankly, I was grateful for the distraction.

By the time I ended my call with Sam, I couldn't say I had everything figured out, but my headache had gone away, so I called it a win.

And in the end, I realized that perhaps I was stressing over something I didn't need to stress about. Maybe I'd never see Cash in the flesh again.

CHAPTER 8

Cash

"ANY LUCK?"

I looked up from the bacon cheeseburger and fries on the plate in front of me and brought my attention to Walker.

I was sitting with him and Killian in a diner in New Hampshire. It was late Sunday night, well after dinner, and the three of us decided we needed to get out for a bit.

We'd all gotten back to the hotel late last night, and slept in this morning. Everyone had kind of done their own thing throughout the day, though I'd talked a bit with some of them.

At the question Walker asked, it was no surprise I didn't need any additional explanation as to what he was referring to.

He was asking me about the progress I'd made with Demi. Or, maybe it was the lack of progress with her.

This was proving to be a painstakingly slow process

I sighed and answered, "Not as much as I'd like it to be, but there's been some progress."

"How so?" he asked as he lifted his fork to his mouth. He'd settled on a veggie omelet with a side of hash browns for his meal.

"Well, she didn't seemed repulsed by the sight of me *all* night last night," I shared after taking a sip of my milkshake. "We even had a civil conversation or two."

I plucked a fry off my plate, dipped it into some ketchup, and popped it into my mouth as I thought back to the good moments I had with Demi last night. It was nice, for once, to not feel so much animosity between us. It was even better to feel her body against mine, even if it had only been brief because I was trying to stop her from falling.

"You only have a few days left," Walker reminded me. "Are you planning to do something to speed up the progress?"

Nodding, I confirmed, "I'm going to go back to Granite tomorrow."

"And you think that's going to work?" he questioned me, his eyes wide. "Do you really think she's going to like having you just show up there? Didn't you say that this was going to be her first day working at a new job? How well do you think that's going to go over?"

I could understand his shock. I probably would have reacted the same if I saw him or any of my bandmates in a similar situation. The thing was, I hadn't let them in on my plan just yet. Unfortunately, this was where I was going to need to get their help again, and I only hoped I could get them to agree once more.

"Well..." I trailed off, wondering how to best approach the subject. I wasn't sure there was a right or wrong way to share it, but I figured I'd go with nostalgia. It'd be my best chance at making this sound appealing. "So, I was thinking about how everything went down last night. I feel like we've become so accustomed to playing sold-out shows at massive venues or huge arenas. Granite was a completely different vibe for us."

"I'm with you on that," Killian chimed in, after taking a sip of his drink before returning to his California chicken club sandwich. "It was awesome having that intimate setting again. It kind of reminded me of the old days before we got so big."

Yep. Nostalgia was definitely the way to go.

Walker and I both nodded our agreement. There was no doubt about it. Last night had been great for all of us. Throughout the day today, I'd talked to Beck, Roscoe, and Holland. They had all felt the same.

"Alright, so how does any of that pertain to you getting on Demi's good side?" Walker asked, cutting to the chase. It wasn't unlike him to find a way to get us back on track. He did the same when it came to making new music, too.

I had just sunk my teeth into my burger. But after I had chewed, swallowed, and taken another sip of my milkshake, I answered, "It doesn't have anything to do with me getting on her good side. I'm just going to use it as my excuse to visit her at work tomorrow."

"You're going to offer to have the band play at Granite again, aren't you?" Killian asked, lifting a triangle of his sandwich in his hand for another bite.

Sitting up straighter, leaning against the back of the booth, I said, "That was my hope. I know I need to talk to everyone else, but what do you guys think? Would you be up for another performance here in New Hampshire after we finish the tour?"

"I'm down," Walker immediately responded.

I had a feeling he would be an easy sell. He was laid back and rarely turned down an opportunity to play.

My eyes shifted to Killian. "I'm down, but don't you think it's a bit much?" he asked.

"What do you mean?" I retorted. "One more show is not going to send us over the edge."

Killian shook his head. "That's not what I meant," he said.

"Then what are you talking about?" I questioned him.

He shrugged as he sat back. "I don't know. I just don't see what the outcome is going to be here," he started. "I mean, don't you think you've gotten in way over your head with this whole situation? Is this woman really worth all this hassle?"

I had to tamp down the immediate and overwhelming anger I felt at Killian's questions.

On the one hand, I wanted to knock him out for indicating that Demi wasn't worth this, but on the other hand, I had to wonder if he had a point. I didn't know Demi all that well just yet to make any determination about her being worth it, but I knew I couldn't deny the way she made me feel.

"I think so," I answered him honestly.

What else could I say? There was no guarantee about her; however, I liked to think that the intense attraction and inability to think about anyone else but her meant she was worth the effort I was prepared to put in to get her.

"It seems to me that it'd just be better to move on to the next woman," he reasoned. "At least if you did that, you could hook up with someone who is actually interested in you."

That's where he was wrong, and I felt compelled to set the record straight.

"The biggest problem with that is that I'm not interested in anyone but her right now," I began. "The other thing is, Demi is interested."

That was a fact. I could tell by the way she looked at me. There was no way she, or anyone else, could deny the attraction we both had to one another. Maybe she liked to pretend she wasn't interested, or maybe she liked playing hard to get. I didn't know. But I knew what her eyes told me, what the changes in her voice revealed when she spoke to me, and how her body melted briefly against mine last night.

"It's interesting you say that, Cash, because from what we've all seen or heard, Demi hates your guts," Killian declared.

I let out a laugh. It would have certainly seemed that way on the surface considering Demi had no issue going toe to toe with me. That was the other thing. The woman made me laugh. If that wasn't another reason for me to believe she was worth the effort I was putting in, I didn't know what would be.

"Demi just hates who she thinks I am," I insisted, brushing off his assessment of the situation.

I watched as confusion washed over not only Killian's face but Walker's as well.

When they said nothing in response, I set down my burger and explained, "She doesn't know me well enough to make that determination. She only knows what she has seen from interviews I've done or reports online. None of that means anything. Until she's talked to me and gotten a chance to know me, she can't possibly hate me."

Having finished his sandwich, Killian threw his hands up in the air in surrender and declared, "Look, I'm not going to tell you what to do. You do what you want and what you think is best. But if you want my advice, I just think you're wasting your time. If it were me, I'd walk away. Life's too short to fight for someone who really isn't showing much interest and continues to turn you down."

That was about what I expected from Killian. He preferred not to deal with bullshit. I'd known that about him from the time we used to practice in my parents' garage when we were all kids. He'd proven it to Walker when he'd walked up one summer day and told us we needed a drummer. That was just who Killian was, so anything that felt like a waste of time to him wasn't something he'd give a second thought to.

"I disagree," Walker chimed in. "If you really do feel strongly for Demi and believe she's worth it, I don't think you should give up. And if us coming back here and playing another show at Granite helps make that happen for you, you can count on me."

I should have anticipated that response from Walker, too.

It was almost a good thing I'd come out with Killian and Walker. They were so vastly different when it came to a situation like this. Then again, none of us had ever really been in a situation like this before, so I couldn't say for sure. But the truth was that we'd been around each other enough over the years we'd been in this band. We know how everyone in the group worked.

When it came to women and sex, Killian rarely turned down a willing participant. He was living the life. For the most part, I'd been the same until I met Demi.

Walker wasn't like us in that sense. In fact, while he joined us for a night out and partied with us whenever something was happening, he didn't hop from one woman to the next. Come to think of it, I couldn't recall ever seeing him with a woman. Not in a serious relationship and not even making out in a bar.

Then again, thinking about everyone else in the band, the same could have been said about Holland. She and Walker always seemed to be all about the music. They enjoyed a night out just as much as the rest of us, but they never let it get out of hand.

Don't get me wrong. They adored our fans and appreciated them as we all did. It was just that they showed that appreciation in the form of words of thanks, autographs, and pictures. They didn't ever cross that line with the fans. When it really came down to it, Holland and Walker were focused on their careers.

Or, so it seemed.

Now that it was hitting me, I realized I hadn't ever considered that whole scenario before. Unfortunately, I wasn't going to sit around pondering what it all meant right now either. I had my own shit to worry about.

"Well, I appreciate the support from both of you," I started. Then I directed my attention to Killian and continued, "Even if you don't agree. Now, I just have to hope I can talk the rest of the crew into coming back here for a third time."

"They will," Walker insisted. "At least, I know Holland is rooting for you. That's why she orchestrated the whole T-shirt deal. And even though he won't admit to it, Beck would probably love to come back and see how that single mom is doing, assuming he can find her. Roscoe is the only one who is really going to need some convincing, and the truth is, if you just make sure there's a good time waiting for him, he's not going to say no."

I couldn't stop myself from grinning. Everything Walker had just said was the truth. Holland was supportive from the beginning, and Beck was still caught up in Chasey—even though he denied it. Roscoe just wanted to have fun; he didn't care where it happened.

"You're right," I replied, feeling a bit of relief. "Now all I need to do is go in there tomorrow and see if I can get us on their schedule. I know we've got people who handle that for us, but I think I'm going to take the reins on this one since I've already got an in with the girl in charge."

Killian scoffed, "I don't know if I'd say you've got an in with her, but I don't think anyone is going to fight you on taking the lead here either."

"Oh, I've got an in," I announced. "Give me some time, and it's going to be a whole lot more than that."

Killian rolled his eyes at me. Walker shot me a look of approval.

With that, the conversation surrounding Demi shifted into talk about the rest of our tour as we finished up our food. We had fifteen more weeks of shows, and it was a pretty tight schedule. I wouldn't have the opportunity to come back here until it was over. That meant I had to make sure I got Demi's number.

I didn't think I'd be able to manage not seeing her or hearing her voice for that long.

The guys and I finished up, paid our bill, and made our way back to the hotel.

When I got into bed that night, I couldn't stop my thoughts from drifting to Demi, which was where they'd been for days.

I needed her to soften just a touch more. If I could manage that, I could get her number. And if I got that, there might be some hope for something more than just banter between us.

As much as I loved her sassy mouth and witty remarks, I wanted more. I wanted to keep that and get more of the sweetness I'd gotten from her after our show at Granite.

After I realized she had that soft side to her, it became clear that she was the whole package. So, even though I knew it wasn't going to be easy, I believed it was going to be worth it.

I might not have gotten lucky enough to convince her to give me a shot. It might take some time, but I had to keep trying.

The promise of all that she was… I would have been a fool to give up now.

CHAPTER 9

Demi

A KNOCK CAME AT THE DOOR.

I looked up from the computer in front of me and saw Cal standing in the doorway. I was in the back office at Granite, and today was my first official day at my new job.

I was excited to be here and thrilled to finally be out of my old job.

It was late afternoon, and I'd already put in quite a few hours of work today. I had quickly learned that a lot of what I needed to do for this position did not require me to be here in the physical sense. Obviously, whenever a live performance was scheduled, I'd be here at Granite in the thick of it, but the brunt of the work I was doing could have been done from home.

Cal wouldn't care, and I'd eventually talk to him about making that change. But for now, I was simply grateful to be anywhere that wasn't the hotel.

"This is your bar, Cal," I greeted my cousin. "You don't need to knock to enter rooms in your own building."

"I'm being professional," he told me.

"Yeah, yeah," I returned. "So, what's going on?"

"Well, we just had someone walk in looking to play here, so I wanted to make sure you were free to meet now," he explained.

Wow.

This was fantastic news.

The truth was, when My Violent Heart played here on Saturday, it put Granite on the map. People from other bands or solo artists wanted to come and play here as well. We weren't some huge arena, and the fact that such a huge name in the music industry had played here meant that others wanted to as well. And it blew my mind that we were already seeing this response.

"Sure," I replied. "This is honestly incredible."

Cal smiled, nodded, and said, "Great. I'll send him down."

"Perfect."

My cousin walked away, and I spent the few minutes feeling excited about what was happening. There could not have been a better way to start my new job.

A moment later, my mood went to shit.

"What are you doing here?" I asked, my tone clearly indicating my annoyance.

Not the least bit fazed by my irritation, Cash walked into the room and moved toward me as he declared, "And there she is."

"What is that supposed to mean?" I questioned him.

Making himself comfortable, Cash settled himself in the

chair on the opposite side of the desk and explained, "The girl from the hotel is back. You know, the one who claims to despise me. I thought she was gone or, at the very least, softening a bit toward me when I was here on Saturday. I can't tell you how happy I am to know the spicy side of you is back."

I cocked an eyebrow. "Spicy?" I repeated.

Cash nodded, but he didn't offer any additional clarification.

"Look, I don't know what you're expecting or hoping for here, but I'm at work," I began. "You can't just keep showing up everywhere I work expecting to monopolize my time."

"Oh, well, I mean, I'm more than happy to meet up with you once you're finished with work," he offered. "What time are you off?"

Crap. I should have thought that one through.

"Never," I immediately replied.

"Ouch. You're brutal," he said.

I let out a deep sigh. "What do you want me to say, Cash?" I retorted. "Cal might be my cousin, but I'm not going to take advantage of that. I'm at work."

"But that's a good thing, Demi," he assured me. "Because I'm here on official My Violent Heart business."

"Oh? And what's that?" I asked.

Cash sat back in the chair, crossed his ankle over his opposite knee, and shared, "We want to play here again."

My brows shot up in response. "You do?"

He dipped his chin. "Yep."

"But… but we're just a small—"

"That's what we like about this place," Cash cut me off. "I've already talked to everyone in the band, and they're all down for it."

Wow.

Wow.

This was *huge* for Cal, for his employees, and for Granite. Plus, I had no doubt the locals would love to know that this band was going to be back.

"When would you be looking to do this?" I asked.

"Once the tour is over," he said. "We've got another fifteen weeks or so of touring, but this will be a great way to close it out."

Fifteen weeks.

Fifteen whole weeks before he'd be back.

Maybe I'd given Cash a hard time about being in my space, but at that moment I realized how much I would miss it.

And that made absolutely zero sense to me.

"So, where does that put us?" I asked.

"Us? Like you and me?" he returned.

Shaking my head, I clarified, "I meant for time. When would you be back here?"

The corner of Cash's mouth tipped up. "Are you asking for scheduling purposes for this performance, or are you asking for yourself? Because I'll be honest, if you want me to come back again sooner for you, I'll do it."

Why?

Why was he doing this to me?

I'd resolved myself to the fact that I'd likely never see him in the flesh again, and for some reason, he just kept popping up.

How was I supposed to forget he existed and move on when every time he was around me I felt as though the fortress I'd put up around me was crumbling?

"Sorry, I was asking for scheduling purposes," I told him.

"Right," he mumbled. "We play the last of our shows the last week of October, so it would need to be any time after that. We could do as early as the first week of November."

It was only the middle of July now.

I held Cash's gaze as I allowed that information to penetrate. November seemed like a lifetime away.

For a long time, I didn't respond.

Fifteen weeks of him being on tour. Fifteen weeks of him singing for other women. Fifteen weeks of not seeing him smile at me. Months without being able to have his scent invade my nostrils.

Why did I even care?

"Demi?" Cash called, interrupting my thoughts.

"Yeah?" I replied.

"Is everything okay?" he asked.

Cash's face was filled with what looked like genuine concern. I didn't know he had it in him to look at me like that.

Quickly, I did my best to recover. "Yeah. I... I'm fine," I insisted. "And the beginning of November will work perfectly. We're not booking anything that far out, so it's all yours if you want it."

Cash's foot went to the floor again and leaned forward, pressing his elbows into his thighs. "I definitely want it," he said, the tone of his voice conveying so much more than the words.

I ignored the way that made me feel and looked away. "Perfect. I'll get you guys on the schedule, and then once it gets closer, it'll probably be a good idea to touch base."

"So, you'll be giving me your number then?" he asked.

"Don't you have someone who is going to take care of the logistics of this for you?" I retorted.

Nodding, Cash confirmed, "Normally, we do. But this is something we decided to add on, and I already told them I'd handle this. So, I'm your point of contact on this one, firecracker."

Great.

Just what I needed… more contact with Cash that would leave me feeling confused and frustrated.

Well, it was time to make him feel just as frustrated.

"Fine. So, you'll be able to reach me via email here," I began. "For now, I'm working here in the bar, but it's likely I'm going to transition out and work from home. Obviously, my intention is to be here for the live performances we book to make sure everything is running smoothly, but I can do most of what is necessary via email."

Cash's lips twitched.

I wanted to kiss him.

Damn it, Demi. Pull yourself together, I thought.

"I can do email," he said, not seeming the least bit upset that I was doing my best to make it inconvenient for him.

"Great. Did you have any other questions?" I asked.

"Just one."

"Which is?"

"Would you join me for breakfast tomorrow morning?" he asked.

"I'm sorry. What?"

"Breakfast. You know, the meal you eat in the morning when you wake up," he clarified.

My eyes narrowed on him. "I know what breakfast is," I assured him.

"Okay. So, will you have breakfast with me tomorrow morning before I have to leave?" he pressed.

"Why?"

"Because I'd like to see you one more time before I go back on tour," he answered.

He wanted to see me one more time before he went back on tour. I didn't know what he was up to, but I didn't think it was wise to entertain his request.

"Cash, I—"

"It's just breakfast," he said, cutting me off. "As tempting as it would be, it's not like I'm going to kidnap you and take you on tour with me."

"I don't know," I murmured.

Cash shot me a look of disbelief. "Please," he pleaded. "Just breakfast before I have to go without seeing your beautiful face for nearly four months."

My heart pounded in my chest as my lips parted. He sounded like he was in anguish.

Could I do this?

It was just breakfast.

Breakfast before he took off for months.

"Okay. We can do breakfast tomorrow morning," I agreed.

"Really?"

I nodded.

"Are you going to let me pick you up?" he asked.

I shook my head. "I'll meet you. Eight o'clock in the morning at the Finch Café."

Instantly, Cash stood up and moved to the door. Stunned by his response, I called, "Cash?"

He stopped at the door and turned toward me. "Yeah?"

"What is the matter?"

"Eight o'clock at the Finch Café," he replied. "I'm leaving before you have the chance to change your mind. And I've decided I'll give you my number the moment you meet me there."

Wow.

He really wanted to have breakfast with me, and it was clear he didn't trust that I wouldn't try to find a way to back out. That was presumably why he was going to make me wait until tomorrow to get his number. He was convinced I'd call and cancel.

Feeling a bit bad, I decided not to give him any more reason not to trust me. If there was one thing that could be said about the woman I was, it was that I followed through on my promises. So, my voice dipped low, nearly to a whisper, and I said, "I'll see you tomorrow, Cash."

"Tomorrow," he repeated. "And Demi?"

"Yeah?"

"Thanks for giving me a chance," he said.

Before I could respond, he turned and walked out.

I sat there, staring at the space where he'd been standing for a long time after he left.

I was going to be having breakfast with Cash Morris tomorrow. Maybe I showed him I was uninterested and didn't care what he did. But the somersaults happening inside my belly told me that what he said was true.

I'd been lying to myself this whole time.

Cash

"Back so soon?"

That came from Killian.

"That can't mean good things," Beck declared.

I'd just walked into my hotel suite I was sharing with Roscoe. Killian and Beck were both there.

"I know it might seem that way," I started. "But I'm not sure things could be any better than they are right now."

"This ought to be good," Roscoe said. "What happened?"

I walked over to the mini-fridge, pulled out a beer, and sat down on the couch with a grin on my face. After taking a pull of my beer, I announced, "I've got a date tomorrow morning."

"She agreed to that?" Killian asked.

I nodded proudly.

"It was only a matter of time," I reasoned. "It pays to be patient."

"How did you manage that?" Beck questioned me. "I thought she wanted nothing to do with you."

"It's my charm," I reasoned. "It was bound to wear her down eventually."

"Yeah, right," Roscoe scoffed. "She probably just agreed to it so you'd leave her alone."

I shrugged. That might have been the case, but I didn't care. I finally had a date with Demi. I'd wanted her number all this time. Instead of asking for that, I should have asked her out during my first trip here weeks ago.

Granted, I hated that I was going to have that date with her tomorrow only to have to leave hours afterward. But

I was going to take the good that I could get and hope I'd be able to convince her to see me just a little bit differently than she did.

"I guess we'll see what happens tomorrow," I said. "For now, I'm soaking this feeling up."

"On the bright side, at least this trip wasn't a complete waste of time," Beck muttered.

"No luck with Chasey?" I asked.

He shook his head. Beck had been trying to locate the woman he'd met weeks ago. Despite the fact that he'd been convinced she'd reach out to him, she hadn't. This was a small town. He came here hoping he'd run into her somewhere. Unfortunately, it seemed that wasn't happening.

"Sorry, man."

"It's not a big deal," he brushed it off. I could tell he didn't mean it. This was a very big deal to him. "I only wanted to check in on her and make sure she was doing okay. It is what it is."

Not wanting to make him feel worse than I was sure he was already feeling, I decided to change topics.

"We should go out tonight," I declared.

"What?"

"This is essentially the last night we've got before we start traveling again. It'll be a nice way to end the break."

"Works for me," Roscoe said.

"Me too," Killian added.

My eyes slid to Beck. "It's not like I have any other plans," he noted.

I nodded my head. "Great. Where's Walker and Holland?" I asked.

"No idea. Maybe in their own rooms?" Beck suggested.

Roscoe and I had been sharing a room, and Beck and Killian were in another. Since Holland always got her own room, that meant Walker would have had his own as well. In this case, though, his brother was going to be staying with him tonight. Walker's brother, Raid, was our road manager and had been with us from the very beginning. He'd gone home to Pennsylvania when we left our last show before the break and decided to meet us here in New Hampshire before we would leave tomorrow to continue to the tour.

"You know, I've been thinking about them," I said.

"Who? Holland and Walker? What about them?" Beck asked.

"Did you ever notice that they're both always so focused on either just the music when we're all together or whatever is going on with any of us?" I questioned them. "Do you also notice that Walker doesn't ever hook up with anyone while we're out? Holland doesn't either."

"You think they're hooking up with each other?" Killian asked.

I shrugged. "I don't know. I don't want to start making assumptions, but nothing else makes sense."

"Shit," Roscoe hissed. "Would they cross that line?"

"I'm not sure, but if they are, it could be a big problem down the road if things were to get dicey between them," Beck noted.

Nodding my agreement, I said, "Yeah. I just can't believe Walker would do that with Holland. I always thought of her like a sister to us."

"Yeah, same here," Killian shared.

Roscoe and Beck both wore expressions that indicated the same.

"I don't think we should give them any shit about it now just in case we're reading too much into something that isn't true, but I think we should all prepare ourselves for the fact that something could be going down between them right now and that there could be a fallout from it," I advised. "We need to be prepared to help them through it if that's the case."

"Losing either of them in this band isn't going to be good for any of us, the two of them included," Beck said. "Let's just try to keep our eyes and ears open."

Just then, a knock came at the door.

I got up, moved to it, and opened it. Walker was standing there.

"Hey, what's going on?" he asked.

I stepped back and allowed him to come in. "Nothing yet," I answered. "Just hanging."

"How'd it go with Demi this afternoon?"

"I've got a date with her tomorrow morning."

A look of approval washed over him. "Nice. Congratulations."

"Yeah, well, we'll have to see where it goes," I said. "In the meantime, the guys and I were just talking about you and Holland."

"What about us?" Walker asked, something strange moving through his expression.

"We were just thinking about going out tonight and wanted to see if you two were up to it," I told him.

"I'm down," he agreed.

I had suspected that much. Walker rarely turned down a night out together with the band, even if he didn't go to the same lengths we did when we were there.

"Cool. Have you seen Holland?" I pressed.

Walker shook his head. "No."

Odd.

No sooner did he get the word out when another knock came at the door. I turned and opened it.

Holland.

"Is everyone in here?" she asked.

"Yeah, come on in," I said. "Where have you been?"

Her eyes slid to Walker briefly before they returned to me. "Um, I was just hanging in my room," she said.

Right.

Yep.

There was definitely something going on with them. Time to let it go for now.

"Well, we're going out tonight. You coming with us?" I asked.

She smiled and answered, "Of course."

With that, Walker and Holland joined the rest of us in the suite. I gave them both a beer, and they comfortably settled in as they always did. If the rest of us hadn't just been discussing it, I never would have given it a second thought.

Now, I had to wonder. And I could see the rest of the guys were thinking the same thing.

Luckily, for the time being, we all just let it go.

And I filled what could have potentially been awkward silence by telling Walker and Holland the news about our final performance when the regular tour was finished as well as my breakfast date for tomorrow morning.

As much as I loved performing, there was no comparison. My date with Demi had me feeling a level of excitement that none of the stops on the tour could even come close to. I couldn't wait.

CHAPTER 10

Demi

I CAN'T BELIEVE I'M DOING THIS.

Then again, I was talking to myself.

It was early Tuesday morning, I was in my car on the way to the Finch Café, and I was really starting to wonder if I'd officially lost my mind. That notion was only reinforced by the fact that I was completely torn.

On the one hand, I was convinced that this was the worst idea I'd ever had. I'd never done anything this crazy. And while having breakfast with someone wouldn't normally be considered outrageous, it was in this case. In fact, this was technically my first official date with anyone.

Even calling it a date made me feel antsy.

Because I didn't do this kind of thing.

I had always done what I needed to do to take care of myself. I didn't need all the bells and whistles. Dinner dates, flowers, and having the guy pick me up was just unnecessary because it was all bullshit.

I didn't need someone to put in all the fake effort to win

me over when the reality is that he only wanted one thing. If there was a guy I liked enough to want to take that step with him, I did. I did not want all the lies and false promises that came along with the chase.

But on the other hand, right now, I had this little voice in the back of my head telling me to do this and not give it another thought. That voice was telling me to enjoy myself and stop preventing myself from having these experiences.

For the most part, I hadn't really felt compelled to have this experience before Cash. I wanted to believe that meant something, but I couldn't ignore the fact that it felt like a huge risk. Bigger than it would have been with anyone else because this was Cash Morris. Then again, I was trying to remind myself of Sam's words a couple days ago.

I could stop fighting this and give myself the chance to get to know Cash better. In a worst-case scenario, I'd learn that we weren't compatible, and all I would have lost is some time. In a best-case scenario, I'd learn that he isn't the man I perceive him to be. Of course, if that were the case, I still stood to lose a lot.

So, it was no wonder I felt as though I was losing my mind.

The moment I pulled into the parking lot at the café, I spotted the man who was responsible for all of the emotional turmoil I felt. And the second he noticed me, his face lit up as he waved.

This was dangerous territory.

A man like him, looking at me like that... yep, this was definitely my worst idea.

I parked my car and tried to ignore all the weird and

unfamiliar nerves I felt in my stomach. I had no doubt that was because my body knew this was not smart.

Just as I turned off my car and reached over to grab my purse, my car door opened.

"You made it," Cash declared.

I got out, looked up at him, and said, "I told you I'd meet you here. Why wouldn't I have made it?"

He shrugged. "I was worried you'd change your mind."

"I always follow through on my promises," I told him.

Cash smiled. "Good to know."

He might have liked hearing that bit of information, but if I had any hope of making it out of this with my dignity and heart intact, I wouldn't be making any additional promises to him.

After Cash closed my car door and I locked it, he held out a piece of paper to me.

"What's this?" I asked.

"Just me following through on my promise to give you my number today," he replied.

I opened the small piece of paper, fell in love with the handwriting, and folded it again before slipping it into my purse.

"Thanks," I said.

With that, Cash and I fell into step beside one another as we walked toward the café.

A few minutes later, we were seated at a table inside and had given our orders to the waitress.

"So, you're heading off to the west coast next, right?" I asked, believing it was best for me to steer the conversation in the direction I needed it to go.

Cash nodded and answered, "Yeah, we'll be there for

three weeks before we head back to the east coast for a few more weeks."

"Is there a location where you're most excited about playing?" I questioned him.

"You mean, other than coming back here to play at the end?" he countered.

I rolled my eyes and smiled. "Yeah. Other than that."

"Probably the show at a venue only twenty minutes from where we grew up in Pennsylvania," he said. "That's the first show we play when we head back to the east coast."

"You guys all live there, right?" I asked.

"Yep."

"Well, it should be nice to finally have some time at home then," I reasoned.

Cash dipped his chin. "Unfortunately, it's not as much time as we'd like, but it's the longest we'll be in any one location on the remainder of the tour."

If there was one thing I found interesting, it was that Cash and the remaining members of My Violent Heart had homes in Pennsylvania. It struck me because on the surface, they seemed to fit the bill for typical rock stars. Or, most of them did anyway. So, to know that they all still held their hometown close in their hearts was special.

I spent so long pondering this that Cash asked, "What about you?"

"What about me?"

"Has this place always been your hometown?" he clarified.

I nodded. "Born and raised."

"Do you like it here?"

Now it was my turn to shrug. "I wouldn't say I'm

attached to the place," I started. "It's my family and friends that I love here."

"So, Cal is your cousin. Do you have any siblings?" Cash asked.

Just then, our waitress returned with our orders. After she set them down and walked away, I said, "I'm an only child."

Cash grinned at me. "Same here."

At his declaration, I couldn't help but feel anything other than happy. This wasn't nearly as bad as I thought it was going to be. I had been worried the entire date—if that's what it could be called—would be filled with us just bantering back and forth. This was anything but that. It was... nice.

For the remainder of our breakfast, Cash and I continued to have an easy conversation with each other. There was no pressure, and none of it felt forced or awkward. It surprised me, and I genuinely enjoyed myself.

But then we finished breakfast and things took a turn.

"I had a really great time with you this morning, Demi," Cash shared.

"Yeah," I agreed. "I had a nice time, too."

"I know I probably sound like a broken record at this point, but I have to give it one last shot," he started. "Is there any chance you've reconsidered and will give me your phone number?"

I tipped my head to the side. He had been really sweet this morning, and I liked that we were getting along well with each other for an extended period of time.

But I couldn't honor his request.

"I'm sorry, Cash," I lamented. "I really don't think that's a wise idea."

"Why not?" he inquired.

"You're going away on tour," I answered. "You'll have moved on to the next city, and life will be back to normal. Why would you want my number?"

Cash held my gaze a long time. I started squirming in my seat, seeing the intensity of it.

Following a long pause, he deadpanned, "I like you."

"It's never going to happen between us," I told him, my voice quiet.

"Why not?" he asked, a genuine curiosity in his tone.

"I'm sorry to disappoint you, Cash, but I can't do whatever it is that you want," I answered. "I'm not looking for a one-night stand with you."

"Maybe I don't just want a one-night stand with you, either," he countered.

He couldn't be serious.

Perhaps this was his way of making sure he had a woman in every state he and the band toured in. It seemed ridiculous for him to put in this much effort to make that happen, though.

I looked away from him as I tried to figure out how to best respond. Part of me wanted to throw caution to the wind and just do this while the other part of me knew it would be the biggest mistake of my life.

It wasn't about the phone number. The problem was that in giving it to him, I worried what I'd be setting myself up for. The only thought running through my mind was that someone like Cash had the power to completely destroy me.

I'd already seen a level of destruction like that before, and I never wanted to witness it again, let alone be the one to experience it directly.

"Demi?" Cash called, interrupting my thoughts.

I returned my attention to him and replied, "Yeah?"

"I just want the opportunity to get to know you better," he started. "I won't be back here for months, but I'd like to have that connection to you. I've already explained that you're unlike any other woman I've met, and that makes me like you even more. To me, that's something I can't just let go."

"I feel like you're wasting your time," I said, though I did it without an edge of irritation or snark in my tone. I believed he needed to know the truth. "Look, you are who you are, and I am who I am. I have no doubt that you can head off to your next location and easily find someone else to stay in contact with throughout the remainder of your tour. You're Cash Morris, after all."

"You're right. I could do that," he responded. I smiled at him, happy that he'd finally accepted my suggestion and was letting it go. Or, that's what I thought. A moment later, he added, "But she won't be you."

"Cash—" I started before he cut me off.

"I think you're someone who is going to be worth *all* the hassle you're putting me through right now, firecracker," he began again. "I've done easy before. In fact, that's all I've ever done up to this point. I'm not going to lie and say I haven't had my fun because I have. But I want something different, and I think that's you. I could give up and move on like you're telling me to do. But I feel like if I have to work for this, I might find that it's worth it in the end."

What was going on with him?

This couldn't be real. What did I have to offer him that he couldn't get anywhere else?

I mean, I guess he already explained that. I was offering

a challenge for him, and it seemed that was what he wanted right now.

But what would happen if I chose to play this game with him. What if I believed him when he said he wouldn't give up the prize he won in this game? Where would I be when he realized he needed a new challenge or wanted to play a new game? One that didn't involve me.

No.

No way.

But maybe I should take Sam's advice and take the time to get to know him. This would be the perfect opportunity. Cash said it himself. He wasn't going to be back here for months, so it wasn't like I had to jump into bed with him. I could simply get to know him better. In a worst-case scenario, we could just remain acquaintances.

"Okay, Cash, I'll give you my—"

"Cash Morris?"

I was interrupted by two girls who'd walked right up to our table.

"Yeah?" he answered with an edge of irritation in his tone.

"What are the chances we'd see you two days in a row?" one of the girls asked.

She barely got those words out when her friend said, "Last night was honestly one of the best nights of my life. We had so much fun with you."

My eyes shot to Cash as the first girl asked, "Would you mind taking a photo with us?"

The second girl added, "Yeah, that would be awesome."

"Excuse me?" the first girl asked.

I reluctantly tore my gaze away from Cash and looked

up at her. I was surprised to see that she'd managed to look away from him and was focused on me.

"Yes?" I responded.

"Would you mind taking a photo for us?" she asked me.

This was just what I needed to snap me right back into reality.

Last night.

He'd had *so much fun* with these girls last night, which would have been only hours after I'd agreed to this date with him and only hours before I pulled into the lot outside to meet him here.

Then again, I shouldn't have been so foolish as to assume this was an official date. I mean, he was Cash Morris. He could have had anyone. He didn't choose me because he liked me. He chose me because this was definitely a game for him.

These two girls walking up to the table was precisely the wake-up call that I needed.

I smiled at the girl and answered, "Sure."

She held her phone out to me. After I took it, she and her friend positioned themselves on either side of Cash. A strange expression had washed over his face, but I couldn't read it. It didn't matter though. I was giving up on trying to figure him out.

"Smile," I urged everyone.

The girls' faces lit up. Cash smiled, too.

Once I'd snapped a few pictures, the girl took her phone back and returned her attention to Cash. "If you ever want to hang out again, you know where to find us," she said.

Before Cash could even respond, the girls took off.

For several long moments, we both sat there staring at one another.

"I'm really sorry about that," Cash said.

Unfortunately, at the same time he apologized, I declared, "I think it's time for me to go."

"What?" he asked.

I pulled my purse into my lap and started rummaging through it. I grabbed my wallet, pulled out some money to cover my portion of the bill, and threw it onto the table.

Standing from my seat, I looked down at Cash. "Good luck on the rest of your tour," I rasped.

Cash opened his mouth to speak, but I turned and ran out of the café. I could hear him calling after me, but I didn't stop to look back.

I thought I was quick, but apparently, I wasn't fast enough.

I made it to my car just in time to have Cash stop me from opening the door.

"Demi, wait," he pleaded.

"I have to go, Cash," I told him.

"If this is about those girls," he began.

"It's not about them," I lied. "I just… I'm not the girl you're looking for."

Something washed over him before his voice dipped low. "You're exactly who I'm looking for, beautiful girl."

I needed to go now before I burst into tears and humiliated myself more than I already had.

"Right. Well, then I guess I'm sorry to tell you that I'm not cut out for this."

At that, I yanked open my door, got inside, and took off.

I didn't dare look back into my rearview mirror because I was afraid of what I'd see.

I stared at the computer screen in disbelief.

It had been three days since my mostly good but suddenly turned awful breakfast date with Cash.

Three days of remembering exactly why I avoided things like that at all costs.

I'd hoped—and possibly even expected—that Cash would understand that I was no longer interested in playing this game with him. It was so obvious that I was done, and I had to believe he knew why. I mean, obviously, he didn't know what my exact reasons were, but he had to know what triggered my desperation to get out of there that morning.

Or, I thought he did.

Staring at my computer screen now, it appeared he didn't.

Or, maybe that was all just part of the game to him.

I came into work today and found a couple of calls waiting for me as well as a bunch of emails.

One of those emails was from Cash.

You haven't called. I miss you. -Cash

I wanted to laugh. Miss me?

Cash didn't miss me.

He missed not being able to receive his own form of entertainment. Maybe that was the life of a rock star. They spent so much time entertaining others that they had to come up with ways to amuse themselves.

Well, I refused to be the butt of a bad joke.

No thanks.

Part of me wanted to ignore his email. Maybe I should have done just that considering he was emailing me at work about something unrelated to his band performing at Granite.

But if there was anything I learned about Cash, it was that he didn't quit. So, if I didn't respond, he'd likely just call me here.

On that thought, I tapped out a response and hit the send button.

Then, I smiled.

That would show him.

CHAPTER 11

Cash

I HAD BEEN SO CLOSE.

So close to getting in there, even if it was just inside the door.

To say I was frustrated at this point would have been an understatement because I thought I'd finally made some real progress with Demi.

That progress started with somehow getting her to agree to go out with me for breakfast before I left to continue on the tour with My Violent Heart. The progress continued when we, for the first time, had a civil conversation while getting to know one another. There was no sarcasm behind any of the words we spoke to one another. We simply talked.

And it was nice.

Damn, it was so nice to have that with her.

The progress had reached a point I never expected it would when Demi decided to give me her number.

And then it all came to a grinding halt.

Because I had fans.

I never had to remind myself to feel gratitude and appreciation for my fans. The band was blessed with the best fans in the music industry, and I knew they were the reason I lived the life I did doing the thing I loved most in the world.

But ever since I watched Demi run out of the café that morning and tell me that she wasn't the girl I was looking for, I had struggled with my thankfulness for the fans.

She might have said differently, but there wasn't a doubt in my mind that the reason Demi left was because of those two girls walking up and interrupting our date.

The last thing I wanted was to feel animosity toward the fans, but it was hard not to feel just a little bit of it.

Demi left because of what happened that morning. And I couldn't begin to understand it, especially considering she seemed more than willing to take the photos for the fans.

Actually, that's not true.

I had a feeling that for her to see it play out in front of her affected her differently than when she was just making assumptions about how my life was. Then again, there had been that moment in the hotel weeks ago when a couple of fans walked right up to me and requested an autograph.

Obviously, Demi and I hadn't been out together at that time, so beyond that, I couldn't see how this situation was any different.

I felt miserable the last few days, hating that we didn't get the opportunity to say goodbye to one another and that things didn't end on a good note.

I hated not having that connection with her.

But last night, in the middle of our show, I remembered I had her email. So the minute I was off stage and able to send one, I shot Demi that email. Initially, I had grappled with what to say to her considering the way things were left that morning. I ultimately decided it was best to give her a bit of myself that she was used to while also giving her a dose of something more.

It felt like a lifetime had passed waiting for a response. Now that one had just come in, I was struggling to open it.

I couldn't imagine what her response was going to be.

I took in a few deep breaths and finally opened Demi's email.

Give it a few cities. You'll forget all about me. -Demi

I wished.

I wished it was that easy.

This would have been much nicer if I could have done what Killian and Roscoe had urged me to do from the beginning when they gave me their advice suggesting I just move on.

But I couldn't.

Wanting to look on the bright side, I felt happy about the fact that Demi had at least responded, even if I didn't like what it said.

Beyond that, she hadn't told me to eat shit, so there was an upside.

The lines of communication were still open, and that meant I wasn't going to give up on her.

I tapped out a response and sent it.

That's where you're wrong. You're unforgettable, firecracker. And I'll prove it to you.

-Cash

PS Do you have any tattoos?

I threw in the tattoo question because I figured it wasn't invasive. Generally, people who had tattoos loved to talk about them, and those who didn't either talked about the ones they wanted to get or unequivocally answered no.

The answer to her question didn't necessarily matter to me. I mean, obviously, I was curious. But the truth was that I just wanted to get her to open up to me again. And if I kept the entire email string on the fact that I missed her, it was almost certain that we'd get nowhere.

That wasn't an option for me.

I don't know why I assumed that Demi would respond to me immediately. Maybe I was secretly hoping that she was sitting around waiting to hear from me.

It had been nearly two full days before Demi responded to me. I'd gone almost a week without talking to her.

I'd never really had a problem with confidence before, but now, that self-assurance was starting to fade.

Damn, this was hard.

But there was one glimmer of hope.

Because even though her response hadn't come back as

quickly as I would have liked, I got something else. A bit of playfulness. And that was enough to put a smile on my face and remind me of one of the reasons this woman had captured my interest.

Still remember me?

-Demi

PS One tattoo.

After reading her response, I came to the conclusion that she was doing this on purpose. Either she wanted to give me more time to miss her, or she genuinely believed she was forgettable.

I hoped it was the former because the latter was just plain sad.

And since I wanted her to know that I hadn't been joking around, I immediately send her a response.

I thought you forgot about me.

-Cash

PS What and where is it?

After sending it off, I sat back and thought about how I was going to get through the next two days without hearing from her again. I had a show tonight. We were currently in New Mexico. Tomorrow morning, we'd head off to Arizona.

We had two shows to play in Phoenix before we took off to Nevada.

Mostly, I was enjoying the tour, but the second half of it was proving to be a lot different from the first half for me. I still enjoyed time with my bandmates when we had an extra day between shows, but I really didn't find myself interested in going out to party.

And I hadn't had sex in weeks.

If that wasn't depressing, I didn't know what would be.

What I'd learned was that my dick was only functional around Demi or at thoughts of her. The mere thought of putting my cock in someone else did nothing for me. It wasn't that I hadn't seen pretty women since we left New Hampshire. I had. It was just that none of them were her, so I never even attempted to go there.

Maybe that was another reason I was hoping I could get Demi to open up to me once more. I couldn't go the rest of my life never having sex again. Surely, I wouldn't survive.

Of course, that was merely me joking. The truth was, I didn't just want her for sex. There was so much more I liked about her.

With all of my pent-up sexual energy, I decided I needed to handle business myself. It was still early, and I was in my bed.

Just as I closed my eyes, envisioned Demi's beautiful mouth, and reached down to stroke myself, my phone chimed, indicating I'd received an email.

My hand stopped where it was as I reached for the phone with the opposite one.

Holy fuck.

She responded in a matter of minutes.

Nope. And it's a single word tattooed on the inside of my right wrist. That's all I'm giving you.

-Demi

She didn't forget about me. That was promising.

I didn't hesitate to hit the reply button.

I guess I'll have to wait to see it in person. How is the new job coming along? Have you booked a lot of bands?

-Cash

This wasn't exactly how I had hoped things would go, but if this was the only way I could have her, I'd take it.

As I stayed in bed, with my phone in one hand, I returned the other to my cock. I started envisioning Demi's body in that dress she wore weeks ago when I first showed up at Granite. I was instantly hard at the vision in my mind. I hadn't stroked more than twice before my phone rang in my hand.

Shit.

Shit.

Shit.

Was she calling me?

I tried to take a calming breath before I answered, "Hello?"

"Cash?"

It was her.

"Demi," I stated, not needing to ask if it was her.

"Yeah, I'm taking my lunch break right now and thought it'd be easier to talk this way instead of through email."

I wanted to laugh. That was precisely what I had wanted to do this whole time.

God, the sound of her voice again just felt so good.

Apparently, I was too lost in that and my shock over the fact that she'd called me that I'd taken too long to respond.

"If this is a bad time, I can let you go," she said.

"No. No, not at all. I'm just… I didn't expect you to call," I returned.

"Well, don't get your hopes up. I called you from the bar, so you still don't have my phone number," she teased.

She was definitely teasing because the sound of her voice was light and carefree.

Wow. I hadn't realized how much I missed that.

"I'll take whatever you'll give me, Demi," I told her. "If all you want is emails and calls from the bar phone, I'll be happy with that. So, how is it going there?"

There was a brief pause before she answered, "Good. I'm really getting into the swing of things, and we've had a ton of interest since My Violent Heart played here. The interest has come not only from bands wanting to play but also a lot of patrons who want to know if and when you guys are coming back to play again."

"I wish we could come back sooner," I told her.

And I did. It was just that my reason for going back had nothing to do with music and everything to do with seeing her.

"I'm sure the time will fly by for you," she declared. "How's the tour going?"

"It's good. Having that little break was nice for us, and everyone is stoked to be back doing what we love. Plus, the crowds have been unbelievable, so that's been a big bonus."

"I can't even imagine what it must be like to see you all perform live in a big venue," Demi shared.

I immediately took advantage of that and insisted, "I can get you tickets to a show. You tell me what venue you want to see us at, and I'll make it happen. Hell, I'd fly you there."

Demi huffed. "You're crazy."

"Crazy about you."

"Cash..." She trailed off.

Worried that I might have crossed a line, I backtracked. "I'm just being honest, but I'll stop if it's going to make you hang the phone up on me or something," I said.

"I'm not going to hang up," she started. "But do I get to ask a question?"

"What do you mean?"

"I mean that you asked me about tattoos," she began again. "I feel as though it's only fair for me to have a chance to ask you something personal."

I smiled.

She couldn't see me. Nobody could.

But I was smiling from ear to ear. The fact that Demi wanted to ask me a personal question made my day. Heck, it had made my week. I'd be willing to go so far as to say that this was going to be the best day I'd had since I left New Hampshire.

"Ask away, firecracker. I'm an open book," I told her.

"Really? Because I feel like you don't give a lot of information in your interviews," she stated.

"So, what you're saying is that you've been reading up on me?" I countered.

"What? No. I mean, well, I might have looked at one or two of them," she admitted.

Yeah.

I knew I hadn't been wrong. Demi was just as attracted to me as I was to her. The only difference was that I had no problem sharing how I felt, and she was wound up tight. In time, I'd definitely find a way to get to the bottom of that. For now, I'd enjoy this.

"Okay, so what's the question?" I asked, deciding to let her off the hook.

"Alright. Well, what would you say is your worst trait?" she asked.

"Damn. Do you always like to focus on the negative?" I retorted through my laughter.

There was a brief pause before she answered, "I feel as though it's always best to know the worst up front."

I had to wonder what she needed to know the worst for. Did she have plans on finding out the good and realizing she wanted it?

Fuck, I hoped so.

"Hmmm. My worst trait," I repeated. "I don't know. I guess maybe that I'm impatient."

"So, it's true then?" she questioned me.

"What?"

"You want what you want when you want it," she clarified. "It's good to know I wasn't wrong about that assumption."

It was no secret that Demi had made assumptions about the kind of guy I was. I didn't know what they all were, and I certainly hadn't expected that she'd thought this about me. All I could do now is hope that any of the worst conclusions she'd drawn about me based on whatever she read online or saw in interviews could be proven wrong with time.

"Dare I ask what else you think of me?" I wondered aloud.

"You can, but I don't think I'm going to share just yet," she said. "I'd rather wait and see."

I'd take that, too.

Because if she was willing to wait and see, that meant she planned to communicate regularly with me.

Or, at least, more than we had since I left New Hampshire.

On that thought, I smiled and settled in for more conversation. "Alright. So, what bands have contacted you? Are there any I know?"

"I don't know. Do you keep abreast of the little guy in the industry? Because I can tell you now that there was nobody as big as My Violent Heart," she replied.

And just like that, Demi and I fell into a comfortable conversation.

It felt good to have that back, even if I could only see her face in my mind.

I couldn't help myself.

I missed Cash.

There was definitely something wrong with me. After witnessing what I did at the Finch Café that morning, seeing his fans come up and talk about being with him the night before, I never expected I'd feel my heart thaw toward him.

But all it took was a handful of emails for me to reconsider.

The truth was, Cash and I weren't together. Whether he was interested in making that happen or not didn't matter because I hadn't agreed.

So, I really had no place to get upset about anything that he did.

Beyond that, it wasn't as though I'd stuck around long enough to ask about the night he had before we went out to breakfast. Truthfully, I didn't think I could handle it.

Because even though I'd never admit the truth to him, I liked him. Cash made me feel alive. Yes, he was handsome and sexy and had a great voice, but there was something else there. Something that ran much deeper for me. I just didn't know exactly what it was.

And since I felt that pull to him, missed him, and adored the fact that he was reaching out to me the way that he was, I caved.

I didn't think it was the smartest idea. I wasn't sure I'd survive whatever came of this. But I figured it was like Sam said. This would be the safest way for me to get to know Cash better. I wouldn't be distracted by the sight and scent of him.

The best part of all was that if Cash was genuinely serious about his interest in me, he'd have to work hard to prove it.

Part of me had wondered if I was caving too quickly. Should I have continued to let things play out via email?

Maybe.

But hearing his voice again for the first time since that morning at breakfast was like music to my ears.

I hated that that's how it was for me, but I couldn't change it.

So, I did what I always did. I gave myself what I wanted and needed, and I'd deal with whatever the fallout was later.

For now, Cash had made it so that I didn't regret anything just yet. Only time would tell if that was going to change.

CHAPTER 12

Demi

"Hey, Mama, how's it going?"

I walked into the kitchen of my mother's house after having just let myself in the front door. She'd been expecting me, so it wasn't like my visit was unannounced. Then again, that could have been the case, and it would not have mattered. My mom loved when I came by for a visit. I enjoyed my time with her, too.

The two of us had come a long way since that horrible, horrible day all those years ago. No matter how much I had wanted to forget what I saw—and trust me, I wanted to forget it—I hadn't been able to.

In fact, even until this very day, every time I saw my mom, I couldn't stop myself from remembering that night and the days that followed.

Initially, I'd been so shocked by it. Maybe I shouldn't have been. I mean, my parents fought so much. But the reality was that I couldn't think of any kid or teenager who'd want to learn that one of their parents was being unfaithful.

Add to that the fact that I'd managed to not only learn that it was happening but also that I witnessed my father in the act, and I was beyond disgusted.

After vomiting on the floor right at the entrance to his room and locking myself in the bathroom until the next morning, I wrestled with what to do. Initially, I blamed my inaction on being sick, but I knew that wasn't it.

I just didn't want to break my mother's heart.

But once I'd turned the corner on the stomach bug I'd gotten, I took stock of the situation and realized I didn't want my mom to look like a fool.

Who knew how long my father had been cheating on her?

So, I told her the truth. My parents ended up splitting up. I always found it strange that there wasn't more of an argument between them once I'd shared the news. I didn't understand it. Perhaps my mom realized deep down that it wasn't worth her time to fight with someone who had already checked out.

My father was probably grateful that she didn't seem to put up a fight. He'd made his choice, and we weren't part of it.

After their separation, I chose to live with my mother. Unsurprisingly, my father didn't put up a fight. Of course, that only made things easier for him. He could fuck his mistress without any worry of his daughter walking in on him.

Maybe it was because I knew it was going to hurt for a bit for the both of us, but we'd have each other. And we did for a very long time.

To this very day, we still do, even though our visits with one another are few and far between. Once I had graduated from school, gotten a job, and had gotten out on my own, my mom ended up moving about an hour away from where I was.

I didn't blame her. It was probably too painful to stay in the place where she'd gotten her heart broken. It was a wonder I could stay because I felt that heartbreak right alongside her.

But things were great now.

She was happy, and I was happy for her. After everything she'd endured, my mom had managed to get herself to a place where she started to put herself out there again and start dating. She never settled down with anyone again, but she found companionship when she needed it.

I guess we were the same when it came to that. Neither of us was prepared to suffer through that kind of heartbreak.

And she had a couple of great girlfriends who lived close who she often spent some of her free time with.

Every so often, I came to visit, and my mom soaked up that time with me, making the most of it.

Today was one of those days.

As I sat down at the island in her kitchen, my mom finished preparing lunch. That was one thing I'd learned about mothers. It didn't matter how old their children got, it seemed a mother's biggest worry was whether or not her child had enough food to eat.

I always came with an empty stomach because I knew she'd have that need to fill me up.

"I'm doing great, Demi," she answered. "I spoke with Pat earlier in the week, and she said things were going well for you at Granite."

Pat was my aunt. She was my mother's sister and Cal's mom. They spoke frequently, so I wasn't surprised to hear that the news of my employment had traveled so quickly.

"Yeah," I confirmed. "I am so happy to be away from the

hotel. It's such a different vibe for me now, which has been great for my mood."

Nodding her head, she replied, "I'd been noticing that about you the last couple of times you visited. You always seemed like you had something weighing heavily on your mind. I'm glad that you're happier now."

"I like it," I told her. "The best part is that I've already talked to Cal about transitioning myself away from being in the actual bar so that I can just start working from home unless there's an event happening. Obviously, I'll be there to help prepare for those, but there isn't anything I'm doing at the bar that I can't do at home."

My mother smiled at me. "That sounds incredible. All that matters is that you're happy doing what you're doing."

I shrugged. I couldn't say that I grew up thinking that this was going to be my job, but I'd always loved music, so this was a much better fit for me than my previous job.

"Yeah, and it's been crazy, too, because My Violent Heart did an impromptu performance just over two weeks ago," I explained. "Ever since, there has been a lot of interest from other bands. Cal does really well on nights when he's got a live band playing, so the more of them we can get, the better."

"Pat mentioned that a big band played there," Mom returned, passing a plate in my direction. "Were you there for that?"

"Thanks," I replied, pulling the plate closer to me. "And yes, I was there."

I wanted to tell her that the reason they played there was because the lead singer had negotiated it after he showed up there looking for me, but I didn't think that was the way to bring up the subject of Cash.

"That must have been so exciting to see them perform live," she started. "I don't listen to their music, but I have heard the name. They're a big deal, aren't they?"

Yep. They were.

And she was going to go crazy when she learned that I was on a first-name basis with Cash.

"They are," I confirmed. "They're actually in the middle of a tour right now, but they're coming back to Finch to play at Granite once their tour is over."

"Wow. I don't think Pat knew that. She was still gushing over how great it was going for Granite, in general, and of course, the fact that Cal is now officially with Sam."

I let out a laugh.

My mom met Sam a couple years ago. From the very beginning, she said that she thought Cal and Sam would make a great couple. Apparently, Aunt Pat felt the same.

We all did.

Because the love they had for one another was unlike anything I'd ever seen in my life. That kind of love was rare, and I couldn't have been happier that the two of them found it.

"Well, Sam's T-shirt business is doing incredibly well right now, too," I shared. "Cal had her bring a bunch of shirts to the bar that night, and then two members of My Violent Heart ended up wearing them on stage. One week later, things exploded for her. That's another reason I'd like to start working from home. What I'm doing for Cal doesn't require eight hours of work, five days a week. I can help Sam with getting some of her administrative stuff handled."

I lifted my sandwich to my mouth and took a bite as my mom responded, "That's incredible. Who would have thought?"

"I know," I replied through a mouthful of food.

As we ate our sandwiches and finished up our lunch, my mom filled me in on everything that had been going on in her life since the last time we had the chance to sit down and talk like this.

Not much had changed in her world. She still went to work, did her thing, and kept herself busy. Earlier this year, she'd taken up gardening and was enjoying learning all the ins and outs of her new hobby. It was really great to see her face light up when she talked about all the things that she'd grown in the last few months.

After we finished our food and she'd shared all that was going on in her life, my mom asked, "So, what else is going on with you besides work?"

This was the golden opportunity. When I'd reached out to my mom and told her I wanted to come visit her today, I did it not only because I missed her but also because I wanted to ask her something. I just hoped what I wanted to discuss wasn't going to upset her.

"Can I talk to you about something?" I asked.

"Anything. What's going on?" she responded.

I hesitated briefly, wondering if this was smart. The last thing I wanted to do was bring up painful memories for her, but I needed her advice. I wanted her perspective. I knew what she went through following my father's cheating because I watched as she worked through that heartbreak. But now that I had this whole situation with Cash, I felt compelled to get her opinion.

"Was it worth it?" I finally said.

A crease formed between her brows. "Was what worth it?"

"Risking your heart and losing it all to my father," I clarified.

Her head tipped to the side as her features softened. "Oh, Demi, where is this coming from?" she asked, her voice gentle.

"I just want to know," I rasped.

"I have you," she declared.

"Okay?" I responded, curiosity in my tone. That didn't explain anything.

Luckily, she realized I was confused and explained, "I'd go through the pain of your father's infidelity a million times if it meant that I was going to have you in the end."

Well, there it was.

She'd risk her heart like that to have me.

"Demi?" she called.

"Yeah?"

"What's going on?" she pressed.

I took in a deep breath and closed my eyes as I blew it out. When I opened my eyes, I swallowed hard and focused my attention on her. Then I shared, "There's a guy that I think I like, but he terrifies me."

"How so?"

Shaking my head, I said, "I don't trust any of them. Men, that is. You know that. If Dad couldn't be faithful, why would anyone else?"

My mom reached out and grabbed ahold of my hand. Squeezing it, she rasped, "Demi, I'm so sorry about what happened. I don't think I ever told you that. You never deserved to go through that, and you definitely didn't need to walk in on it."

I let out a laugh. "I don't think you're the one that needs to apologize for it," I noted.

"But I'm your mother," she said. "And it was my job to protect you from that. I can't go back and change it, and I wish I could. Not for myself, though. I'd want to fix it for you. Because I've seen what it did to you. The fact that you've gone all these years and never had a serious boyfriend and that you're now asking me if taking that risk was worth it."

"I don't want to get hurt," I admitted, my throat tight.

Nodding her understanding, she replied, "I know. Nobody does. But falling in love is beautiful."

I was so far away from falling in love. The thought terrified me.

"It's scary."

"Of course, it is. That doesn't mean you shouldn't experience it. If there is one thing I want for you in this life, Demi, it's for you to experience romantic love," she said. "I know what happened when you were just a teenager changed the way you look at love, but I promise you it can be worth it. Even after all that happened, I still don't regret falling in love with your father."

I let out a huge sigh. Over the years, I'd purposely avoided talking to my mom a whole lot about what happened. While it was always a very horrible memory for me to recall, I assumed it was painful for her.

I'm sure it was.

But to know now that she didn't regret all that she'd had with him made me feel a little bit better. The bottom line was that she was here now, and she was doing well. So while she had gone through something horrible, she still came out the other side with a smile on her face.

Following a long stretch of silence, my mom urged, "Tell me about this guy."

Instantly, I felt a smile tug at the corners of my mouth. "You're never going to believe this," I told her.

Her brows shot up, silently questioning me.

I ignored that and shared, "He's probably the worst possible choice I could make for myself considering my current stance on romantic relationships."

"Why?"

"Because he's Cash Morris, the lead singer of My Violent Heart," I told her.

My mom's eyes nearly fell out of her head. "Are you serious?"

I nodded. "Yes."

"What? How?"

Shaking my head slowly because I understood her disbelief, I said, "I've turned him down so many times, but he's a persistent man."

She grinned at me. "I love that."

"I was kind of hoping you'd tell me that I need to be careful and really reconsider even thinking about proceeding with him," I pleaded.

"No way," she declared as she sat up taller with a smile on her face. "No way am I going to tell you that this isn't a good idea because I'd be lying. Why would you want me to do that?"

"Because not only would this be brand-new territory for me, but it's also brand-new territory *with* a man like him," I answered. "I feel like this could have a very bad outcome."

My worries didn't seem to affect my mother's mood in the slightest. In fact, this whole conversation had taken a turn I hadn't expected.

"So, are you officially dating him?" she pressed.

"No. I just... well, we've spoken on the phone a few times over the last week or so," I started. "Initially, I communicated with him via email because I had refused to give him my number. But I eventually realized how tedious that was going to be, so I called him from the bar."

"You mean, he still doesn't have your number?"

I shook my head.

"Why not?"

Shrugging my shoulders, I answered honestly, "I'm just being stubborn at this point."

And I knew that I was.

I didn't know why. I guess I was trying to hold on to some sliver of control because I felt like I didn't have any when Cash was around.

But the truth was that now that I'd talked to him on the phone several times over the last week, the more I felt like I wanted to give him my number.

Part of me wanted to take a chance and give myself the opportunity to see what he'd do with it. Would he put in the effort to call? Would he reach out at least as often as he sent me emails?

I never thought in a million years that I'd ever get to a place where I wanted to have a man woo me, but here I was, wanting that from Cash.

"Take a chance, Demi," my mom urged. "It could be the best decision of your life."

"It could also be the worst," I countered.

She shook her head. "It won't ever be that," she insisted. "Maybe it won't work out, but I promise that if nothing else, you will learn something from it. Truthfully, if this guy has any brains in his head, he won't do a damn thing to screw it up because you are the best he'll ever get."

"He's a rock star, Mom," I reminded her. "He could have just about anyone he wants."

"Yep. And you're the best he could ever hope to get," she maintained.

I rolled my eyes at her, but I did it with a smile on my face.

Before I could say anything in response to that, my mom demanded, "Okay, show me some pictures of this guy. I don't listen to their music, so I don't think I know what he looks like."

And just like that, the conversation that I thought might end up with at least one, if not both, of us, in tears was anything but.

We laughed.

We joked.

We had the best time.

Hours later, when I got in the car to head back home, I pulled out my phone and tapped out a text.

Me: I hope your show goes well tonight. -Demi

There.

I did it.

Cash had my number. There was no turning back now.

Surprisingly, as I drove home with a smile on my face, I realized I didn't want to anyway.

CHAPTER 13

Cash

"I'M BEAT."

That came from Walker.

"Agreed," I said from beside him.

We had all just piled into the limo that was taking us back to our hotel for the night. We'd just played our fourth show in five days. It was Sunday night, or technically, early Monday morning, and we'd all decided that after tonight's performance we needed to head back to our hotel.

Not only were we exhausted but we were also leaving California early Monday afternoon and beginning our trek back to the east coast. If there was any hope of making sure we were all ready to go on time, we couldn't risk a night out.

Then again, with the exception of Roscoe and Killian, I wasn't sure anyone could have handled an all-nighter. Maybe handle wasn't the correct word. I had no doubt that any one of us could manage it, but the reality was that we didn't want to.

Of course, a lot of it made sense now. Holland and

Walker often called it quits early; though, I think they'd put some distance between their departure from a night out so nobody got suspicious.

For me, I'd always been right there alongside Roscoe and Killian. But now that I'd met Demi, I no longer had that same desire to go out on the prowl.

And Beck... well, he could go either way. Some days he was all about it, and other times, he wasn't. It just depended on what his mood was like.

"I think these last few days were the worst of it for us," Beck chimed in.

"Yeah, and it'll be nice to have a slightly longer stretch between shows once we make it back to Pennsylvania," Holland added.

"At least the fans here made it all worth it," Killian declared.

There was a round of nods from all of us as I said, "No arguments there."

That had been the case. Obviously, we all loved what we did. But in the moments when we started to feel the strain of a long tour, we had to find ways to look at the positives. More often than not, we always found that with our fans.

It was hard to be upset, frustrated, or anything but grateful when we were able to live out our dreams of being on stage when we had thousands of screaming fans who were excited about seeing our performance.

"And the groupies made it even better," Roscoe blurted.

At that, we all burst out laughing. That was Roscoe. He had zero problem finding the absolute best in every situation. As was not uncommon for him, as long as he had music, booze, women, friends, and fans, he'd play music every night.

The man enjoyed this life in every aspect and loved all that came with it. Sometimes, it was a little too much love.

Though, right now, I felt the tiniest twinge of jealousy. There hadn't been a shortage of physical intimacy for Roscoe on the tour. On the other hand, I was in a drought. I felt like I'd been stranded in the middle of the desert for months. I just wanted one tiny sip of water.

"Holland's right," Walker began after we'd all settled down. "Even though we still have a couple shows, it'll be nice to be back home and have those few days to relax and enjoy some time off."

While I didn't disagree with the sentiment, I couldn't help but notice how he had brought Holland into it. Had he always done that?

It was far too late, and I was entirely too wiped out to think about it.

"Anyone up for a beer in the hotel bar?" Roscoe added.

Killian immediately answered, "I'm down."

"Ah, why not?" Beck agreed.

It was like they'd all done a one-eighty.

"I'm out," Walker said.

"Me too," Holland replied.

When all their eyes came to me, I shook my head.

"Fuck, Cash, are you still holding out hope that Demi's going to change her mind about you?" Killian asked.

"She has," I declared.

"What?" Holland gasped.

Shaking my head because I knew she misunderstood, I explained, "Technically, she hasn't. But I have been talking to her on the phone for the last week."

"Really?" Walker asked.

I nodded.

"After all this time, she finally gave you her number," Roscoe proudly announced. "I'm so happy for you."

"Thanks, jackass," I shot back.

I couldn't bring myself to tell them that Demi hadn't technically given me her number. God, that would have been embarrassing. It hadn't ever taken me this long. Hell, it hadn't ever come close to being this long. The more I thought about it, the more I realized that I had to have set some world record. Surely, this was not normal.

A few minutes later, we pulled up outside the hotel. We'd barely gotten out of the limo when a group of women came up to us.

We entertained them for a few moments, taking pictures and signing autographs. Eventually, we made our way inside, where Beck, Roscoe, and Killian took off toward the bar while Holland, Walker, and I made our way to the elevators.

Once it had made it to our floor and the doors opened, I had to go in one direction while they went in the other.

"See you in the morning," I said.

"Good night, Cash," Holland replied.

"Later," Walker returned.

I started moving down the hall and felt the corners of my mouth twitch. Walker and Holland had us all fooled. Or, they used to.

Whatever.

Right now, things were good in the band. If they were happy and whatever they had going on between them wasn't affecting the rest of us, more power to them.

I made it to my room, pushed inside, and let out a deep sigh.

My goal was to shower, pack up my things, and get to bed. I didn't want to have to worry about packing in the morning because Demi typically called me on her lunch break, which was early morning here. There was not a chance I was missing her call or being distracted when it came in, especially when I hadn't had a chance to talk to her all weekend. Since she didn't go into the bar on the weekend to work, unless there was a band playing—in which case she'd be tied up with that—I quickly became aware I wasn't going to hear from her on Saturdays or Sundays. That realization yesterday morning had been humbling, to say the least.

Oddly enough, getting those calls from her over the last week had been some of the best moments I'd had on this part of the tour. Yes, it was great being on stage and performing for the fans, but having the chance to talk to Demi simply made my day.

I couldn't wait until I could see her again.

And I hoped that when it happened a few months from now that she and I would be in an even better place than we were right now. As much as I would have liked to push for more now, I figured there was no point in rushing it.

I wasn't going to see her until we returned to New Hampshire in the fall, so I'd take this time now to form a deeper bond with her. Up to this point, our conversations had been mostly lighthearted and surface level. We hadn't gotten into anything really deep, but I was okay with that for now. We had the time to take it slow.

My only hope was that this time was going to help us foster a healthier relationship once we were face-to-face again. We couldn't continue to go at each other the way we had in the beginning.

Not quite an hour after I'd gotten back to my room, I'd showered and packed. Just as I was about to get into bed, I decided to take a quick look at my phone. Sometimes, especially right after a performance, there'd be news reports. There was occasionally something worth reading.

But the moment I picked up my phone and put a knee to the bed, I froze.

A text from a number I didn't recognize.

But that didn't matter because the sender had included her name.

Fuck.

Demi had texted me. That meant she wasn't on the phone in the bar.

Had she just given me her number?

Needing a minute to come to terms with it, I slowly twisted my body and fell to my back in the bed.

I was making progress with her.

My firecracker.

If the old Cash could see me now he'd be laughing at me for thinking of a girl as mine.

My firecracker.

I didn't care. She was.

And I intended to see to it that she didn't regret taking this step.

Even though I knew she was probably still sleeping, I had to respond to her message wishing me a great show earlier that evening.

Me: It did. And now my night has just gotten better. We're down to thirteen.

With that, I set the phone on the nightstand and rolled to my stomach in an attempt to find sleep. Just an hour ago

I'd felt exhausted. Now, my body was buzzing with excitement. Demi and I had turned a corner.

I couldn't wait to see what the morning brought.

"You're only hours away now."

That came from Demi.

It was Thursday morning, and I'd just had the best week of my life. Well, it hadn't been a full week just yet. Ever since Demi texted me on Sunday night, nothing had dampened my mood.

I no longer had to wait for her to reach out to me when I wanted to talk to her. If it was in the middle of the day and I thought she might be busy at work, I could simply shoot a text off to her and share whatever was on my mind.

Sometimes, it was a simple text telling her about whatever was happening with the band. Other times, I'd ask how her day was going. Mostly, I used the texting just to let her know that I was thinking about her.

I tried not to be so obvious about it.

Because the truth was that if I reached out to her every time I was thinking about her, I'd have a constant open line to her.

I hadn't been this consumed by someone ever. It was a strange feeling for me, but it was one that kept me excited.

"I know," I responded with a smile on my face. "I can't wait to get back home."

"You realize you're heading home to Pennsylvania but that the tour isn't over yet, right?" Demi asked.

Letting out a laugh, I answered, "I know. But we're that much closer. It's almost twelve weeks until I'm back in New Hampshire."

"Is that really all you're looking forward to?" she questioned me.

I was done with holding back.

Demi had opened the door a few days ago by reaching out with her text. We'd communicated regularly in the days that followed.

She knew where I stood; she knew I wanted her.

And even though she didn't verbally indicate that the feeling was mutual, she definitely didn't hand me the same attitude she had the very first time I'd gone to New Hampshire and saw her working at the hotel. That told me that perhaps her perspective was shifting, and I had to believe that she wasn't the kind of woman who'd string someone along if her heart wasn't softening just a bit.

Her heart.

Never did I think I'd be considering the state of a woman's heart like this.

"It's not so much about the location for me. It's about who's there that makes me wish I was flying there instead of a few states south later today," I shared.

In her typical fashion, unable to accept the truth of what I was saying, Demi said, "Oh, yeah, I mean, everyone at Granite is so excited for you to come back. I can see why having that level of appreciation would draw you back here. Cal and Sam are particularly excited."

I loved it.

I loved that she tried to do anything she could to avoid admitting that perhaps she was looking forward to seeing me just as much as anyone else, if not as much as I was looking forward to seeing her.

"What about you?" I asked, wondering if I might be pushing it too much.

"What about me?"

"Do you feel even a smidgen of excitement about seeing me again?" I asked.

Demi hesitated to answer. I held out, waiting for her to respond. Eventually, she did, and she didn't fail to make me laugh.

"My Violent Heart is going to be playing again at Granite," she started. "Why wouldn't I be excited about seeing one of my favorite bands play live?"

"You'll do anything to avoid admitting you like me, won't you?" I pressed.

"I like your music, Cash," she insisted.

"That's all?"

She huffed. "Okay, fine, I'm excited for you to get here in a couple months so that I can make sure you know how to keep your clothes on," she said.

"Excuse me?"

"I saw the pictures from your last two performances," she shared. "You took your shirt off somewhere in the middle of it."

I grinned. She was keeping tabs on me.

Yep.

Demi liked me.

She just didn't know how to handle it.

"And you're saying you don't think that was a good look?" I replied. Demi didn't respond. When too much time passed without a response, I guessed, "Or maybe you think it's a great look, and you don't want to share what's for you with the world."

"I never said that!" she gasped.

"You don't have to. Your silence said everything. But don't worry. I'm a changed man, firecracker. If it makes you uncomfortable, I'm keeping my shirt on for the remainder of the tour."

"Cash, I didn't—"

"It's done, Demi," I cut her off. "No sense in arguing. I'm saving my body for the next time I see you. The fans might be disappointed, but all I care about is making sure you're satisfied."

Following an extended silence, she murmured, "You're crazy."

"Only about you."

"Does it get tiring?" she asked, catching me off guard.

"What?"

"Carrying that big head of yours around all day long," she replied.

I burst out laughing.

The feeling that this woman gave me in just having a phone conversation was unbelievable. I never knew it could be like this with a woman.

In all fairness, I hadn't ever given it the chance with anyone else, but that didn't matter to me now. I had her, and she was definitely more than enough for me.

As soon as I pulled myself together, I said, "Fuck, I can't wait to see you."

"So, let's make it happen," she challenged.

"What?" I asked, my body going solid.

"Tomorrow. After your show," she suggested. "We can video chat... unless that's not good enough for you."

I went from feeling excited to feeling high. I'd always been grateful that nobody in the band had gone down that road and gotten hooked on drugs. But right now, I understood the allure.

Demi was like a drug for me.

I'd do anything for more of her.

"Tomorrow," I rasped, my throat tight at the prospect of what tomorrow would bring.

"I probably should get going now," she said softly.

"Right. Yeah. Okay. I'll talk to you tomorrow," I told her.

"No. You'll see me tomorrow," she reminded me, her voice sultry and seductive.

Jesus. She was so fucking sexy, and I wasn't even looking at her.

I was going to need to take care of business with my hand *again* before I walked out of my hotel room to get on a plane to head home.

"You definitely will," I promised.

"Oh, wait. Before I forget," she declared. "Can you do me a huge favor and ask Holland to give me a call?"

"Sure. Is everything okay?" I asked.

"Yes. Um, well, Sam came up with a few new T-shirts and wanted to see what Holland thought about them."

"I could give you my opinion," I offered.

Demi let out a quiet laugh. "I appreciate that, and I'm sure Sam does, too, but these are women's shirts. I get that you're into being half naked all the time, but you don't strike me as the type who wears shirts that are cut for women's bodies."

Well, there went that opportunity. "Right. I'll give Holland your number and have her reach out before we get on the plane."

"Thank you."

"You're welcome."

"Have a safe flight," she said.

"Thanks. See you tomorrow."

"Bye."

With that, Demi and I disconnected.

I already had my pants unzipped and my cock in my hand before I even set the phone down. This woman was going to be my undoing.

How the hell was I going to last another three months?

CHAPTER 14

Demi

"BUT YOU'RE SAFE, RIGHT?"

"Yes, I'm safe, Sam," I promised. "Everything is fine, and I'm just going to finish getting myself ready right now."

"I can't believe you're doing this," my best friend said.

"That makes two of us," I declared.

"I'm sure it's going to be perfect," she insisted. "Have a great time, and make sure you reach out to me some time tomorrow. I can't wait to hear all about it."

Nodding my head even though she couldn't see me through the phone, I assured her, "I'll call you tomorrow."

"Good luck!"

"Thanks," I murmured.

A moment later, I disconnected the call and tossed my phone down onto the bed.

I had lost my mind.

I didn't know what I was thinking, but I knew this was well beyond anything I had ever done.

No, that's not entirely true.

I knew exactly what I was thinking.

I had been thinking for days now that I wanted something different. I wanted to give myself the opportunity to experience something more than what I'd been giving myself all my life.

So, I came up with a plan and put it in motion.

And now, it was early Friday evening and I found myself back at the one place I dreaded. The hotel.

Only, the hotel I was at currently was not the same one I used to work at in Finch, New Hampshire.

Nope.

I was at a hotel in Pennsylvania.

Yes, that's right. I decided to drag my ass all the way down to the venue just outside of Cash's hometown to watch My Violent Heart play tonight.

Actually, that's not entirely true either.

I was definitely going to go to watch My Violent Heart play tonight, but that wasn't the reason I came here.

I came because I missed Cash, and he hadn't stopped talking about how much he couldn't wait until he'd be able to see me.

Things had changed between us over the last couple of weeks, particularly over the last few days, ever since I texted him from my personal phone.

Talking to him every day had become something I hadn't expected. I didn't think that it would feel a whole lot different than when I'd picked up the phone to call him from the bar.

But it was.

Because now that he had a way to reach out to me that was far more convenient than email, Cash didn't hesitate to remain in constant contact with me. We talked on the phone, but I also got those texts from him at random times throughout the day about anything and everything. I could often tell that they were things he'd just thought of on a whim to share. That's when I realized he had things happening around him, and in those moments, I was the person he thought of to share them with.

All I knew was that if this was a game for him, maybe he deserved to win. He was making all the right moves.

Of course, I hoped he wanted more than to just win the game. I still hadn't forgotten what he'd said to me weeks ago.

When I win this game, I intend to keep the prize.

While I didn't think of myself as a prize to be won, I appreciated the sentiment behind his words. It would be nice to know that he truly felt that way.

It was nearly time to find out, too.

I had arrived here last night after talking to Sam and Cal about my plan. I told Sam because she was my best friend. I told Cal because I was just as close with him, and I wanted him to know that I'd still be working here today and possibly Monday. I didn't know how long I'd be staying, and luckily enough, Cal didn't mind. In fact, he told me not to worry about work at all. I couldn't bring myself to do that, but I appreciated his leniency.

The only other person who knew that I was here was Holland.

I didn't like having to lie to Cash the way that I had, but it was all in the name of pulling off what I hoped would be an epic surprise.

And Holland was ecstatic the moment I told her what my plan was. She immediately offered to help me pull it off, which is why I was now here getting ready in this hotel knowing that somewhere in this town, Cash was getting himself ready, too.

I had presumed he was at his own home still since the venue was only about twenty minutes away from his house.

Cash's house.

The place I'd be going to tonight.

It seemed impossible and completely surreal that I had the address to Cash's house.

I didn't know if it was a good idea for her to give it to me, but Holland insisted Cash wasn't going to be upset when I spoke to her on the phone before she hopped on the plane to come back to Pennsylvania.

"Are you sure he won't mind?" I asked her.

"Demi, trust me," she ordered. "The man is going to be over the moon that I gave you his address. You have nothing to worry about."

"I'm just... I'm nervous about showing up unannounced," I confessed.

"Don't be. I don't know what it is, but something has changed with him ever since he met you," she shared. "I can't imagine there is any reason why he wouldn't want to see you in the flesh if the highlight of his days right now has been when he gets to talk to you on the phone."

The minute she shared that, all of my nerves about Cash being upset that I was just showing up to his place unannounced had vanished. Of course, that meant those nerves were replaced by the ones created when Holland communicated that the highlight of his days was when he got to talk to me.

Had he really changed?

He had said it. Holland had said it.

I was praying for it.

On that thought, I finished getting myself ready. The first part of my plan was to go to the concert and watch. When it was over, I was going to wait for Holland to reach out to me to let me know that Cash had left the venue and was on his way home. She and I were both reasonably certain that Cash wasn't going to hang around afterward since he and I had decided to video chat tonight.

When I had gotten myself ready, I gathered up my bags and left the room. With any luck, I wouldn't be coming back to the hotel, so I didn't want to leave anything behind.

Before I knew it, I'd made it to the venue and was watching the droves of people walk through the massive parking lot to get indoors. It was crazy to think that this many people were there to see Cash and his band. I knew how big they were—or, I thought I did—but to see this in person was astonishing.

I made my way to the will call window for my ticket. Holland had managed to reserve one for me. I wanted to be discreet, so she promised a ticket that wouldn't put me front and center and ruin the surprise.

The arena held twenty-thousand people, and I had no doubt once I had made it inside and took in the crowd that every seat as well as the standing area would be packed.

I didn't know why I was worried.

Cash would have never been able to spot me with this many people.

Before too long, My Violent Heart took the stage. It took me a matter of seconds to realize that what we did at Granite didn't even come close to comparing to what this was. Tens of thousands of screaming fans were riveted to the sight before them, and the band hadn't even started playing yet.

They were larger than life.

Cash was larger than life.

The music started—Walker on the drums and Killian on the guitar—and everyone went crazy.

I didn't.

Because I knew that I was going to hear his voice in a matter of seconds.

Sure enough, the moment he opened his mouth and sang the first few lyrics, I was rendered motionless. With each word that moved past his lips, I grew more and more turned on.

He was breathtaking. Jaw dropping. Magnificent.

His voice moved through me in a way it hadn't when he performed at Granite. It moved through me in a way it hadn't when he was talking to me on the phone.

Maybe because it was different now.

Maybe because I'd finally admitted what I'd been so afraid to admit before.

This man was everything I never thought I'd want. I had been so focused on who I thought he was that I missed feeling this. And while it still terrified me to think that I'd risk my heart with someone like him, I couldn't deny it any longer.

I wanted to give him the chance to change my mind about men.

I wanted him to show me that this was about so much more than just having a warm body in his bed.

I wanted him to make me believe that a real, honest, and genuine man existed.

Watching Cash on stage, hearing his voice, I wanted him to prove that he was that man for me.

Anticipation.

I thought that the feeling I got before we released a new album was untouchable. Never did I think I would ever feel something that came even remotely close to that level.

The energy and excitement had been buzzing through me for more than twenty-four hours now.

Ever since Demi told me she wanted to video chat with me tonight after we performed, I felt like I'd been unable to think about anything else.

It was a wonder I could even get on stage and perform tonight.

Even that felt different tonight.

Just when I believed I'd gotten used to the eager feeling, I stepped out on that stage and something else moved through me. I didn't know what it was. I couldn't explain it.

But if there was one thing I did know for sure, it was that Demi was absolutely the reason behind why I just had my best performance ever.

With a crowd of twenty thousand people, it would have been easy to give them the credit. No doubt they helped, but that wasn't what it was.

It was her.

It was the promise of her.

It was knowing that I was finally going to be able to see her for the first time in weeks, even if it was only through a screen.

I hadn't ever felt this energetic and alive before.

Coming from someone who lived a life that took him all over the world to perform for sold-out crowds, that was saying something. And what it told me was that Demi was meant to be someone special in my life.

I needed to do whatever I had to do to make sure I didn't screw this up with her.

I'd just made it back to our dressing room, and it was clear everyone else was running on the same high.

"There's nothing quite like performing at home," Killian declared.

"Agreed. That vibe was crazy tonight," Beck added. "Cash, man, you were on fire."

"Yeah, you were," Holland agreed. "What got into you tonight?"

Did I tell them? Should I let them know that the whole reason I was 'on fire' tonight was because I couldn't stop thinking about Demi.

My Violent Heart was good. I knew we were good.

But had my ways all this time held us back from being the best we could be?

Before I could answer, Beck joked, "It was the best performance we've ever had, and Cash didn't even need to take his shirt off."

Shit.

When everyone had their eyes on me, I shrugged. "I don't know. Maybe it was a fluke. Or, it's like Killian said. It's just something about being home. I can't really explain it, but something just felt different when I stepped out on the stage tonight."

I was glad that they all felt the same high I was feeling, but I didn't want to take credit for how everything went tonight.

"Didn't you guys all feel it, too?" I asked.

"We felt it, Cash, but it wasn't us that made it happen like that tonight," Roscoe offered. "Tonight was what it was because of you."

I didn't know what to say.

Tonight felt like the perfect time to celebrate with my band. Something incredible had happened tonight, and I truly believed it wasn't wise to just overlook it.

But I didn't want to bail on Demi.

I knew she was the reason I had done so well tonight.

I wasn't going to not have that call with her tonight, but maybe I could delay it for just a little bit longer.

"Why don't we go out for a bit and celebrate this?" I suggested.

"No!" Holland yelled.

Stunned by her reaction, everyone's eyes turned toward her.

"What's going on?" Walker asked her.

Shaking her head, she insisted, "Nothing. I just… I just think that maybe we shouldn't jinx it. Tonight was good. Great. The best ever. But Cash hasn't been going out regularly lately. Maybe that's why tonight was what it was."

She made a valid point.

I'd been spending as much time as I could talking to Demi.

And I'd just admitted that I needed to do whatever I

needed to do to not screw it up with her. Delaying that call to her probably wasn't a smart idea.

"We can plan a barbecue or something like that while we're home for these few days, but I don't think we should go out tonight," Holland added.

"I'm going out," Killian announced. "I'm not going to let this feeling go to waste."

"Same here," Roscoe said.

"I'll go," Beck remarked. "I told my sister I was going to stop by and visit her tomorrow after I go see my mom. Sadie was bummed she couldn't make it to tonight's show, so I want to take her out tomorrow afternoon and do something to cheer her up. Plus, I need to take her out for her birthday since we'll be on tour, and I'm going to miss the actual day this year."

Walker cleared his throat. "I'm calling it quits here tonight," he started before turning his attention to Holland. "You'll let me know what you figure out for a barbecue? I'm definitely down for that."

Her worried eyes went to his, and she nodded. "Yeah. I'll work it out and let everyone know the details tomorrow."

"We can do it at my place," I offered. "Anytime you want works for me."

"Okay."

"You going to come out with us tonight, Cash?" Beck asked.

I thought a moment. I did. I really did.

But I'd made a commitment to Demi. If I was a changed man, I needed to follow through on the promise I made.

I shook my head and answered, "No, I think I'm going to head home tonight."

"You sure?" Killian pressed.

I nodded.

At that, I got to work on gathering up my things and getting ready to head out. After saying goodbye to everyone, I took off.

Twenty minutes later, I was finally back home.

Now that I'd made the decision to follow through on my original plans for the night, I thought it was wise to reach out to Demi ahead of time.

Me: Hey, I just got back home. I'm going to hop in the shower quick. I'll call you in five. Does that work?

I set the phone down on the sink in my bathroom and started stripping. I'd just barely gotten all my clothes off when I heard the chime of an incoming text.

Demi: That's perfect.

I smiled at the phone.

Normally, I would have spent some time lingering in the shower after a show, but I wasn't going to do that tonight. I had waited long enough.

As quickly as I could, I did what I had to do and got out. After toweling myself off, I pulled on a pair of loose, gray sweats.

Just as I settled them on my hips and prepared to go get my phone, my doorbell rang.

Fuck.

At this hour of the night, I couldn't imagine who would be stopping by. Unless, of course, one of my bandmates found it easier to crash at my place instead of making their way to their own. This wouldn't be the first time that happened.

Instead of checking my outdoor camera to see who was here, I just went to the door.

When I opened it up, I received the shock of my life.

"Demi," I gasped.

"Hi, Cash."

I blinked in surprise. "What… what are you doing here?" I asked.

"I missed you, too," she admitted, her voice hoarse.

It took me a moment to come to grips with the fact that Demi was standing right there in front of me, close enough to touch.

Close enough to touch, I thought.

I reached out to her and demanded, "Come here."

Demi didn't hesitate to fly forward into my chest. While keeping one arm firmly around her back, I used the other to close the door and lock it.

Once I had both arms around her, she tipped her head back and looked up at me.

"What is it?" I asked, seeing the strange expression on her face.

She swallowed hard before she begged, "Please don't break my heart, Cash."

With that, she pressed up on her toes and touched her lips to mine.

Just like that, I was gone.

CHAPTER 15

Demi

WHY HAD I WAITED?

Why did I hold back?

For far too long, fear had consumed every part of my being and prevented me from doing something that felt this natural.

Just one touch of my lips against Cash's lips was all it took.

Heat and desire flooded me. Desperation took over, and it felt as though I couldn't get close enough. I couldn't touch enough.

My moans filled the air as Cash claimed my mouth in an all-consuming kiss. It was hot, deep, and wet.

And the way his arms and hands held me—like he never wanted to let me go—felt like he was telling me he'd be sure to do just as I had asked him.

He wouldn't break my heart.

The front of my body plastered against his, my hands drove into his hair until they reached the back of his skull.

Cash had moved his arms from around me and brought both of his hands up my body. One drove into my hair while the other landed just beneath my jaw, curling around the side of my throat.

Allowing my tongue to sweep into the warm recesses of his mouth, I tasted the man I'd fantasized about for weeks now. And I did it as he spun me around and backed me up against the wall.

I couldn't even begin to comprehend how he kissed. It was far beyond any expectations I had. If I wasn't so caught up in how good this was already, I might have questioned whether or not I could even hold a candle to that level of kissing.

When another moan tore up my throat, Cash pulled his mouth away from mine.

His forehead was just inches from mine, and he was staring me in the eyes. "What are you doing here?" he asked, his voice low and husky.

I didn't hesitate to answer him honestly. "I'm risking it all."

The intense, heated look on his face faltered, and I instantly regretted saying those words. Just as he parted his lips to speak, I pleaded, "Not now, Cash. I just want to feel good right now."

Cash wavered for all of a few seconds before he captured my mouth again. I couldn't have been more grateful he didn't push to talk.

That was the last thing I wanted to do right now.

I didn't want to talk. I knew if we did, it'd lead to painful discussions that would put a halt to this. And I absolutely did not want to risk not having this with Cash.

We could talk later.

I'd discuss it all with him if he wanted to know it.

But right now, I just wanted him.

I'd been yearning for this for days now, and the minute I made the decision to come to Pennsylvania to see him, the anticipation and longing grew tenfold.

I didn't even know how I made it through the performance earlier tonight. He was amazing on stage, and I wondered if I'd missed that when the band played at Granite because I'd been so caught up in trying to protect myself from a man who seemed, at least for now, to want to change for me.

God, I hoped he was serious.

Unable to control myself, I began kissing Cash's naked torso and allowing my hands to roam over the smooth skin of his chest. I moved to one side, brought my mouth to his nipple, and tipped my head back to look up at him as I swirled my tongue around it.

His hand put a bruising grip on my hip and he groaned.

Somehow, I managed to push my back away from the wall and turn so that Cash's back took my place there.

I kissed his mouth once more before moving down his body. I ran my mouth over his broad shoulders and spanning chest. I licked his nipples again as I felt him squeeze my biceps when I did. My mouth moved down his abdomen and trailed along the skin toward his hip, where there was the unmistakable beginning of the V, which disappeared beneath his gray sweats.

Seeing him in those sweats, I realized it was a thing.

A pair of gray sweats slung low on the hips of a man like

Cash was the kind of thing that could make a girl forget she ever had any worries in her life.

And considering Cash's sweats weren't just showing a bulge but a rather impressive erection instead, I thought I was a very lucky girl.

Wanting to tease him, I tipped my chin up, looked at him through hooded eyes, and curled my fingers around his hardened length. Gripping him tightly through his pants, I asked, "Is this for me?"

"Jesus, fuck," he hissed. "You're incredible."

I smiled at him.

There was one sweet moment that followed as his hand came up to the side of my face, captured a lock of hair between his fingers, and pushed it away.

No sooner had he done that when I could no longer prevent myself from allowing the clean, masculine scent of him to push me to drop to my knees. My hands went to the sweats at his hips and yanked them down his legs.

I watched as his cock sprang free, jutting out from between the tops of his legs, and licked my lips.

He was perfect.

His penis was perfect.

Beautiful.

Long, thick, and very, very hard.

I tilted my head back one last time to look up at him. The moment our eyes locked, Cash rasped, "You're so fucking beautiful. I could come just looking at you like that."

Feeling like I was on top of the world, I reached my hand out and curled my fingers around the base of his cock. Then I brought my lips to the tip, parted them slightly, and slowly took him in my mouth.

I kept my eyes on his just a bit longer and was overcome with emotion at the intensity of his stare. It was as though having my mouth on him was his every wish come true. Seeing that only encouraged me to continue.

For the next several moments, I focused all of my effort on giving him pleasure. My hand held him firmly while my tongue glided along the velvety soft skin of his hardened length. Initially, I had only allowed my mouth to cover little more than just the tip. But once I'd had my fill of teasing him, I parted my lips again and took as much of him as I could into my mouth.

The sound that came from him as a result was gratifying. He was loving everything about this.

All I wanted at that moment was to give him more.

So I did.

I worked him hard. My jaw began to feel the effects of it, but I didn't care. I wanted to give this to him.

My free hand had moved from its place on his thigh to his hip. The moment it landed there, Cash's hand covered it.

And as I continued to suck and lick and tease and taste, the pressure his hand and fingers put on mine alternated. It went from soft and delicate to hard and bruising.

I hadn't gotten anywhere near enough of him when he was suddenly no longer in my mouth. Cash had pulled his hips back, bent down, and lifted me up under my arms. He dragged my body up along his, captured me behind the head with one hand, and planted his other firmly on my ass.

"You're remarkable, firecracker," he praised me just before he took my mouth. He kissed me in a way that communicated his appreciation for what I'd just done for him. I was simply grateful he had a solid grip on my ass because I would have surely melted into a puddle at the heat and building desire I felt. When Cash gave a gentle tug back on my hair and separated his mouth from mine, he added, "I've fantasized about this mouth from the very first day I saw you. Now that I've experienced the real deal, the things I'd do for this mouth border on criminal."

"Cash," I whispered.

He spun me around and pressed me up against the wall before he smiled and said, "It's my turn to have a taste."

For the next several moments, I waged a war within my body. Part of me was caught up in what he was doing while the other part of me was struggling to remain standing.

Cash's mouth left mine, and his lips trailed down my throat toward my chest as his hands began tugging at my clothing. It was clear the material was in his way, and he wanted access immediately.

I would have helped, but I couldn't.

I was too far gone, lost in the feel of having him near me like this.

Kissing me.

Touching me.

Somehow, he managed to get my clothes off so that all I was wearing was a sexy bra and a G-string.

Yes, I planned for this, and the last thing I was going to do was have him see me naked for the first time wearing a pair of full-bottomed cotton underwear.

No way.

I was going for seductive.

I wanted his heart pounding in his chest at the sight of me.

Truthfully, if he had been experiencing any of this the

same as I was, his heart started pounding right about the time he opened the door.

For a brief moment, Cash stepped back and looked at me. My upper back was leaning against the wall, my hips pushed forward. My body was mostly on display, and Cash stood there completely unabashed by his nakedness as he allowed his eyes to roam over me. He made no secret of the fact that he liked what he saw.

"How are you this beautiful?" he asked, his tone ragged. "Are you even real?"

Cash didn't give me a chance to respond. He closed the distance between us and yanked the cup of my bra down to expose my breast. His large hand caught the soft, rounded flesh as his mouth descended on it.

Wetness pooled between my thighs as his tongue teased my nipple. His free hand unhooked my bra with expert-like ease before reaching up to the strap at my shoulder and pulling it down my arm.

The bra fell to the floor, and Cash moved his mouth to the other side. He lavished the opposite breast with the same attention he'd given the first side. All I could do was moan, claw my fingers through his hair, and roll my hips in the air in search of something to give me relief.

There was none to be found.

And just when I thought I'd die of desperation, Cash's mouth began moving farther down my body. His hands left my breasts and started sliding down my sides. His lips trailed a path down my abdomen and over to my hip as he settled himself on his knees.

One of his hands gently stroked over the skin of my ass while he continued to kiss all along my outer hip.

And then, it happened.

Suddenly, Cash's hand that had been gripping the front of my thigh on the opposite side moved up and slid underneath the flimsy fabric of my G-string. With one quick yank, he tore it off my body.

He tore it off my body.

"Cash," I gasped.

He looked up at me with a devilish look in his eyes. He grinned and declared, "It was in my way."

"I liked that one," I told him, even though I had just realized that his worst trait of impatience really wasn't a bad thing.

"I'll buy you a hundred more," he promised.

It seemed it was now Cash who wasn't interested in talking because no sooner did he get those words out when he put his mouth between my legs and started eating.

My head dropped back against the wall as his talented tongue and mouth devoured me.

Nobody.

Nobody compared to him.

Nobody even came close.

Cash was on a scale all by himself.

I was ruined.

Completely, totally ruined.

If he didn't fall in love with me and keep me forever, I was certain I'd never find anyone who would measure up to what this man could do to me.

Everything about it was raw, passionate, and animalistic.

Instinct, no doubt, was pushing us both to do what we were doing. There had been so much licking, touching, and tasting, and we were only just beginning.

I'd been so turned on from the moment I saw him step on the stage earlier that it barely took a few minutes of having his mouth between my legs to bring me to the brink of an orgasm.

My breathing grew shallow, and I started to whimper.

Cash groaned between my legs, and I could feel the vibration of it run through me.

"Fuck, baby, I'm going to come," I warned him.

His fingertips pressed in harder at my ass just as violent tremors tore through me. My body shook with the force of each wave of pleasure, and Cash continued to work me through it.

When it finally left me, Cash pressed several sweet kisses to my inner thigh before trailing another path up my body. His lips made it to my mouth.

"You taste even better than I thought you would," he shared, his voice soft.

Then he kissed me, allowing me to taste myself on him. After the orgasm he'd just delivered, I didn't know how it was possible to already feel turned on again, but I was.

Without breaking the connection between our mouths, Cash lifted me in his arms. I wrapped my legs around his waist, loving the feel of his heated, solid body against mine.

How he did it so effortlessly without being able to see, I'll never know, but the next thing I knew, Cash had placed me in his bed. He stood at the side, tearing open a condom packet.

As he sheathed himself, his eyes never left mine.

The exchange between our gazes was hot and intense, and while I wasn't sure I could read it, I loved everything about the way his expression made me feel.

The slight edge of tenderness I saw on his face lasted a

brief moment because everything turned frantic a few seconds later.

Cash drove in fast, hard, and deep. My head flew back, pressing deeper into the mattress and exposing my throat.

Everything between us became a mix of fiery and lust-filled moans, fervent and greedy caressing, and desperate, unhindered movements of our hips. The sound of our skin slapping together, the heady scent of sex in the air, and the undeniable sparks flying between us every time our eyes locked was lifting me higher and higher.

Though the force of each stroke of his cock into my body was wild and powerful, I couldn't help from feeling as though he was worshiping my body. He'd made me feel that way from the moment our mouths connected just inside his front door.

But it hit me then that this was all about the two of us finally coming together and sharing our bodies with one another after weeks and weeks of me denying that where I was right now was precisely where I had wanted to be all along.

At that realization, feeling just a twinge of guilt, I felt compelled to give it my all. Lifting my head and torso slightly, Cash understood what I wanted. He rolled to his back, took me with him, and allowed me to take charge.

Then I went to work.

I pressed my palms into his chest, leaned my weight into them and my knees at his sides, and worked my hips over him. For a while, I was simply caught up in the feeling. His erection was thick, large, and pulsing, so it was hard not to just be consumed by the physical pleasure.

The way Cash could make my body feel with his body alone was indescribable.

But it was when I tipped my head forward and saw the look on his face that I realized the physical pleasure he could deliver was nothing compared to the feeling one single look could give me.

God, I wished I knew what it meant. There was so much there, and if I had to guess, I would think it was a mix of amazement, adoration, relief, joy, and something else. That something was the thing that made me lose all sense of control.

I slowed my pace, took in that something, gobbled it up, and savored the feeling it gave me. Before I could stop myself, I lowered my torso down until my breasts were pressed against his chest. Continuing to move slow, I brushed my lips against his.

Cash was patient, giving me the opportunity to lead the way. But when I felt the beginnings of my orgasm starting to splinter across my body, he knew I needed him to take over.

And he did just that.

One hand on my ass, the other at the back of my head, Cash powered his hips up. I threw my head back as I felt every inch of his cock moving inside me.

"Cash," I groaned, my legs shaking on either side of his body.

"That's it, Demi," he encouraged me gently. "This is all yours. Take it."

I took it.

I took all of it and tucked it away somewhere deep in my heart.

And just as I started to come down, Cash demanded, "Look at me, baby."

I looked at him, and then I saw the most beautiful thing

I'd ever seen. Cash came apart beneath me. His chest, neck, and face grew flushed as the muscles delineating his impressive body flexed with the force of it. It was breathtaking. But it was the look on his face that did me in.

I couldn't look away.

I couldn't think about anything else.

All I could do was watch him in utter amazement and feel nothing but overwhelming joy and gratification.

This had been the right thing to do. Coming here, being with him, was the best decision of my life.

On that thought, as he started to come down, I lowered my mouth to his and kissed him.

Cash didn't hesitate to kiss me back.

CHAPTER 16

Cash

If I thought everything I went through in my life up to this point was the result of being very lucky, I had no words for what I'd just experienced.

Could this actually be described as luck?

Maybe everything before now was simply the result of hard work and dedication. No. No, I knew it was more than that. There was good fortune there. I was a talented singer, born that way. That had to be considered lucky.

And if that was the case, I just couldn't come up with the right word to express what I just had with Demi.

Unforgettable. That's for sure.

But it was so much more.

It was life changing, earth shattering, and all-consuming.

I knew that I was already so incredibly fortunate to be living the life that I was living, doing something I loved with people who were like family to me.

Why I got that *and* I got Demi, I'd never begin to comprehend. It seemed [illegible] unfair.

Of course, I wasn't complaining. I'd take all the good that this life had in store for me and never do anything to jeopardize it. It all meant too much, and I realized that not everybody had the opportunities that I did.

I wouldn't squander this life.

As I walked from the master bathroom back to the bed and saw Demi on her side looking at me, I couldn't stop myself from smiling.

She was perfect for me. There wasn't a single thing about her that I didn't like, not even her sassy attitude the very first day I met her.

In fact, it was her mouth that I was probably most attracted to.

Her mouth was paradise.

Whether I was kissing her, whether she was kissing my body, whether she was talking, or whether she had my cock in it, I loved everything about her mouth.

Climbing into the bed, I was still having a tough time wrapping my head around the fact that she was here.

Demi was here.

In my bed.

I had so much to talk to her about, so many things I wanted to discuss, and it didn't matter that it was the early hours of the morning and that I still hadn't slept.

Rolling to my side, my front to hers, I dove right in.

"How are you here?" I asked.

"I drove the rental car from the venue to your house," she answered.

Okay. So, she was taking this literally.

I let out a laugh and replied, "There are a lot of questions that follow that. First, let me say that I'm not in any way complaining, but how did you find out where I lived?"

"Holland."

Suddenly, it all made sense.

Holland knew what Demi had planned, which was why she insisted I not go out to celebrate tonight. I'd always looked at Holland as the sister I never had, and in that moment, I couldn't have been more grateful for her. I was definitely going to have to do something to show her my appreciation.

It dawned on me that Demi said she came from the venue.

"Wait. You were there?" I asked. "You watched the show tonight?"

"Yeah," she answered softly. "You're incredible."

"It was you," I blurted.

"What?" she asked.

I couldn't believe it. This had to be the craziest thing I'd ever experienced. I was sure if I told anyone, probably even Demi, they would think I'd lost my mind. But I knew it was the truth.

"The minute I stepped out on the stage tonight, something felt different," I confessed. "Everyone knew it, and we even talked about it after the concert. I tried to brush it off as us being home and playing at a place that was so familiar to us, but in the back of my mind, I thought it was because I'd been feeling so excited about having a video chat with you tonight. Now, I realize it wasn't any of that."

Confusion washed over her. "What was it?" she wondered.

"You," I told her. "I know that probably sounds crazy, but I'm convinced that's what it was."

Demi shifted her body closer to mine and said, "I don't think it's crazy at all."

Feeling her close to me like that and hearing her response, I had to know more.

"How did this happen? What made you decide to come here?" I questioned her.

Something moved through her expression, and I could tell she was struggling with how to answer me. I didn't want to put her in a tough or uncomfortable spot, no matter how much I wanted to understand what changed. If she needed more time, I could give her that.

Just as I was about to tell her she didn't have to answer just yet, Demi replied, "I denied how I felt for too long, and I thought it was time to be honest with myself."

I didn't know what I thought her answer was going to be, but it definitely wasn't that. "How do you feel?" I asked.

Demi's hand came up and cupped the side of my face, right at my jaw. Her thumb stroked along my bottom lip as her eyes followed the movement. I didn't dare move because I loved what she was doing. Feeling her hands on me was something I enjoyed a lot more than I ever thought I would. And I had already thought I was going to enjoy it tremendously.

After a long pause, she shared, "That I'm just as attracted to you as you are to me, and that your persistence in trying to connect with me made me feel good. I liked that you didn't give up no matter how many times I insisted there would never be anything between us. But most of all, it's what I felt after I started to cave just a little and started to get to know you."

"And what was that?" I pressed, feeling like I was hanging on to every word she said.

"Whenever I wasn't talking to you, I missed you," Demi admitted. "I found myself wanting more time to talk with you and started counting down the days until you'd be back in Finch."

Nope.

Not in a million years did I expect that was going to be her answer.

For so long, she'd fought me on this. I was on the verge of losing my mind thinking about how much I wanted someone who clearly did not want me.

Actually, that wasn't entirely true.

I could see it, even if just a little bit. I knew there was a connection there. She felt the chemistry between us.

But for whatever reason, she denied it.

My persistence paid off. There had been a few times when I started to worry that I'd be labeled a stalker or something, but that hadn't even come close to being what Demi thought was happening.

I was so caught up in my thoughts about all of it, Demi continued, "I got tired of pretending."

"Pretending?" I repeated.

She nodded as her hand that had been at the side of my face moved down along my throat to my chest and over my pecs. Her touch was as soft as a feather. "That I didn't want you."

I gave her hip a gentle squeeze. "I'm glad you changed your mind," I said.

Her features softened. "Me too."

"We have to talk about something, though," I told her.

Concern and worry immediately marred her features. I hated seeing her like that, but I really wanted to know what I was dealing with. There wasn't a whole lot that was said, but there had been enough for me to know there was something here I needed to help her work through.

"What is it?" she worried.

"Can you tell me why you begged me not to break your heart?" I began. "I get the obvious reason… nobody wants to have their heart broken. But that's a given, and I have a feeling that's not what's going on with you."

Demi didn't hesitate to respond. "You were my first," she declared.

My body instantly froze.

What?

She couldn't possibly mean that. "Demi, baby, are you telling me you were a virgin?" I gasped.

I didn't necessarily have a problem with her being a virgin, but I'd just taken her, and I wasn't exactly gentle. I mean, I wasn't rough to the point that I'd hurt her, but if this had been her first time, I couldn't understand how she wasn't in any pain.

Not only that, but Demi would have been the world's first virgin who knew exactly what she was doing.

There was no way that was possible.

Laughter escaped her. "No. No, it's not that," she assured me. When some of the tension left my body, she continued, "You were my first date. And I know it probably wasn't really a date per se, but going out to breakfast with you that morning before you left New Hampshire was new territory for me."

Now I was the one who was confused. "In what way?"

Her fingers continued to move over the skin of my chest. I couldn't work out whether she was aware of what she was doing or if it was something she was doing absentmindedly. Either way, it didn't matter. It felt good to me, and she seemed to need to do it.

"I haven't ever gone on an official date with anyone before," she shared. "I'm… I know that must sound horrible. I've never been on a date, and yet, I'm not a virgin."

"Demi, look at me," I demanded.

Her fingers stopped moving, though they remained on my chest, and she directed her gaze to my face.

Once I had her attention, I said, "You are not going to make yourself feel bad about anything. I am not a saint, and I'm not sitting here judging you at all."

"I… I wasn't… I didn't mean to imply that you were being judgmental," she stammered. "I just… I know it's not a good look."

"I get the distinct feeling that you did what you had to do to take care of natural human needs and desires," I started. "I also get the feeling that you had your reasons for doing that. There's *nothing* wrong with it. Okay?"

She nodded, but I wasn't sure she believed what I just said to her.

Deciding it was best to let it go and get back to the conversation, I asked, "So, why was breakfast with me your first date?"

"Because I didn't want to go on dates with anyone," Demi answered.

"So, am I just that charming and irresistible?" I teased.

Demi started laughing, and I let out a sigh of relief. I didn't want her holding on to any tension about whatever choices she made in her life. It was the two of us now, and I was grateful for that.

When she finally settled down from the laughter, she replied, "It was partly that and the fact that you didn't just walk away when I turned you down. You put in effort, so that was a big deal."

"Nobody ever put in any effort with you?" I asked, thinking this wasn't adding up.

"Not the person who should have," she countered.

Her cousin Cal told me she was fragile. I had a feeling whatever she was about to share was going to explain why that was the case.

"I feel like I'm missing something here," I said.

There was another pause, and this one was rather lengthy. Demi got back to trailing her fingers over my skin, and I waited for her to offer some kind of clarification.

Eventually, she shared, "I was just a freshman in high school when I woke up sick in the middle of the night. Actually, it wasn't really the middle of the night. I hadn't been feeling well earlier that evening, so I went to bed early. I thought my stomach was bothering me because my parents had been fighting with each other that evening before my mom went to work. But when I woke up not even two hours later, I realized I was actually sick, so I ran to the bathroom and vomited."

Demi paused a moment, and I could see she was really struggling with something.

Eventually, she went on, "My mom was at work that

night, so I went to my dad to tell him that I was sick. When I opened the door to his room and turned on his light, I found him standing beside the bed fucking a woman who wasn't my mother. To make matters even worse, he turned toward me and was completely naked."

Fuck.

It all made sense now.

Demi didn't trust men because her own father hadn't been faithful to her mother. And to think she walked in and saw it happening.

"Demi, I'm so sorry," I apologized.

"Me too," she murmured. "I lived the aftermath of that. The betrayal. The disappointment. The pain for both my mom and me. The fact that he didn't even try to fix it, not even for me. He was just fine with getting the divorce. My mom deserved better, so I wouldn't have wanted her to stay, but his indifference really just hit me hard. He never even apologized. And I guess it's possible he was simply embarrassed because of how awkward it was for me, but it still hurt."

I couldn't imagine. I mean, I knew people got divorced all the time, and it was never pleasant, but this was just horrible.

"I wish I knew what to say to make it better," I told her.

"You could tell me that this wasn't just a game for you," she responded.

Her?

She thought I was putting in all this effort with her for the fun of it?

"Demi, do you even realize how incredible you are?" I asked. "This was not a game for me. At least, not in the way that you're thinking. Was this challenging for me? Yes. Did

I enjoy the banter between us and the scouring looks you gave me? Absolutely. But I didn't do everything I did just so I could get you in my bed for a night. Not for nothing, but if I just wanted to fuck someone, I could have easily made that happen. I wanted you."

"You did," she said. "Do you still feel that way?"

She couldn't be serious.

"Yes," I deadpanned.

When Demi didn't respond, I decided we needed to have another discussion.

"Look, I know this is *really* early here, but I think it's important we discuss what just happened here tonight and what that means for us moving forward," I started. "I like you, and I want to explore what this is between us. Do you want the same thing?"

She closed her eyes and let out a deep sigh. When she opened them again and looked at me, she said, "I really want to try, but I'm terrified. And I think you need to know what you're getting into with me. I might seem tough on the surface, Cash, but inside, I'm so insecure. I have a terrible time trusting men."

"I understand that, but please believe me when I say that you don't need to be insecure when it comes to me," I pleaded.

I could hear the sarcastic undertone to her laugh as she declared, "You being you makes me feel even more worried than I would if you were someone else."

I didn't quite know how to take that. "Who do you want me to be?"

"That's not what I meant," she insisted. "I just mean that you being this massive rock star makes me more terrified about what I'm getting myself into with you. Jealousy ran through me when I saw the pictures of you without your shirt on at your concerts. All those women had their eyes on you, and I know they were thinking the exact same thing I was."

I smiled and asked, "What were you thinking?"

"That I wanted to be right where I am now. That I wanted what just happened between us to happen… repeatedly."

"Repeatedly?" I said.

"Yes."

I pushed a lock of her hair back from the side of her face and promised, "I'll be sure to make that happen right away. But first, I want you to know that I understand where you're coming from, and I want to do everything I can to make you feel comfortable and secure."

"It might take me a minute to feel that way," she stated.

"I expected that much, and I promise to be patient with you," I told her. "The last thing I want is for you to feel like you've come into this risking it all and feeling like it wasn't worth it. I want it to be worth it for you."

"Thank you."

"You're welcome. And just for the record, I want you to know that nothing ever happened with those girls who walked up to the table when we were out at breakfast. The whole band was there, and it's not uncommon to have groupies hanging around. I promise you, I did nothing with any of them."

"I appreciate you clarifying that, even if I wasn't in a position where it should have mattered," Demi said.

For a few minutes, we stayed there like that, Demi continuing to run her fingers over the skin on my chest. I was comfortable in the silence with her, just happy being beside her.

Eventually, she called, "Cash?"

"Yeah?"

"Will you kiss me?" she asked. "I hesitate to tell you this since I'm sure you already know it, but your mouth is unbelievable."

I burst out laughing and buried my face in her neck as I rolled her to her back. If Demi was frustrated by my reaction, I didn't know it because all I could pay attention to was the fact that her naked body was beneath mine and she had wrapped her legs around my waist.

It wasn't until she spoke that I had to redirect my focus.

"What's so funny about that?"

I lifted my face from her neck, stared at her, and said, "I thought the very same thing about your mouth from the first day I saw you. And I've got a boatload of reasons why I like it so much."

Demi cocked an eyebrow. "Really?"

I nodded.

"I think you should kiss me now, Cash," she urged.

I'd waited weeks for this. I was not going to delay.

At her request, I lowered my mouth and touched my lips to hers. That was just the beginning of a very long and satisfying round two. Suffice it to say, we didn't get to sleep until just before the sun came up.

CHAPTER 17

Demi

"IS EVERYTHING OKAY?"

That question came from Cash. I had just walked into his kitchen to find that he'd made food for us. Lots of it, too. Seeing it, I stopped moving and remained frozen to the spot.

Is this what it's like?

That was the only thought running through my mind as I took in the scene before me. For the first time ever, I'd spent the night with a man—one who meant something to me—and I'd just walked into his kitchen the next morning to find that he'd made breakfast.

Or, I guess, it should probably be called brunch considering the time.

Either way, I was only slightly bummed about the fact that I'd denied myself from experiencing something like this for so long, but given that my first time it was happening was with Cash made it all worth the wait.

Then again, there wasn't much that hadn't been worth

the wait when it came to him. The only real issue I had with any of it was that I'd been the one to hold back with him for so long. I was not, in any way, disappointed that I held out for so long waiting for him to come along.

I hadn't expected him to come down and do all of this for me. It was just that I needed to make a phone call this morning.

Cash and I had woken up this morning and immediately gotten distracted with sex, which was no less fabulous than the first two times we'd had it last night. Afterward, we'd discussed what was happening over the next few days.

"You flew here, right?" he asked when we were curled up in bed with one another earlier this morning.

"Yeah."

"Is there a return flight scheduled?"

"Sunday night," I told him.

There was not an ounce of hesitation in his voice when he requested, "Would you mind canceling it and staying longer?" When I didn't respond because I was still trying to process the fact that he wanted me to stay longer, he added, "I'll cover any of the costs for switching the flight."

"It's not the money I'm worried about, Cash," I said.

"What's wrong then? You seem troubled," he noted.

Smiling at him, I shared, "You want me here."

Confusion washed over him. "You say that like it's a bad thing."

"It's not," I assured him, shaking my head. "It's just taking me a minute to catch up. You're so sure about everything, and I'm just—"

"Worried?" he guessed, cutting me off.

I shrugged. "Maybe a little," I admitted.

Cash, who had been on his back in the bed while I sat up beside him, tightened his abs and came to a seated position beside me.

"Demi, I didn't think that wanting more time with you would be the kind of thing that would make you scared or nervous," he began. "I'm not trying to make you uncomfortable or move faster than you're prepared for. I just... I have to get back on the road soon, and I'm not ready to let you go just yet."

When he put it like that, I couldn't say no. He wanted more time with me. It wasn't as though I didn't feel the same. The fact that I completely did not want to even think about him getting back on the road while I made my way back to New Hampshire was weighing heavily on my mind, too. It wasn't something I wanted to even think about at the moment, so I simply leaned closer and said, "I need to make a phone call. I want to let Cal know that I'm going to be staying a few extra days."

He smiled against my mouth, brushing his lips back and forth against mine. Then he said softly, "Okay. You make your call and meet me downstairs."

"My phone is lost somewhere down in the pile of clothing at the front door," I informed him.

He reached out to the side, grabbed his phone off his nightstand, and said, "You can use mine."

"Are you sure?" I asked. I didn't know how he felt about members of the general public having his number.

"Are you calling your cousin?" he countered.

"Well, I was going to call my best friend first," I confessed. "The likelihood is that Sam is with Cal anyway, so I could kill two birds with one stone."

"I don't think Sam is going to go distributing my number to anyone, so it's cool," he insisted. "Use my phone and make your call. The code is zero nine zero seven."

"Okay," I agreed.

With that, Cash gave me a kiss before he twisted his body and heaved himself out of the bed. I watched as he paraded in his birthday suit across the room to pull on a new pair of gray sweats.

Yum.

Then he moved to the closet, disappeared behind the door for a moment, and came back toward the bed. He tossed a T-shirt down in front of me. "You can wear that for now if you're interested in covering up," he offered. "Though, I will say that I'm entirely alright with you remaining naked."

I tried to scowl at him, but my efforts were futile because he simply laughed as he started walking away.

"You owe me a pair of panties," I reminded him.

He moved to the doorway, stopped, and looked back at me. "If I recall correctly, firecracker, I said I'd buy you a hundred pairs."

"One would be sufficient," I insisted.

"Not if I plan to rip more of them off your body," he returned.

My mouth dropped open at his brazen comment, and I didn't get the chance to respond because he laughed again and walked out.

I took a moment to allow myself to remember how it felt when he'd ripped my panties off me last night, and then I picked up his phone to call Sam.

Now, I was standing in his kitchen, wearing his T-shirt, and I couldn't stop the good feelings from overwhelming me.

"Demi?" Cash called when too much time passed without a response from me.

"Yeah?"

"Did everything go okay with Sam?" he asked.

I shook off the thoughts I'd been having and moved toward the table, where he was sitting.

"Yeah," I answered as I came to a stop beside him.

Cash's eyes roamed over me, moving from head to toe and back again. When they stopped on my face, he reached his arm out, curled it around the back of my waist, and urged me into his lap. Once I was settled there, he pressed, "Are you sure?"

I nodded. "Yes. In fact, everything was better than okay. She's beyond excited for me. Well, and for you, too, but mostly for me."

"That's great news. Is Cal cool with you staying longer?"

I didn't want to tell Cash exactly what Cal had said because I thought it was a bit presumptuous. Instead, I answered, "Cal is more than okay with me staying longer. Besides, I was already working from home, so I can still take some time to answer emails while I'm here."

Cash grinned. "Cool. Are you hungry?" he asked.

"Yeah," I said, as I made the move to stand and sit at the chair on the opposite side of the table.

Cash's arm tightened around my waist, holding me in place, as he used his other hand to pick up his fork and spear a strawberry with it. He brought the fork to my mouth.

"Open," he said softly.

I parted my lips and Cash slid the fork inside. When my mouth closed around the fork, he pulled it back, leaving only the sweet fruit behind.

I chewed slowly as he watched.

Once I swallowed, he said, "I'm really glad you came here, Demi."

"Me too," I rasped.

He lifted another strawberry to my mouth. I opened my mouth, accepted it, and chewed again.

"Do you like pancakes?" he asked.

"Only if you've got syrup on them," I answered.

He reached out, plucked a pancake off the stack at the center of the table, and set it on his plate. Then he drizzled syrup on it, used his fork to cut it, and brought a bite to my mouth.

Without needing any instruction, I parted my lips once more, and Cash slid the pancake in my mouth. Syrup ended up on my lip, so after I chewed and swallowed, I licked my lip. Cash's fingers tightened at my hip, his focus never leaving my mouth.

"Kiss me," he urged.

I didn't hesitate. He was feeding me, and he was doing it in the most seductive way. Why would I not kiss him?

For more than an hour, Cash and I stayed there, eating breakfast, kissing, and teasing. It was, by far, the most erotic experience of my life.

I loved that Cash was the one to give it to me.

"Are you excited?" Cash asked.

"For the concert?" I retorted.

He laughed, reached his hand out to mine, and held it. "For the backstage pass," he teased.

"Oh. Yeah. Of course," I told him, doing my best not to freak out about the fact that Cash Morris was out in public with me holding my hand. "I've loved My Violent Heart for years, so this is definitely up there on my list of things I never thought I'd ever experience."

"Good to know."

It was a few hours after Cash and I had our pancake, syrup, and strawberry brunch, and we had just arrived back at the same venue My Violent Heart played at last night.

They were playing a second show tonight before they had a break. Apparently, they were planning to spend that break—or, at least, part of it—with each other because tomorrow afternoon, the entire band was going over to Cash's place for a barbecue.

Cash led me down a long corridor, claiming we were heading toward his dressing room. When he came to a stop, I looked up at the door and saw his name on display.

Just as he put his hand on the doorknob so we could enter, the door for the room across from his opened.

"Yes!"

Cash and I spun around and found Holland there grinning at us. I had a feeling she was celebrating the fact that she not only saw me there with Cash but also that he was holding my hand.

"What's going on?" Cash asked her.

Her face lit up. "You two are so adorable," she beamed. Then she reached out, curled her fingers around my wrist, and ordered, "And considering I know that you've now had

Demi in your presence for hours, I'm taking her into my dressing room for a bit."

Cash's grip on my hand tightened. "What?"

Holland rolled her eyes before she insisted, "It's okay, Cash. I promise I'll bring her back in a little bit."

I looked up at Cash and smiled. He looked sad. "I'll be back in a little bit," I told him.

"Promise?" he asked.

I didn't want to laugh, but I couldn't help a small chortle from escaping. He looked like a guy who'd just lost his puppy.

"I promise."

Accepting that, he pressed a kiss to my cheek before he let my hand go. Then Holland dragged me into her dressing room.

No sooner had she closed the door when we walked deeper into her dressing room and I saw a woman sitting on the couch.

"Demi, this is Sadie," Holland introduced us. "She's Beck's younger sister and my best friend. Sadie, this is Demi. And I'm hoping she's ready to spill all the details of her night with Cash."

Sadie and I exchanged pleasantries and greetings. Holland walked over to the vanity where she'd set out all of her makeup when she started speaking again. "I've been *dying* to know how it went for you last night," she began. "I thought I was going to lose my mind because Cash started talking about going out to celebrate how well we did. Of course, getting Roscoe or Killian to turn down a night out is like pulling teeth, so I had my work cut out for me."

"Oh, I'm sorry," I lamented, hating that I'd put her in that position.

Holland shook her head. "It was nothing. I was happy to do it. Besides, it seems like it all worked out for you anyway," she returned.

I nodded and smiled. "It did. Thank you for helping me facilitate this whole surprise."

"It was so much fun," she replied. "I liked that I had this little secret that I knew was going to just make Cash's night. He's been so different ever since our first trip to New Hampshire."

This intrigued me. While Cash had said himself that he was a changed man, it was entirely possible that he was making it seem more drastic than it actually was. For Holland to be hinting at something similar, I thought it was a good thing.

"How so?" I asked.

She finished putting her eyeliner on, turned back to me, and thought a moment. "I don't know," she answered. "He's just not the same, but I mean that in the best way possible. It's been really nice to see him sort of change his mindset. Cash has always been like Roscoe, Killian, and even Beck when it comes to living the rock star lifestyle. For the guys, that comes with a lot of women." I started to feel some uneasiness settle in my stomach as she paused a moment and shook her head. Then she continued, "Cash isn't interested in that anymore. In fact, even if he was interested, apparently, it wasn't possible for him to follow through."

"What does that mean?" I questioned her.

She grinned at me. "He told us you broke his dick."

I gasped. "What?"

Sadie burst out laughing. When she got it under control, she immediately lamented, "I'm sorry. It's just that…

well, I've known Cash a long time, and that was completely unexpected."

Holland giggled, and while I was only slightly relieved she found this funny, which indicated it couldn't be all bad, I was still very much alarmed.

"After we left New Hampshire, he was a mess," she started. "Women flashed him or came up to him and grabbed his crotch. It did nothing for him, apparently. That's the reason we came back to your hometown for our break. Cash needed to see you to make sure he wasn't permanently damaged."

Oh my God.

I did my best to ignore how it made me feel to hear that women were flashing Cash and grabbing his crotch and instead focused on the bottom line of what Holland shared. Cash wasn't turned on by these women, and he believed I was the reason for that.

A coy smiled flashed across my face, and I shared, "Cash's dick is not broken or even remotely damaged."

Holland laughed. "I figured that much, which is why I told him we needed to go back to get you. He just needed to give his penis what it wanted, and that, my friend, was you."

"I'm so happy for him," Sadie added. "And I think it's great that he's settling down."

That felt good to hear.

As Holland got back to her makeup, the three of us talked a bit more about how things had been for Cash over the last few weeks. Talking with her had really opened my eyes up to how horribly I'd judged Cash. Of course, they hadn't hidden—neither had he, for that matter—what his life was like before I came along, but it was nice to know that there was far more to the man than what could be found online or in interviews.

Once Holland was done getting ready, she stood and declared, "Come on. It's pre-show ritual for me to join the boys. We just have to figure out whose dressing room they're in today."

"Okay," I agreed.

With that, we left Holland's dressing room and didn't need to search very hard. The noise coming from across the hall was enough of an indication of where the rest of the band was.

She knocked and cracked the door open. "Are we good?" she asked.

"All clear, Holls," someone answered from inside.

Holland looked at me and said, "I entered without knocking once and saw more than I cared to see."

Understanding dawned, so I nodded.

We walked inside, and the room instantly grew silent. My eyes went to Cash. His face lit up at the sight of me, and I started to feel all warm inside.

"Everything cool?" he asked.

Before I could answer, Holland did. "Oh, it's fine, Cash," she started. "What do you think I did to her?"

He shrugged. "I don't know. Could be anything," he replied.

Holland shook her head. "Nope. We were just discussing the fact that it's a great thing your penis isn't broken," she said. "I'm so relieved for you."

Cash dropped his head back and looked to the ceiling as the rest of the guys laughed. I didn't know if I should, but I moved across the room toward him. I slid my arms around his waist and felt one of his slip around my back.

When his eyes came to mine, they were shining.

I felt incredible seeing him like this.

A moment later, he said, "Demi, I want you to meet the rest of the band." I turned slightly in his hold and directed my attention to the remaining members. Then Cash said, "Demi, this is Beck, Roscoe, Walker, and Killian. Guys, this is Demi."

"It's nice to meet you all," I said as I got similar responses and chin lifts in return.

When another knock came at the door just a few seconds later, everyone directed their attention there. Someone popped their head inside and said, "You've got fifteen."

"Thanks, Raid," Killian said.

"Hey, Raid," Cash called.

The man I now knew as Raid peeked farther into the room and brought his attention to Cash. "Yeah?" he replied.

"This is my girl, Demi," he started. "Demi, this is Raid. He's Walker's brother, and he's our road and tour manager. He handles everything with regard to our stage set up, lighting, and a multitude of other things, including our tour schedule, accommodations, and travel plans. If you need anything while we're on stage tonight, he can help you out. Right, Raid?"

Raid nodded. "You got it," he confirmed.

With that, he backed out of the room and closed the door. The rest of the band fell into their own conversations. I turned back into Cash's hold and squeezed my arms around his waist.

"I'm sorry," I apologized.

"For what?" he returned.

I bit my lip to stop myself from laughing. When I thought I had it under control, I whispered, "I didn't mean to make your cock stop working."

His lips twitched. "Correct me if I'm wrong, but it worked just fine last night and earlier today, did it not?" he countered.

"It did," I assured him.

"Good. Then let's not bring this up again," he begged.

I giggled and buried my face in his chest.

Cash brought his other arm around me and hugged me tightly.

I never felt happier in my life.

CHAPTER 18

Demi

"AND HERE I THOUGHT THIS LIFE WAS ALL GLITZ AND GLAM for you."

Cash looked up from where he was sitting on the couch in his great room with a pen and a notepad in his hands and smiled at me.

"Hey," he returned as he set the notepad and pen down and held out his hand to me.

Just like that. No matter what he was doing, he dropped it all so he could hold me in his arms. I loved it.

Not wasting any time, I moved toward him and settled myself in his lap—something I'd learned rather quickly that Cash preferred. Truth be told, I didn't mind it so much either.

It was late Sunday morning, and we were expecting his bandmates to arrive soon for the barbecue. We hadn't woken up that long ago because we'd had another late night.

Following their incredible performance, which affected me much like the one the previous night had, we made our way backstage. There was a common area set up for the band that had a bunch of booze, food, and comfortable seating. Very comfortable seating.

Initially, I thought it was strange. After playing a show, I would have thought they'd want to head home and get some rest, especially considering they'd played two nights in a row.

That wasn't the case.

And not more than a few minutes after we'd arrived backstage, the door to that room opened and a bunch of people had entered. Most of the people were women. It seemed My Violent Heart didn't just give a backstage pass to the girlfriend of the lead singer. Passes were also given out to fans.

I understood that, and I guess I kind of already knew and expected it. But it definitely caught me off guard, and I certainly wasn't prepared for it.

Things had started off innocently enough, especially because the fans were slightly cautious when they first entered. But the band was extraordinarily welcoming toward their fans; they always had been. Because of that, things quickly escalated from simple and innocent things, like pictures, autographs, and conversation to things that were much less virtuous, like excessive flirting, touching, and even kissing.

Luckily, Cash was incredible. He made me feel safe and comfortable, and beyond the pictures and autographs he offered for the fans, he kept his focus and attention on me the entire time.

But I'd have been lying if I didn't admit to myself that I wondered how things went down with him when I wasn't around. Would he be just as disinterested in the company in my absence as he was in my presence?

Unable to stop myself, I asked, "Do they ever come back?"

"Who?"

I jerked my head backward while directing my eyes toward the fans and said, "The groupies. Like after a show, do they ever come back with you guys to the hotels when you're on the road?"

"Yes," he answered.

Something tightened in my belly at his admission.

Cash must have known I was reacting to that information because his voice got gentle and he promised, "That's not for me anymore, Demi. But I'm not going to lie and say that it hasn't happened in the past. I'm with you right now, though, and I'm very happy."

I nodded slowly, trying to indicate that I understood, but I still felt wary. I had a feeling I would for a long time.

"I promise you have nothing to worry about," he added.

"Okay," I replied because I didn't know what else to say.

And considering he hadn't given me any reason to doubt him, I had to at least take him at his word. Yes, I knew my jealousy wouldn't just stop right there, but for now, I was with him, and he was being beyond attentive.

By the time we left and got back to his place, I'd forgotten all about my worries regarding that because the sexual tension between Cash and me was running high. It was a wonder we even made it back to his place before tearing our clothes off.

In fact, the drive back was a little spicy. I spent the vast majority of the drive with my mouth on his neck, his cheek, his jaw, and his ear while one of my hands massaged his inner thigh and occasionally gripped his cock.

We barely made it inside the house before we were

clawing at each other's clothes. I ended up losing another pair of panties in the process, too.

I loved the fire that blazed between us. There always seemed to be such passion and emotion bottled up on both sides that when we had the chance to be intimate with one another, we just ignited.

We eventually got to sleep, and once again, we slept in this morning. Shortly after we woke up and had something to eat, I told Cash I wanted to take some time to go through my emails for work. He didn't seem to have any problems agreeing to give me that time and offered up a quiet space in his house to do it.

Now I was here, and I hadn't expected to find him like he was.

"Why does it seem like you're concentrating so hard?" I asked. "Isn't today your day off? I feel like you work harder than your job implies."

Cash laughed at me and asked, "What does that mean? What do you think my job is all about?"

"Having a lot of fun," I guessed.

"Well, that's certainly part of it," he assured me.

"It's exhausting," I declared. "I don't understand how you do this. Performing, traveling, and partying. It seems like you're constantly on the go, even when you're supposed to have some downtime."

He peppered kisses on my bare shoulder for a few moments before he insisted, "It's not that bad."

"I'd hate to see what you define as a demanding schedule," I mumbled. Directing my attention to the notepad on the table, I asked, "What are you doing now?"

"Right now, I'm trying to figure out if I can get a quickie

in with you before everyone gets here," he started. "Before you entered the room and sat your sweet ass in my lap, I was just working on a few lyrics."

My eyes widened. "You're writing a song?" I exclaimed.

Cash laughed and reminded me, "Not anymore."

"Are you heading back into the studio to record a new album?" I wondered.

He shook his head. "No. Not yet anyway. In fact, I don't typically work on lyrics or new music while we're on tour, but sometimes, when the inspiration hits in moments of downtime, I can't really ignore it. So, I'll typically just jot down a few words so I have them there when we're ready to start writing more."

"That's incredible. Can you sing what you just wrote for me?" I pressed.

"It's not done yet," he replied. "But once I finish it, I'll sing it for you."

"Promise?"

He nodded.

I sat there and stared at him, searching his face. It felt like he was doing the same, and I couldn't quite work out what was happening between us. Even still, I knew we both had something running through our minds.

For me, it was still just a whole lot of disbelief that I was even here and had followed through on taking this step. While I still had some anxiety and reservations about whether this would turn out the way I wanted, I was thoroughly enjoying where we were right now.

"So, what do you think?" he asked.

"About what?"

"Do you think we can get a quickie in?"

I narrowed my eyes. "You're insatiable," I declared.

His hand on the arm that had been draped over my thighs began drifting up my abdomen toward my breasts. He made it there, gently cupped my breast, and stroked his thumb over my nipple. "And you're far too tempting," he countered.

"You can't withstand temptation?" I asked.

"Being able to and wanting to are two very different things, firecracker," he noted.

I began squirming in his lap because his thumb hadn't stopped moving and his voice was doing very delicious things to me. It didn't take long for me to feel Cash grow hard beneath my ass.

That was all it took. His voice, his hand on my breast, and his erection beneath me.

Before I knew it, I had shifted my body in his lap so that I was facing him. Cash didn't waste any time. He lifted my shirt up and over my head. Then he buried his face between my breasts while both of his thumbs stroked over my nipples. I rolled my hips over him.

With little time to spare, he brought his hands to my waist, pulled on the waistband of my shorts, and urged me to lift my hips so he could pull them off. Once they were gone, he tore off his shirt and his bottoms before reaching for his wallet on the end table. Pulling out a condom, he immediately sheathed himself.

"Come here," he encouraged softly.

I positioned myself over him. Cash captured my mouth, one of his hands going behind my head, the other going right between my legs. Two of his fingers slid through the wetness and gently rubbed me there. When his hand gripped my hair at the back of my head and tugged back, he plunged a finger inside my vagina and said, "You're so wet, and I've barely touched you."

"Cash," I rasped, unable to get out anything more as I began riding his finger.

A second finger entered me, and his thumb pressed firmly against my clit.

My head flew back as I moaned and Cash's free hand squeezed my breast. He gave me a few minutes to ride his fingers, and just as I thought he'd send me over the edge, he pulled them from between my legs, positioned himself, and urged my body down over his.

"You feel amazing, Demi. I don't think I'll ever get used to how incredible you feel," Cash declared, his voice thick with emotion.

I dropped my head forward to look him in the eyes, and that's when I realized the emotion wasn't just evident in his voice. It was written all over his face.

Something profound was moving through Cash.

I would have thought that seeing it would have resulted in me being unable to move, but that wasn't the case. I ended up planting my hands on his shoulders and riding him hard, my eyes never leaving his.

My fingertips pressed in deeper, my hips moved faster, and my breathing quickly grew labored.

I didn't care that I was out of breath.

I didn't care that my hips were starting to fatigue.

I wanted to do this.

I wanted to continue to do whatever it was that was making him look at me like that.

It was so intense, so powerful, that well before I wanted it to happen, I was just seconds away from climaxing.

"Baby," I warned, one of my hands moving into his hair and landing at the back of his head.

Something new washed over him, his expression changing from what it had been to something much more intense.

I didn't understand how that was even possible. And it wouldn't have mattered if I wanted to figure it out because I couldn't anyway.

Because a moment later, Cash groaned and said, "Come with me."

That was all I needed. My body was completely overcome by the force of my orgasm, and for the first time since I'd made the connection with his gaze, I broke it. My eyes squeezed shut while my hand at the back of his head pulled him closer to me.

Cash didn't waste the opportunity. With his face in my chest as we both went soaring, he captured my breast in his mouth and offered just a bit more sensation to my trembling body.

We both worked hard to get through our orgasms and to the other side, and when we did, Cash declared, "You're in charge of quickies from now on."

My body started shaking with laughter, but I couldn't come up with a witty reply. I was too exhausted. Too sated. Too satisfied.

"You know I'm perfectly fine with keeping you right where you are all day long," Cash stared, his fingers tracing gently up and down my spine. "But I need to know if I'm going to have to call everyone and postpone the cookout?"

The apple of my cheek was resting on his shoulder, and

I knew I could easily stay like that forever. But at his question, I lifted my head so I could look at him.

Shaking my head, I answered, "No, I'll be okay. I just need another minute."

He grinned at me. "Okay."

I ended up taking two or three minutes, but I eventually pulled myself together. Cash and I gathered up our clothes that were strewn all over the couch and floor, removing any evidence of our late morning romp, and went upstairs to clean up and get ready.

An hour later, things were in full swing. Not only had the entire band come over to Cash's place but so did the rest of their crew from the roadies to personal security and even some guests for those guests. Beck brought his sister along, two of the roadies had brought their girlfriends, and a few others just brought some friends.

I'd met more people who ran in Cash's circle, and I appreciated that he took the time to introduce me to those he spent time with. From the start, he'd been very open with everything and easily and seamlessly brought me into the fold. I liked that he was taking the time to let those around him know that I was somebody in his life that was important enough to him for them to know.

For a while, it was all about good food, great conversation, and simply kicking back and relaxing.

Assuming I hadn't prepared for this, Holland even came up and handed me a swimsuit. "I brought over one of mine for you to wear because I figured you didn't pack one," she said. "We can lay out, catch some sun, and even go for a dip. Everyone else will eventually join in."

"Thanks," I replied, taking the suit from her.

On my way back inside the house to change into it, Cash stopped me and asked, "Where are you going?"

I held up the suit and explained, "Holland brought me a bathing suit."

Cash tipped his head to the side. "Is it a two-piece?" he asked.

I took the top in one hand and the bottom in the other before I replied, "It would seem so."

Cash groaned. "Great. Now what am I going to do?"

"About what?"

"About the fact that I already have a hard enough time keeping my hands off of you without you being half naked. Do you know what this is going to do to me?"

I smiled and said, "Look on the bright side."

"Which is?"

Leaning in close, I whispered, "You'll have more proof that everything down below is still functioning as it should."

Cash narrowed his eyes on me.

Ignoring his attempt at intimidation, I suggested, "You know, you could always throw on a pair of swim trunks and join me."

With that, I didn't stick around for a response. I went inside and got myself changed. Cash did not put on swim trunks. Or, at least, he didn't do it immediately. Holland and I laid out on the loungers by the pool, and for a while, nobody else made any moves to join us. Eventually, Sadie came up and grabbed a lounger beside us, and it remained the three of us the entire time. But not long after we went for a dip in the pool and started splashing, the others joined us.

For hours, we had a blast, and I had to admit how much

I loved that these people, Cash's people, had accepted me like one of their own.

In fact, they'd done it so well that they didn't even realize that it could possibly be painful. Hours after everyone had arrived, I had gotten out of the pool and moved to the table set up with food on it for a snack. As I stood there loading up a plate with goodies, Walker came up to the table to grab some food as well.

"Hey," I greeted him.

"Hey," he returned. "Having fun?"

I nodded. "I was just telling Cash earlier this morning that I don't know where you guys all get your stamina from. This is exhausting work."

Walker laughed and said, "You do it enough, you get used to it."

"I guess so. I'm going to have to work on it," I told him.

"Are you coming along?" he asked.

"Coming along?" I repeated.

Walker nodded. "On the rest of the tour," he clarified. "We're leaving again on Tuesday afternoon. I can't imagine how Cash will manage without you there."

The minute the words were out of his mouth, I felt my stomach clench. I wanted to focus on the fact that what Walker was saying should have been a good thing. He believed Cash would be better off having me with him. But as much as I wanted to concentrate on the positive, I couldn't. Time with Cash was running out.

"Shit," Walker hissed.

"What?" I asked, feeling worried.

"He didn't ask you, did he?"

I gave him a slight shake of my head. "I couldn't go

anyway," I told him, hoping that eased any of the guilt he clearly felt. "It's just… I've been trying to avoid thinking about having to go home."

Walker gave me a nod of understanding and lamented, "Sorry."

"It's okay. You didn't know."

At that, I took my plate and walked away, even though I was no longer hungry. I sat down and tried to eat, but I struggled.

It was Sunday evening. I had to leave on Tuesday morning because Cash was leaving Tuesday afternoon.

I didn't know how I was going to cope without him for more than two months.

CHAPTER 19

Cash

"I MISS YOU ALREADY."

I watched as the tears leaked from Demi's eyes and spilled down her cheeks. With each one that fell, I felt like my heart was being ripped out of my chest. Seeing Demi so upset simply killed me.

The last few days were some of the best days of my life. Considering what I did for a living—the things I've experienced, the places I've been—I felt it was only a testament to just how special Demi is.

I held her close as we stood at the top of my driveway. It was very early Tuesday morning, and Demi had to leave to head to the airport.

I didn't want her to go. I wanted to take her with me. In fact, I'd finally brought that up to her yesterday morning before we even got out of bed.

"Will you stay with me?" I asked her.

"What?" she replied, her body going rigid.

"I don't want you to leave me and go back to New Hampshire," I told her.

There was a lengthy pause before she noted, "I'm not *leaving* you. I'm just going home."

It felt like she was leaving. I wanted her to feel like her home was wherever I was because I was starting to feel that way about her.

As I sat there contemplating her words, wishing things had been different, Demi spoke again.

"And can I just add that you're also leaving me?" she countered.

"But I'm prepared to take you with me," I noted.

She was silent for a long time before she rasped, "I'd take you with me, too."

We were curled up in bed with her back pressed to my front. At her declaration, I kissed her bare shoulder and said, "If I was the sole member of My Violent Heart, I'd cancel the rest of the tour and go with you."

Demi shifted her body and pushed her shoulder into my chest. I scooted back to give her the space to fall to her back. Then I propped my head up in my hand to look down at her face. When her eyes connected with mine, she said, "You're not serious. Your music means everything to you."

"So do you."

Her lips parted in shock.

Maybe that had been too much for her to hear so soon. I didn't know, and honestly, I didn't care. It was the truth, and if anyone needed to know the truth, it was her.

"Cash..." She trailed off.

I brought my hand up to the side of her face, stroked my thumb along her cheek, and rasped, "I don't know what

I'm going to do not being able to touch you or kiss you for weeks, firecracker."

Her emotions started to get the best of her because her eyes got wet, and she whispered, "We'll figure it out. We can make it work."

I knew we would because not working it out wasn't an option. But it killed me to think we even had to take those steps to begin with.

Unable to stand the sad look in her eyes, I couldn't talk about it any longer. So, I dropped my mouth to hers and kissed her. From there, I took things slow. Everything from the kissing and touching to the penetration and orgasm. I wanted it to last forever; there was no race. We had nowhere to be, and I was going to take my time savoring her, hoping that it would help me cope without her while I was on the road.

Now that we were here outside the house and she was minutes away from leaving, I knew that everything I'd done over the last few days to prepare myself for this wasn't going to be enough. There was no good way to cope with something like this. I couldn't imagine a time when I'd ever want to be separated from her for an extended period of time.

I didn't know how I was going to do this.

I had gotten used to it. To having her there. To having her body beside mine at night when I went to sleep and every morning when I woke up. To having her ass settled in my lap while she let me feed her breakfast. To having her smile at me.

There was so much.

And while there was a lot that was physical between us—we'd certainly had our fair share of sex over the last few days—there was so much more that I enjoyed about being with her.

It was all in the kind of person she was. Deep down, she truly cared about people. She got along well with the rest of the band. I'd even go so far as to say that she and Holland were well on their way to becoming great friends. Everyone liked her. She was interested in me, my music, and my family.

Just yesterday, she asked me about what it was like growing up in Pennsylvania.

"Why are you here?" she asked.

"What?"

"In Pennsylvania," she clarified. "You, and the rest of the band, are here. It's surprising that none of you moved out to Hollywood. Wouldn't there be even more opportunity?"

I shrugged. "Maybe. Probably. We go on tours, and we do the interviews. But the truth is, we're not necessarily interested in the publicity or the fame. We just like making music that people love. Some of what we do is necessary to make that happen. But moving away from what's been home for so long isn't going to change our perspective on that. We can still do everything we do from here. So, from where we stand, why leave the place that we love for a life we don't want?"

"That makes sense. And I think it's really cool that you all have this place that you're attached to," she remarked.

"Unlike you, who is only attached to the people in New Hampshire," I responded.

She grinned. "Exactly."

Recalling that conversation as I held her in my arms this morning, I started to wonder if maybe I'd be able to convince her to come back here with me when the tour was over. She'd already admitted it wasn't about the location for her. And New Hampshire wasn't far from Pennsylvania. We could always go back and forth so she could see the people who were important to her.

I just knew that I was going to miss her too much to maintain something long-distance for an extended time.

And apparently, she felt the same considering she'd just claimed she already missed me and hadn't even left yet.

"I know. I feel the same way," I told her as I held her face in my hands and wiped her tears away.

"I don't want to leave," she whispered.

I tipped my head to the side, simply trying to focus on something else other than the pain in my chest. "So stay," I urged. "Come with me."

Demi's head fell forward and landed on my chest. Her arms grew tighter around me. "I can't," she said. "I've got to go back and work. I can't leave Cal hanging."

I wanted to tell her that I thought her cousin would understand and that she needed to do what was best for her. But I didn't. The last thing I wanted was to make this harder for her.

As much as I wanted her to come with me and make herself happy, she needed to be the one to make that decision.

"I know," I replied, my hands running through locks of her hair in what was a feeble attempt to comfort the both of us.

Eventually, Demi pulled her face back, tipped her chin up, and said, "I have to go now."

I nodded, unsure if I could even formulate a response that wouldn't reveal just how much this was affecting me. I gave myself a few seconds to get my emotions under control and urged, "Call me when you get to the airport, okay?"

"Yeah."

"We'll get through this, Demi. I promise."

She nodded her understanding, but I wondered if she believed me.

A moment later, we were moving toward her rental car. We stopped just beside it and kissed one last time.

Weeks.

I'd have to endure weeks of not having this. Of not kissing her. Of not feeling my tongue gliding against hers.

There was so much I wanted to say but didn't have the time to communicate. I hoped this kiss gave her even just a fraction of what I wanted her to know.

When our mouths separated, she cried quietly, "Good luck on the rest of the tour."

"Have a safe flight home," I responded.

She folded in behind the wheel and looked up at me. "I'll see you soon."

I didn't know if she was trying to make herself or me feel better. It wasn't going to be soon. At least, not soon enough. Even still, I said, "I'll see you soon."

With that, I closed her door. She started the car, turned around at the top of the driveway, and waved at me before she drove to the end of it.

I kept my eyes on the car knowing that I wasn't going to be the same until I was with her again because when she left, she took my heart with her.

Demi

"It sounds like you had the best time."

That came from Sam.

I'd barely been home a full twenty-four hours, and I was sitting beside her on a stool at Granite. It had become our thing over the last few years. When we were both working at the hotel, we'd come into Granite, visit with Cal, and talk about everything that had happened at work that was stressing us out.

Right now, it felt like old times.

I found that surprising considering I hadn't been gone that long.

But my time in Pennsylvania with Cash had been incredible, and all I wanted to do was go back.

Sam hadn't been wrong, I truly did have the best time over the last few days. But now that I was home, something was seriously missing in my life.

Cash.

I hated having to leave. I hated telling him I wouldn't go on tour with him. But I wasn't exactly sure it was what he wanted, so I made up the excuse that I couldn't leave Cal hanging. Truthfully, I knew that Cal wouldn't have cared because when I called him to extend my trip, he told me I should just go on the road with the band. I tried not to think about it after that fact.

Especially because Cash hadn't asked.

And until Walker mentioned something to me at the cookout on Sunday, I hadn't really thought about it again.

It wasn't hard to see how horrible Walker felt that day

for assuming that Cash would have asked me, so when I saw the two of them talking later in the day, I could only assume Walker was sharing what happened.

My suspicions were mostly confirmed the next morning when Cash asked me to go on tour with him. I just couldn't agree to it when I believed that he only asked because Walker told him he should.

I wanted Cash to want me to come with him all on his own, without the encouragement from his bandmates.

And now that I was back here in Finch, I wished I would have just accepted his invitation.

"Do you realize that you're one of the very few people who not only get to go backstage with My Violent Heart but also get to spend days living with the lead singer?" Cal interrupted my thoughts.

"I know. Aren't you jealous?" I teased.

I was doing my best to appear happy because deep down, I was. It had just been difficult to adjust to the separation from Cash.

"I am," Sam declared.

"Yep," Cal agreed.

I grinned at them.

"So, how are you doing now that you're back here?" Sam asked.

I shrugged. "I'm okay. It's definitely not the same lifestyle, that's for sure," I answered.

Nodding, she said, "Right. I get that. But I'm talking about with Cash. I can't even imagine how you two are going to go for weeks without seeing one another."

"We're working it out," I assured her. "We're going to talk every day, and we'll even video chat. I'm sure time is just going to fly by, and before we know it, My Violent Heart will be back in Finch playing here at Granite."

"Well, you're a stronger woman than I am," Sam announced.

If she only knew that I'd spent the night last night struggling not to break down into tears at every turn.

"Demi?" Cal called.

"Yeah?"

"I'm really happy for you, and I'm so proud of you for putting yourself out there," he remarked.

His words made my heart melt. In so many ways, Cal had been like the brother I never had. To know he was proud of me was a big deal.

"Thanks, Cal. I'm proud of myself, too," I responded. "I'm just trying to come to terms with it all."

"What do you mean?" Sam asked.

I thought for a moment about it.

"For so long, I was adamant about never getting into a romantic relationship," I began. "And now that I'm in one, I'm struggling to understand how it's possible for me to feel this happy. How could I go from being so sure I'd never have this let alone want it to now being ridiculously, deliriously happy that I have it? Did I deny myself this experience all this time for no reason?"

Sam shook her head. "I don't think so," she insisted. "In my opinion, this is what it is for you because it's not something you've ever had before. It's that much more special because you've found someone who wanted to put in the work to make you feel safe and secure in him and what he was bringing to the table. I think if you had considered the possibility before Cash, you might not have gotten anything that even came close to resembling what you have now."

I had a feeling she was right.

Nobody else would have ever compared to Cash. And now that I'd had him, I had no doubt that nobody else would ever live up to him.

"Yeah," I agreed just as my phone buzzed on the bar beside me.

A text from Cash.

Cash: I'm about to head out on stage. Wish me luck.

I gave him what he wanted.

Me: You don't need it, but good luck.

Cash: Call me when you wake up tomorrow morning, okay?

Me: I will.

I set the phone down and looked up at the two people in my life that I'd grown to depend on. They were both smiling at me.

"What?" I asked.

"You're so happy," Sam declared.

"I never thought I'd see the day that your face would light up while you text your boyfriend," Cal said.

I wanted to roll my eyes. I should have, but I didn't.

They weren't wrong about any of it.

So, I let it go and smiled back.

And then I demanded a change in topic, which they both easily accommodated.

The truth was, as much as I knew they probably wanted to hear about Cash, I wasn't ready for it. I knew I'd feel good in the moment when I was talking about him, but when I went home and crawled into my empty bed alone, I'd feel the sadness about missing him creeping in. I didn't need to add in anything else that would make that harder than it already was.

And on a night like tonight, I had no doubt it was already going to be difficult. Because he was about to go out on stage.

I couldn't stop myself from worrying about what might happen after the concert was over.

CHAPTER 20

Demi

Three Weeks Later

"ARE YOU WET?"

I was.

Then again, it wasn't difficult to be that way when it was Cash on the other end of the line. We'd been doing this for weeks; it had become the norm for us.

Regular phone sex.

This wasn't ideal, obviously, but it was our only choice. We would have much rather been in each other's presence, but since that wasn't an option, this was the next best thing.

And it wasn't bad at all.

Cash was good at it. Of course, I'd always been fond of his voice when he was talking about anything. When he was talking to me like this, his voice was that much better.

"Yes," I answered, my voice just a touch over a whisper. "What about you? Are you hard?"

"You know I am," he returned. "I'm hard every time I

think about you, so when I know you're in your bed touching yourself, that's definitely not going to be the exception."

"I wish you were here touching me, Cash," I rasped.

"Me too, Demi," he replied. "Put one finger inside your pussy, babe."

I did as he asked and moaned.

"I want my mouth on your cock, baby," I told him. I sounded needy, and at that moment, I was. There wasn't anything I wouldn't have given to have him right beside me.

"My cock wants your mouth," he said. "It's sick of my hand."

"Tell me what you'd do to me if I was there right now," I urged him.

He groaned. "I'd do everything," he began. "First, I'd kiss that pretty mouth of yours. Then I'd strip you out of your clothes and play with your tits for a bit."

"Mmm. Would you lick them? Would you put them in your mouth?" I asked.

"Fuck yes," he confirmed. "I'd suck on one side and use my hand to play with the other. I might even slip my other hand down between your legs. I'd put two fingers inside you and feel how wet you are."

God, I wanted that. If he wasn't all the way down in North Carolina, I would have hopped in my car and driven to him.

"What else would you do?" I questioned him.

"I'd kiss that pretty pussy next," he went on.

Just hearing him say those words, it was like I could feel him doing that to me.

"Baby," I whispered.

"You like that?" he asked.

"Keep going," I begged, feeling myself get more and more turned on as I continued to work my finger in and out of my body.

Cash cleared his throat and continued, "I'd start gentle. Light, tender kisses. Then I'd use my tongue and taste you."

I could hear a mild strain in his voice and smiled. Talking about eating me always got him particularly excited.

"Would you roll to your back so I could sit on your face and lean forward to suck you?" I asked.

"Jesus, fuck, yes," he groaned. "I'd alternate between sucking on your clit and sliding my tongue inside you while your mouth moved all along my dick."

"It's so long and thick and hard, Cash," I said. "Would I fit all of you in my mouth?"

He didn't respond immediately, and I knew he was imagining what would happen. "You'd take as much of me as you could," he finally said. "You'd take me in until I hit the back of your throat, wouldn't you?"

"I'd be so greedy, baby," I declared. "I'd take all that I could get. Would you come in my mouth?"

"Maybe. But if I did, I'd have to give myself a short break and have another go at you because I can't have you in bed with me and not put my cock in your pussy."

"I'd give anything to have your cock in my pussy right now, Cash," I moaned. "Anything at all."

He remained silent, though I could hear his breath quickening.

Feeling myself close and wanting him there with me, I continued, "I'm not sure what position I'd want to be in, but I definitely know I want it hard. I want to feel you pounding into me over and over again, feeling our skin slick with sweat.

Maybe you'd be behind me. Would you like that? Would you like to fuck me from behind with my ass in your hands?"

"Fuck, Demi, I'm going to come," he warned.

"Come with me, Cash," I begged.

The next thing I knew, we were both moaning as our orgasms tore through us. It was never nearly as powerful or satisfying for me as it was when Cash was the one actually delivering it, but it was still enjoyable. And considering it was something I was enjoying with him, I wasn't going to complain.

For the next few minutes, we didn't speak. It was very much like it had been between us when we were together in Cash's bed. We took the time to allow our breathing to return to normal; though, it never took nearly as long as it did in person.

I was the one who broke this silence this time.

"Tell me something."

"What do you want to know?" Cash asked.

"Anything," I answered. "Any random bit of information you want to share with me."

Just like that we were falling into what had become the norm for us when we talked. Having phone sex, having that level of intimacy was important to both of us, but we also thrived on the rest of it, too. There was more to our conversations than just sex.

Truthfully, as much as I missed Cash and wanted to be wherever he was, there was also a small part of me that was grateful for this time apart. Obviously, I would have liked for it to be a substantially shorter period of time, but what was nice about it was that it gave us the chance to really get to know one another better. We weren't distracted by physical intimacy when we weren't in each other's presence.

And for weeks now, we'd done a lot of talking. Sometimes, the conversations were simple and easy. We'd discuss things like our favorite foods or movies. I'd often share whatever was happening day to day in my life or at the bar. Anytime I booked a new band, I'd tell him about it. Cash would frequently share whatever was going on with the band or any funny things that happened while they were performing.

There were times when our conversations went a bit deeper, though. Cash told me more about his childhood and growing up, and how the band all started. I would sometimes share what things were like for me, both before my father's infidelity and afterward. When he knew I was going to visit with my mom one Sunday, Cash urged me to call him when I got home. He wanted to know how it went and what she thought about the fact that I was now officially dating someone.

My mom was thrilled to learn about my new relationship with Cash, by the way. She was beyond ecstatic that I'd finally opened my heart up to having this experience, and she loved that I was as happy as I was.

I couldn't say she was wrong.

Ever since I risked it all and surprised him at his house, I was the happiest I could ever remember being in my life. My father's infidelity had marked me in a way I didn't ever think I could recover from. But Cash had been persistent, unwilling to walk away from me because I would be too much work.

And so, even though there were moments of sadness for me over the last three weeks simply because I missed Cash, on the whole, I just felt like I was on cloud nine. Life was better, and I felt utterly blissful.

What took things up a notch for me was a few weeks ago, not long after I returned from Pennsylvania, when Cash asked me for my address. When I asked him why he wanted it, he told me it was a surprise.

I saw no harm in giving him that information—it wasn't like I didn't know where he lived. I pressed him for more details about why he wanted it, but Cash refused to give me anything. Days went by, and just at the time when I completely forgot about the fact that I'd given him my address, I checked my mail. There was a postcard inside.

There was nothing particularly grand about any of the sentiments written on the card, but it was the idea that he'd taken the time to think of me, buy the card, and send it off to surprise me. With each new city he got to, he sent a new postcard. I had a stack of them now, and every time I looked at them, they made me smile.

Cash was doing everything to make me feel reassured in what we were building together. I appreciated his efforts and felt my heart softening even more toward this incredible man.

And every time we were on the phone and he shared something personal with me, I got more of that reassurance.

I never had to ask for it either. Sometimes he gave me the deep conversation; sometimes he gave me simple and easy.

I had no idea what I'd get now.

Cash was quiet a moment while, I'm assuming, he thought of what he wanted to share. When he finally spoke, I certainly hadn't expected to hear what he gave me.

"So, remember how I told you that I don't typically work on new material while we're touring?" he asked.

"Yes," I confirmed, thinking it was crazy that he thought I'd ever forget anything he said to me.

"Right. Well, at the time I told you, it was the truth," he began. "It's no longer the truth."

"Does that... are you saying—"

Cash cut me off and shared, "I'm saying that I've been feeling very inspired lately, so whenever there's time that I'm not on stage, talking to you, eating, or sleeping, I'm writing new music. And I finished the song I'd been working on when you were at my house with me."

I smiled.

"I would ask you to sing it now, but I think I'd rather hear it in person," I told him. "Will you sing it for me when you finish the tour?"

"Absolutely."

My smile grew huge. I was going to get a preview of new My Violent Heart material.

"But you need to prepare yourself," he warned.

Suddenly, I sat up straighter, and the smile was wiped from my face. "Why?" I asked hesitantly. "For what?"

"A few of these songs will be unlike anything you've heard from us," he explained.

"Is that a good thing or a bad thing?"

There was a brief pause before Cash answered, "For the fans, it could be either. Any deviation from the expectation is bound to be met with some criticism. But I've never felt more sure about any material that we've released as I do about this. I haven't shared any of it with the rest of the band, but I think this one song has the potential to be one of our best if it's got all the right instruments behind it. Bass, drums, and lots of synthesizer. It's going to feel reminiscent of classic My Violent Heart material, but it's going to have a sexier vibe."

That sounded incredible. "I can't wait to hear it," I told him.

"I can't wait for you to hear it," he returned. "Oh, shit, hang on a second."

"Okay."

I heard some rustling around before I heard what I thought was Beck's voice. "Hey, man, sorry to interrupt your call. I was just going to see if you were up for some food? I needed to talk. We can do it later."

"No, no," Cash insisted. "Come in. Just give me a minute."

I heard a door close before Cash said, "Demi, I'm sorry to—"

"It's okay," I insisted, cutting him off. "He sounds like he's got something on his mind."

"Yeah," he agreed. "I'll reach out later today, okay?"

"Okay. Good luck."

"Thanks."

With that, Cash and I disconnected. I hoped everything was alright with Beck. I didn't expect Cash would share any of Beck's personal issues with me, but I had no doubt he'd at least confirm that everything was okay once he knew that it was.

And for me, I was simply happy that I was starting my day off on the right foot. Then again, I'd been doing that every morning since Cash came into my life.

It seemed impossible that things could ever get better than they were right now.

I wasn't wrong.

Things getting better wasn't possible.

What was possible was things getting worse.

Something happened. I didn't know what it was, but there had been a profound change. A bad one. Something that just didn't feel right.

About a week after the call I had with Cash when Beck interrupted us, I noticed the change. I was relatively certain it had nothing to do with Beck because Cash had confirmed for me later that same day that all was good. And for the next few days, everything was as it had always been between us.

So, I had no reason to believe there was anything wrong there.

But there was still *something* wrong.

For the last two weeks, Cash had been different with me. We still had our morning phone calls; though, there had been two instances when I called and Cash hadn't answered. He *never* missed my calls. On both occasions, he did call me back, but he didn't offer an explanation as to why he hadn't answered.

I tried not to think too much about that because it wasn't as though he'd made me wait hours to hear back from him. No more than ten minutes had passed when he returned my call.

It wasn't just that, though.

While we still talked with the same frequency, the conversations were different. Cash seemed distracted, less interested. Phone sex had dwindled.

I was terrified to think what that meant. Cash enjoyed sex. He enjoyed phone sex. The fact was that he wasn't nearly as interested in that nor was he as playful as he had been with me from the beginning, I couldn't help worrying.

The other problem was that he wasn't talking to me. Yes, we spoke on the phone still, but he wasn't sharing whatever was on his mind. Everything was very much focused on facts, not feelings. He'd tell me whatever was happening that day, where they were traveling to, or what time they were heading to the venue.

And finally, one of the things that had really made me think about the state of my relationship with Cash was the postcards. I'd gone from receiving one just about every other day to only once or twice a week.

I didn't understand what happened.

I even tried coming right out with it and asking him about a week ago.

"Is everything okay?" I asked.

"Yes," he replied.

"Are you sure?"

"I'm sure. I just have a few things on my mind that I'm working through right now," he said. "But I'm okay."

I didn't know what I was supposed to say to that. Should I have just called him out for being a liar? He was telling me everything was fine. Even though I knew it wasn't, I couldn't exactly force it out of him.

I wanted to believe he had just had a bad day or two, something we all experienced, but when his mood never turned around, I could no longer ignore it.

So, I thought about it.

The only thing that I could think was that perhaps Cash

was simply frustrated with the distance between us. We'd been talking on the phone every day, but it wasn't the same as being close enough to touch.

Maybe he needed that.

I knew I did.

For the last couple of days, I thought about it and came to a decision. I was going to fly to Cash and meet him at his next location. We'd be in Florida, and they were scheduled to play two shows there with a day off in between. Maybe we could spend that day together getting ourselves back on track.

But because I'd already done the whole surprise thing with just showing up somewhere, I thought it might be better to call him ahead of time. I mean, perhaps the sooner he knew that he'd be able to see me, touch me, hold me, and kiss me, the better his mood would be.

Cash and the rest of the band were currently in Texas. They'd had a show last night, and from what Cash told me, they were going to be flying out later tonight to head to Florida.

I couldn't wait to tell him my plan. It was earlier than I'd usually call him, but I didn't think he'd mind, considering the news I had to share.

And because I wanted to see his face when I told him I was coming to see him, I decided on a video chat.

I tapped the button on my screen to call him, and that was the last moment of peace I had.

Two rings later, I felt sick to my stomach.

My face met that of a woman, and it was clear to see she was in a bed. Staring at her, feeling my heart pound wildly in my chest, I asked, "Where's Cash?"

"Oh, he's in the shower right now," the woman answered.

"Who are you?" I pressed.

"I'm one of the bands biggest fans," she told me. "I came back here last night."

I was going to be sick. I didn't want to believe this. How could he do this to me?

When I didn't respond, the woman sat up in the bed, and I belatedly noticed she was only wearing a bra on her top half.

Oh God.

Oh *God.*

She started walking, and I should have disconnected the call. I'd already seen enough. But something kept my eyes riveted to the screen. Something made me continue clutching my phone in my hand.

She eventually stopped moving outside a closed door. Her face filled half of the screen while the door filled the other. The woman knocked on the door, and I heard him.

"Be out in a minute."

I didn't know why I thought that this woman was lying. I didn't know why I thought he wouldn't be the one to respond.

I was stupid, obviously.

That was the only explanation.

A moment later, my whole world came crashing down when the door opened and the devastatingly handsome man that I'd fallen in love with stood there in a towel, fresh out of the shower. We locked eyes for only a moment, his going wide with surprise, before I disconnected the call, threw my phone down, and ran into the bathroom.

CHAPTER 21

Demi

STUPID.

Stupid. Stupid. Stupid.

I'd spent the last three hours doing nothing but feeling sick and crying. And I hated that. Because I knew better. I knew better than all of this.

I never should have trusted him. I never should have believed the words he said to me. I never should have thought that Cash would be different. More than all of that, I never should have thought that he would ever change the kind of man he was for me.

Hours.

Three long, horrible, tragic hours of seeing that sight in my mind over and over again.

Three hours of feeling my heart break into a million pieces.

Three hours of questioning why I didn't stick to my guns. Why had I given in to him? Why didn't I trust that I already knew how it was going to turn out?

I thought I was good enough. That's all I wanted... to be enough for someone. No. Not someone. Just Cash. I wanted to be all he needed.

And as soon as he hooked me and made me fall in love with him, he destroyed me.

No sooner had I disconnected that horrific call earlier and gotten sick in the bathroom when my phone started ringing again. It was Cash, and I didn't answer because my body was bent over the toilet. By the time I thought I would no longer be sick, ten minutes had passed. I ambled back to my bed and climbed under the blanket.

I hadn't been there more than five minutes with tears leaking from my eyes and pain spearing every inch of my body when my phone rang again. Seeing his name and face on the display, I declined the call and turned off the phone.

I didn't want to hear his excuses. I didn't want to know what he had to say. It didn't matter anymore.

Anything good between us was now gone. I had nothing left to give him, and I owed him nothing.

But it had been three hours since I saw him and his mostly naked body on the phone. That body. That beautiful body that I foolishly thought was mine.

It felt like it had been a nightmare. I was hoping I was going to wake at any moment and realize I'd made it all up in my head.

I knew that wasn't going to happen, though. This pain was too real. Too raw. Too devastating.

Every time I closed my eyes, I saw him opening that door with that woman standing right beside him in her bra.

In her bra.

In his room.

Curiosity got the best of me, and I did another stupid thing.

I turned on my phone.

Within seconds, I received a notification that there was a voice mail message waiting.

I should have deleted it. I should have turned the phone off. I should have just gotten a new phone number altogether.

But I didn't.

Instead of doing any of those smart options, I put the phone to my ear and listened.

Cash's ragged voice came through the line. "Demi, it's not what you think. It's not what it looked like. Please call me back so I can explain."

I could hear the panic and worry in his voice, and I knew it was all because he never thought he'd get caught.

I closed my eyes and sighed.

Just as I was about to put it down, my phone rang in my hand.

His handsome face was smiling at me.

I realized I didn't want to hear what he had to say, but I deserved to tell him how I felt. I needed to be the one to officially end this.

After connecting the call and holding the phone up to my ear, I said, "You can stop calling me. We're done. This game is over. You won. I hope it was fun for you."

"Demi—"

That was all I heard before I disconnected the call and shut off my phone again.

Mere minutes later, there was a knock at my door.

I moved to it, opened it, and saw Sam standing there. One look from my best friend was all it took.

She stepped inside, closed the door, and I burst into tears.

I'm not sure how long it took, but it was quite a bit later when I finally settled down enough to have an actual conversation. With all of the heartbreak I had been feeling, it didn't immediately dawn on me that my best friend just happened to be here right when I needed her. I was about to ask her that when she spoke first.

"Demi, babe, tell me what happened," she urged gently.

"How did you know something was wrong?" I replied.

Sorrow was written all over her face. "He called me."

"I'm sorry he dragged you into it," I lamented.

Shaking her head as she waved her hand through the air, she insisted, "There's nowhere else I'd rather be right now. Are you okay?"

I shook my head. "No."

"Can you tell me what's going on?" she asked.

"You mean, he didn't tell you?" I countered.

"No," she answered. "I saw the call come in, and luckily, I had programmed his number in weeks ago when you called me from Pennsylvania. It caught me off guard, but I answered, and he sounded... he sounded like he was in agony."

If it wasn't so heartbreaking, I probably would have laughed.

Boy, could he act.

If the music thing ever stopped working for him, he could no doubt have a very successful and lucrative career as an actor. He knew exactly what he was doing.

"What did he say?" I pressed.

"Not much. He called about a half an hour ago and just begged me to come and check on you," Sam started. "I asked him what was going on, and he didn't say. He just told me that he couldn't reach you and that you needed someone to be here with you."

Why?

Why would he do that?

What difference did it make to him if I had anyone here for me or not?

"He cheated on me," I told her.

Sam's eyes widened. "What? What do you mean?"

"I mean, Cash cheated on me. He slept with another woman," I said.

Confusion and concern continued to litter her features. "He told you this?" she asked.

I shook my head. "No. No, I called him this morning to tell him that I was going to catch a flight tomorrow morning and meet him in Florida," I began. "I thought it would be fun to see his reaction when I told him, so I opted for a video chat. Unfortunately, a woman who, from the waist up, was only wearing her bra answered the call from Cash's bed."

Sam gasped, "Oh my God. I'm so sorry, Demi."

"Yeah, me too."

"What did he say?" she asked.

I closed my eyes and took in a deep breath. After I blew it out, I opened my eyes and shared, "He was taking a shower while she was in his bed. She told me she spent the night there. And when she knocked on that bathroom door to get his attention, he wasn't even remotely surprised that someone was in his room. Then he opened the door wearing nothing but a towel and saw me on the phone."

"Did he offer an explanation?" Sam questioned me.

The anger was building in her.

Good.

I needed that from her because I was the one who usually got angry. Sadly, in this scenario, I couldn't feel much of anything other than overwhelming devastation and despair.

"I ended the call before he even said a word," I answered.

More sorrow moved through her face. Sam looked like she was experiencing close to the same level of hopelessness that I was.

"I can't believe it," she said. "Why would he do that? And why would he call me to come here and check on you if he didn't care?"

I shrugged. "I don't know," I rasped. "I don't know anything."

"Has he tried reaching out to you?"

"I turned off my phone, but he left a voice mail message telling me that it wasn't what I thought it was and begging me to let him explain," I shared.

"Are you going to let him?"

"Why would I?" I countered. "There was a half-naked woman in his bed. There's nothing to explain. I'm just so upset with myself."

"What? Why would you say that?"

Could I even say the words aloud? If I did, it was only going to make me feel that much worse. But this was Sam. And I figured it was better to tell her now and deal with the emotional turmoil all in one shot instead of holding it in and letting it eat me alive.

"I fell in love with him," I shared. "I knew better, Sam. I knew that a happy ending didn't exist. But I let his charming ways and his persistence convince me that maybe, just maybe, they weren't all the same. I was so stupid, Sam. So, so stupid."

"It's not wrong to fall in love, Demi," she insisted. "It's not wrong to want it, either. I don't know why Cash would do this to you. I'd be curious to hear his explanation, though."

"He knew."

Sam tipped her head to the side and gave me a curious look. "Knew what?"

Tears filled my eyes. "He knew about my dad," I rasped. "He knew why I struggled to open up my heart to him and give him a chance. And only weeks later, he destroyed that. I can't even begin to understand why he needed to do that. If he didn't want me anymore, he should have just told me."

For the next few minutes, the silence stretched between us. The air was heavy, filled with the weight of my sorrow.

"I wish I knew what to say, Demi," Sam said softly. "My heart breaks for you. After all of this time of you being so set on remaining single. I've never seen you so happy like you were whenever you were talking about Cash after you two got together. I hate that he's ruined this for you."

Me too, I thought.

I couldn't even begin to understand why people cheated.

Yes, it would be terrible to suffer through the pain of a breakup, but at least the person would feel a smidgen of respect.

Cash didn't even have the decency to respect what I'd been through. I shared something so personal with him because I wanted to be honest with him. I wanted to give us a fair shot, and I knew my past wouldn't remain hidden. It would come out in all the ways that I experienced jealousy and doubt and worry.

He promised to be patient with me. He promised to

make me feel comfortable and secure. Did he only mean that he'd do that when he wasn't busy fucking other women?

"I have a headache," I said.

Sam jumped up off the couch and replied, "Let me get you something for it. Have you had anything to eat today?"

I shook my head.

"I'll make you something, too," she declared before walking out to the kitchen.

I didn't argue with her, and I didn't stop her.

I wasn't hungry, and I didn't think I could eat without feeling sick.

But for Sam, I'd try.

A couple hours passed, and Sam stayed with me. We watched movies, and she held me when I cried.

Cal stopped by with dinner later in the evening, and he spent time with me, too. He was just as livid as Sam was—just as livid as I would have been if this had happened to anyone else but me.

It was comforting and heartbreaking all at the same time.

When it got late, I said, "You guys should go home."

"We can stay and take care of you, Demi," Cal insisted.

Nodding, I said, "I know. And I appreciate that more than I could ever tell you. But I think I just need some time to be by myself."

"Are you sure?" Sam asked.

"Yeah. I'm just going to try to get some sleep," I answered. "I gave him my tears and my sadness today. Tomorrow, he gets my anger. I figure within a few days, I'll be back to being your favorite cynic."

Sam pushed out her bottom lip, indicating she didn't like that idea and Cal said, "I'm sorry he didn't protect your heart, Demi. If I had known he had it in him to hurt you like this after the way he pushed so hard to be with you, I would have warned you to stay away."

The last thing I wanted was anyone decent and good in my life blaming themselves for what Cash did to me. So, I reassured him, "It's not your fault, Cal. This was Cash and me. I was foolish for believing he was being honest with me, and he was a jerk for doing what he did."

"You weren't foolish," Sam cut in. "You deserve to be happy. And I know that what he did sucks so bad, but when it was good between the two of you, it was everything you deserved to have and experience."

I simply nodded my understanding because they wouldn't want me blaming myself any more than I wanted them feeling guilty about it.

And after a long, tearful round of goodbye hugs, Sam and Cal left.

I made my way to my bedroom and climbed in my bed.

Even though I told them I was going to try to get some sleep, I knew I wasn't going to find much of it tonight.

There were too many emotions and too many unanswered questions swirling in my mind.

In the midst of all my thoughts, Sam's words before she left started to hit me. They were similar to the words my mother had said to me.

If she could do it all over again with my father, knowing she'd experience that heartache in the end, she'd still do it because she knew what it felt like to be in love.

I swallowed hard as the truth and reality of that settled in me.

If I had to do this all over again knowing exactly what the outcome would be, I'd do it.

Because despite the pain that I felt, I'd never been happier than when I was with him. I'd be forever grateful to him for giving me that, but I'd hate him for the rest of my life for taking it away from me.

CHAPTER 22

Demi

I WAS STANDING IN MY KITCHEN WITH MY COFFEE MUG HELD up to my mouth.

I needed the caffeine. For my headache and for the stamina to get through the day.

Sleep eluded me last night. No matter how hard I tried not to think about what I'd witnessed earlier in the day, I couldn't stop myself from seeing it every time I closed my eyes.

I'd looked at the clock several times throughout the night, and all I knew was that time kept passing by.

I wanted sleep.

I wanted to be able to have some time to simply forget what happened.

The last time I recalled looking at the clock, it was right around four in the morning. I still hadn't slept a wink at that point. I must have drifted off shortly after that.

Unfortunately, my slumber didn't last long because I woke again just after six thirty when I had a bad dream.

The worst dream.

In it, I didn't call Cash while he was still in Texas.

Nope.

I decided to surprise him again by simply showing up. So, I hopped on a plane, flew to Florida, and walked right into his hotel room. It was my dream, so the whole thing where hotel staff just doesn't give out that kind of information didn't exist. It was the one time I wished it would have.

When I walked into Cash's room, I didn't find him in the shower while a woman waited in his bed. Instead, I walked in and caught him in the act of fucking her in that bed.

I woke with a gasp, sweating profusely and out of breath.

At that point, even if I could do it easily, I didn't want to go back to sleep. Closing my eyes was apparently the worst thing I could do.

So, I got up and got myself in the shower.

I needed to do normal things. This was how it worked. People went through breakups all the time. Yes, it was hard. Yes, it felt as though my world had ended. But if everyone else could do it—if my mom could do it after having been *married*—I could do it, too.

It would be just like it was for them. It'd be difficult in the beginning. But the more I did what I had to do to return to my normal routine, the better it was going to be.

I'd gone against everything I knew I should that would keep my heart safe, so now I had to bear the consequences of that decision. If no longer living with the pain and heartbreak it caused was my goal, I had a feeling I'd need to pretend for a while.

I knew it was important to sit with my feelings, but I did

that yesterday. I gave myself that opportunity, and I didn't like the way it felt. That wasn't who I was.

I wasn't the girl who was ever going to let a man bring me down.

Things happened.

Life went on.

I'd survive.

As soon as I got myself out of the shower and dressed, I went to the kitchen to prepare some coffee.

Now, I was standing here taking sips of it as I tried to figure out what I'd occupy myself with today.

I'd work, of course.

But I'd gotten myself into a rhythm and routine over the last several weeks and knew that it wouldn't take me more than two hours or so to get caught up with all of my work.

I needed something else to do to take my mind off of my current reality.

Before I could come up with any reasonable options, there was a knock at my door.

Poor Sam. She had been so worried about me last night, it wouldn't have surprised me if she showed up here this morning with a box of donuts and a shoulder to cry on.

Lucky for her, I'd prove that no more crying would be happening.

I set my mug down, made it to the front door, and swung it open. I did not see Sam standing there with a box of donuts to bury my misery in. Nope. Not at all.

Instead, I saw Cash standing there, looking like he hadn't slept in days. Even in his disheveled state, he could still send my heart racing with just a single glance.

I did not like that.

"You need to leave now," I ordered.

Cash didn't remove his hand, which had been resting high up on the doorframe, and walk away like I had demanded. In fact, he completely ignored my request and stepped inside.

"What are you doing?" I asked, my irritation evident. "You need to go. I don't want you here."

"You need to let me speak," he instructed.

I shook my head. "Your chance to speak was… oh, I don't know, sometime over the last two weeks when you were being miserable. Or, maybe you should have spoken to me sooner if this is where things were headed for you. Bottom line, if you wanted to talk, you should have done it before you cheated on me."

"I did not cheat on you, Demi."

I rolled my eyes and walked back away from him. "Okay, sure. And the grass is no longer green, am I right?" I shot back. "Do you honestly think I believe that?"

"No, I don't. But that doesn't mean it's not the truth," he responded.

I stopped walking and spun around. "Really, Cash? You had a woman who was half naked in your bed, answering your phone, while you were naked in the shower," I reminded him. "I'm sorry, but I don't trust a word that comes out of your mouth."

In a flash, Cash reached for my right hand and lifted it up between us. While one of his hands held my palm, his pointer finger from the opposite hand came to the inside of my wrist. "This, right here, is bullshit," he declared.

With a look of disgust, I replied, "Excuse me?"

"You heard me," he seethed. "Trust. You had the word trust tattooed on your wrist, and it's nothing but bullshit."

How dare he?

I'd gotten this tattoo years ago, after my father's infidelity. It had a double meaning for me. The obvious was that it was there to remind me what's most important to me in life and relationships with others. But the deeper meaning was that it was there to remind me to trust myself. To trust that I knew what was right for me and to always follow my gut instinct. For a long time, I had hesitated with making decisions. Once I got this tattoo, I no longer hesitated.

But if Cash wanted to sit here and point out that he thought my tattoo was bullshit, I'd hand it right back to him.

"Exactly," I agreed. "It's bullshit that I thought I could trust you. I was wrong. I don't trust you at all."

"That makes two of us then," he spat. "Because I don't trust you either."

I yanked my wrist from his hold. "Me?" I questioned him. "You don't trust me? I can't even begin to imagine how you could possibly say that when I woke up alone in my bed yesterday and every day before that. In fact, I woke up alone every single day since I got back from your home in Pennsylvania."

At my words, anguish marred his features.

Good.

He deserved to feel a little bit of pain, too.

"You weren't the only one waking up alone, Demi," he insisted, now sounding like he was irritated with me. I couldn't imagine why he thought he had a right to be irritated with me, especially after he claimed I was the one who was untrustworthy. "And infidelity isn't the only way people lose their trust in others."

I crossed my arms over my chest. "Oh yeah? So, enlighten

me, Cash. Tell me how I made you lose your trust in me. This ought to be interesting."

"You cut me out," he said, his voice just a touch over a whisper.

Something in the way his voice sounded made me stop and really listen to what he was saying. I hadn't ever heard his voice sounding so wounded and broken. It was... heartbreaking.

When he realized he had my full attention, he continued, "You saw what you saw, made up your mind about what you saw, and never gave me the benefit of the doubt. You never gave me the chance to explain. I understood your initial shock. I'll remember the look on your face when I opened that door in my towel for the rest of my life. But when I called you back to explain, you didn't give me that chance. You turned your phone off, and all I could do was think about how all these weeks have gone by, and you haven't even taken the time to get to know me."

I blinked in surprise.

What was he talking about?

Of course, I'd gotten to know him. We talked every single day. We shared stories with one another, and we talked about favorite movies and food. There had been so much.

"I don't understand what you're saying, Cash," I shared.

"I'm saying that if you really knew me, or even better, what you mean to me, you would have known that what you thought you saw wasn't even a possibility for me," he explained.

What I mean to him?

"So, you're telling me that you, the famous rock star who could have anyone he wants, expect me to believe that you didn't fuck a woman who was wearing her bra in your bed, answering your phone, and telling me she spent the night there?"

Cash didn't hesitate to inform me, "That's exactly what I expect you to believe."

Nodding my head, I replied, "Okay. I get it. You think I'm stupid."

He shook his head. "No. But I think you're so damn scared of what you feel for me that you're just looking for anything you can right now to end this."

"I didn't have to look very far, did I?" I shot back, completely ignoring his comment about how I felt about him.

"Jesus, Demi, would you listen to yourself for a minute?" he huffed. "Or better yet, would you listen to me?"

"Why do I feel like you're trying to blame me for what *you* did?" I asked.

"I didn't do anything!" he shouted. "Fuck, you're so set on believing that every man out there is going to be like your father, you won't open your eyes and see what's in front of you. God, it doesn't matter how much I fucking love you, if you're never going to let go of what he did and give yourself the chance to truly be happy, I'm wasting my time."

He loved me?

I stood there staring at him, unable to respond.

Why was he saying he loved me?

If he did, he wouldn't have cheated on me.

Tears filled my eyes and rolled down my cheeks as I stared at the man who'd stolen my heart and turned my world upside down.

"I know you're hurt, Demi," Cash said, his voice now as

gentle as ever. "I'm sorry you saw what you did, but I didn't do anything with that woman."

"Why was she in your room?" I rasped.

"Killian, Roscoe, and I were in a three-bedroom suite," he began. "After the show the night before you called, the guys brought a couple of women back to the room. Three women came back. We all hung in the common room for a few minutes before Killian took the woman he was talking to back to his room. Roscoe took the other two women to his. I went to my own room and crashed."

Cash paused, allowing me some time to digest all that he'd just shared.

When he'd given me enough time to do that, he continued, "I woke up yesterday morning, knew you'd be calling me, and decided to take a shower before your call came in. You called earlier than usual, which is beside the point. When I heard a knock at the door, I had just assumed it was Killian or Roscoe. I was just as surprised to find that woman, who had been one of the two women that disappeared into Roscoe's room the night before, standing there in her underwear with my phone in her hand."

He didn't cheat.

Cash didn't sleep with that woman.

I tried to let that news penetrate into my brain when Cash went on, "Demi, I saw the horrified look on your face, and it haunts me to know that you think I could do that to you. I can't even begin to tell you how sorry I am about what happened yesterday morning. After I kicked that woman out of my room, I tried to call you back, and when you didn't answer, I knew you gave up on me. You gave up on us."

Tears continued to stream down my face.

Could I trust that he was telling me the truth?

If I chose to believe him and he was lying, I'd look like a fool when something like this happened again. But if he was telling the truth and I doubted him and sent him on his way, I'd lose the very best thing that had ever happened to me.

"You're supposed to be in Florida," I murmured.

Cash shook his head. "I'm supposed to be here, with you," he corrected me. "I'm not going to Florida until I know we've worked this out. I've already told them to cancel tonight's show."

My eyes widened.

Holy crap.

He canceled a show on his tour to come and work this out with me?

"Why would you do that?" I asked.

"Because I made a promise to you," he answered. "I told you that I wasn't going to allow you to feel like you had risked it all for it to not be worth it. I promised to be patient with you while you learned to trust and have faith in me. And because I made a promise to myself to protect your fragile heart."

Oh my God.

I didn't think there was any hope of me being able to withstand all that.

He couldn't be making this level of emotion up. If he really didn't care about me, he wouldn't have come here now to try to fix this.

Maybe he was right.

Maybe I refused to give him the chance to explain what happened yesterday morning because I was terrified of the way I felt for him.

"Do you really love me?" I asked.

"Yes."

"How much?" I pressed.

"Pardon?"

"Earlier, before, you said it didn't matter how much you loved me if I wasn't willing to let go of what my father did and give myself the chance to be happy. So, I'm asking you... how much do you love me?"

For the first time since I yanked my wrist out of his hand, Cash touched me. He brought his hand up to the side of my face and used his thumb to wipe away the tears that had fallen.

After he allowed his eyes to roam over my face, they settled on my gaze. Then he whispered, "Enough to give up everything I've worked for my whole life."

My lips parted in shock. "What?" I rasped.

"Demi, I've been so out of sorts the last few weeks because I can't cope with how much I miss you," he shared, his voice strained. "About two weeks ago, there were talks of scheduling another tour. For now, it seems everyone in the band is on board with it, but I'm not. I want time off because I don't want our entire relationship to be phone calls and video chats. I don't want to just sit in my hotel room writing songs about you while I wait for your call. I want to take you on dates. I want to wake up with you in my arms every morning. I want to make love to you before we go to sleep every night. I want to feed you breakfast. I just want you. And I didn't want to disappoint the rest of the band, so I was struggling with what to do."

"You've been writing songs about me?"

"Either about you or inspired by you," he told me without an ounce of hesitation.

That's what he'd been working on that day at his house. He was writing a song about me. I didn't even know what to do with that information. I didn't know what to say in response to that. But what I did know was how it made me feel.

Unless Cash was writing a song about how he screwed up with the girl who got away, which I didn't think was the case, there was no way he cheated on me.

So, in that moment of clarity, I acted on what I was feeling.

I lifted one of my hands to the side of Cash's face, stroked my thumb over his cheek several times, and slid my fingers back into his hair. I was acutely aware of the fact that Cash had stopped breathing while I did this.

When my hand landed at the back of his head, I pressed up on my toes, leaned my body into his, and kissed him.

I could feel the relief sweep through Cash as he wrapped his arms around me and deepened the kiss.

And it was then that I started to feel the pieces of my broken heart mend themselves back into place.

CHAPTER 23

OBODY HAD EVER MADE ME FEEL THE WAY DEMI DID.

Yesterday had been the worst day of my life, bar none. All day long, I had been caught between feeling r and panic. I didn't know which was worse.

3ecause the anger was so consuming, I lost control in e moments after Demi disconnected the call. And the c left me feeling hopelessness and despair as I scrambled ıd a way to get back here to New Hampshire so I could e things right with her.

Losing Demi was not an option.

wouldn't survive that.

Luckily, I got on a plane and made it here.

Luckily, she opened the door.

Luckily, she didn't kick me out.

Luckily, she listened.

And luckiest of all, she believed me.

knew the last had to be true because she was now in

my arms, kissing me. I've never felt more relieved in my life than I did at this moment.

Feeling her pressed close, taking in the light, feminine scent of her, and hearing her moan while we kissed was what I'd needed for weeks now.

God, I had missed her so much.

Demi started backing up, taking me with her. I followed, not wanting to lose that connection to her mouth.

Before I knew it, she was pushing me down onto the couch. The moment I was seated, she climbed on top and straddled me.

Demi didn't wait for me to take action. She lifted her shirt over her head and tossed it to the side. She hadn't been wearing a bra, so I immediately captured her breasts in my hands and dropped my mouth to one.

As I tasted and teased her on one side, she rolled her hips with such need and desperation over me. My cock was rock hard, and with the way she was moving, I wasn't sure I'd be able to last until I was inside her.

There was no doubt this was going to be quick. It had been far too long for the both of us.

"Baby," she breathed. "I need more. I need you."

"Take off your bottoms," I urged. "Do you have condoms?"

Her eyes widened as she froze. "Shit. Shit, no."

"It's entirely up to you," I started. "If you're covered for birth control, you'd be safe with just me. Even though I've never not worn protection, I still get myself tested regularly. I did that not long after I met you, and I haven't been with anyone but you since."

"I'm covered with birth control," she confirmed as she

stood and pushed her pants down her legs and shimmied out of her panties.

While she did that, I kept my eyes focused on her and stripped out of my own clothes.

A moment later, I could barely contain the emotion building inside me at the feel of her soft skin against mine.

It had definitely been way too long.

"Demi, I'm not going to last long," I warned her before I was even inside her.

She smiled and shared, "Neither am I."

I slipped my fingers down between her legs, touched her there, and found she was already wet.

I played only for a few seconds before she lifted her hips away, curled her fingers around my cock, and positioned herself over me. The next thing I knew she slammed herself down on my erection.

"Damn, firecracker, you feel amazing," I said.

"I missed you, Cash," she replied. "I missed having this with you."

Demi didn't give me a chance to respond.

She went to work and rode me hard. There was no hesitation.

I was mesmerized by her.

Her tits were bouncing, her eyes were intense, and her lips were parted.

She was extraordinary.

"Fuck me harder," I urged her, my fingers pressing in deeper on one of her hips.

She did precisely as I asked, and I couldn't get enough of her. I reached up with one hand, squeezed her breast, and watched as her head fell back. I leaned forward, ran my tongue along her collarbone, and up along the front of her exposed throat before I nipped at the skin there.

"Cash," she whimpered.

That's when I knew she was close and decided to help her out. I moved both hands back to her hips and encouraged her movements, making them a bit faster and much more frantic.

Seconds passed, I felt myself ready to explode, and demanded, "Come with me, Demi."

She didn't need the instruction because she was already there. As I shot inside her, Demi moaned through her orgasm as her legs trembled wildly on either side of my body.

I loved that, too.

I loved knowing that I was able to make her body quiver like that.

When we both made it to the other side, Demi's body slumped forward. Wanting her to be a bit more comfortable, I managed to hold her in place while I swung my legs up to one side of the couch and lowered my back to the opposite side.

I closed my eyes and simply relished the feel of having her like this.

Naked, spent, and sated.

For a long time, we stayed like that, just enjoying having it again. Quite frankly, I didn't feel any need to talk. I wasn't opposed to it, but I'd said all I needed to say. Even though it was early in the morning, I was completely content to fall asleep right where I was.

But that didn't happen because Demi broke the silence.

"I called you earlier than normal yesterday morning because I was so excited," she started. "I wanted to let you know that I was planning to meet you in Florida today so we could spend some time together."

Shock moved through me, and my body went solid.

She was going to come to Florida to see me.

I didn't know if she realized how much it was affecting me or not, but she added, "I fell in love with you, Cash. And it was hurting my heart to know that there was something weighing on your mind. For two weeks, I saw you struggling with something, and I just wanted to do something to make it better."

She wanted to make it better.

This was it.

She was all I would ever need.

She loved me.

I knew I'd treasure that gift for the rest of my life.

"I love that you feel that strongly for me," I told her. "If it's any indication of how much you mean to me and how much I feel for you, I almost beat the shit out of one of my best friends."

At my admission, Demi's face shot up off my chest. "What?"

I shook my head, feeling disappointment along with a smidgen of regret. "If Killian hadn't been there, I have no doubt that either I would have landed in jail, Roscoe would have been in the hospital, or both."

Worry littered Demi's expression. "I don't understand," she said.

"It was the look on your face in that brief moment right before you disconnected the call when I heard the pained cry come from you," I started. "That set me off. I yanked my phone from that woman's hand and told her to get the fuck out of my room. I tried to call you back, and when you didn't answer, I lost it. I threw on some clothes and started shouting as I went in search of Roscoe. He came out of his room half a second after Killian came out of his. And then I charged forward. Killian caught me before I got close enough to land a punch."

"Oh my God. What happened?" Demi asked.

"Roscoe and Killian were both trying to figure out what happened, and I told them," I began again. "There was a lot of words said, but the basic gist of it was that if I couldn't make things right with you, I was holding him personally accountable."

"It wasn't his fault," Demi reasoned.

I could tell she was simply trying to get me to calm down. Even though she was here now, and we'd worked it all out, it still made me angry when I thought about the whole situation. Roscoe's negligence could have cost me the best thing that had ever happened to me.

"It was," I insisted. "Those women were there with him. I'm not going to judge him on what he chooses to do in his personal life. That's his choice. But when what he does starts to affect me, that's where I draw the line. It wasn't his job to just fuck them and let them do what they wanted. He needed to make sure that they were accounted for at all times. He didn't, and you got hurt in the process. That is *not* okay. That woman was being a bitch just for the sake of it. She had no right to come in my room, especially not without her clothes on. And she definitely had no right to answer my phone and make you think that there was ever anything between her and me."

Demi absentmindedly ran her fingers through my hair.

Her expression turned curious, and she asked, "How did you leave things with them?"

"Well, I told them I was coming back here to work this out with you," I explained. "They knew we were going to have to cancel tonight's show. I also told them that if I couldn't get you to listen to me and we couldn't work it out that I wouldn't play another show."

"Cash... you can't do that," Demi remarked.

"Luckily, I don't have to since we worked it out," I countered. "But I'm not joking, Demi. You mean that much to me, and I'm not about to have someone else ruin what we have."

She didn't respond with words, but she smiled at me.

"Do you still want to go to Florida with me?" I asked.

Her smile grew. "I'd love to," she rasped.

I nodded. "I should probably call and let everyone know that we're on for the second show," I told her.

"That's probably a good idea," she agreed.

I returned her smile and took in her beautiful face. Then I said, "I love you, Demi."

"I love you, too."

With that, she touched her mouth to mine before we both got up to get cleaned up. After we accomplished that, I called Beck to let him know all was well and that I'd be there before the next show. Once Demi and I got a flight sorted and had some breakfast, we had some time to kill. So we made our way to her bedroom and used that time wisely.

Demi

"I've never seen him so distraught."

That came from Holland.

I was in Florida with Cash, and they were getting ready for their show. Holland saw me when Cash and I arrived, and much like the last time, she kidnapped me and whisked me into her dressing room.

I didn't mind because not only did I really like Holland, but it also seemed I was going to get a bit more information on how things went down with Cash.

"Really?" I replied.

She nodded. "I mean, I'm so glad you two worked it out because I don't think he would have ever been the same," she shared. "I love him like a brother, and it was so hard to see him that devastated. He was sure you'd never speak to him again."

My heart hurt hearing all of this.

It was making me wish I hadn't been so quick to assume the worst. I mean, in my defense, I didn't know he was staying in a three-bedroom suite, and a half-naked woman *had* answered his phone while she was in his bed.

But still.

I couldn't even begin to imagine how bad it was for Cash. Even with everything he'd told me and what Holland was telling me now, I was certain it didn't compare to how it all felt in the moment.

"I jumped to conclusions," I admitted.

Her brows shot up, and she shot me an incredulous look.

"I would have, too," she assured me. "Don't feel bad about that."

I nodded because I didn't know what else to do.

"It was heartbreaking, though," she said. "For a man who is always so confident, he was utterly broken."

"You're going to make me cry, Holland," I told her.

"I'm sorry," she lamented. "It's good. Everything is good now. You're both here, and you're both happy. That's all that matters."

"Yeah," I agreed.

"You ready?" she asked, jerking her head to the dressing room door.

With a downward jerk of my chin, I confirmed that I was.

At that, Holland and I left her dressing room and made our way to the one with the guys in it. No sooner did we knock and get ushered inside when I realized it was the first I was seeing any of the guys since before the whole situation went down.

Nerves suddenly shot through my body.

Would they hate me?

I glanced cautiously around the room as all their eyes landed on me. I avoided making eye contact with them, sought out Cash, and took a step in his direction. Before I could take a second step, a solid mass filled my vision. I tipped my head up and saw Roscoe looking down at me.

Swallowing hard, I waited for him to share whatever thoughts he had about me with me.

"I'm sorry," he apologized.

Blinking in surprise, I returned, "What?"

"I'm sorry for what happened and that you were hurt by

it," he clarified. "I was careless. It was never my intention to have something like that happen. You didn't deserve whatever you went through because of it."

Well, that was unexpected.

And it was really nice of him.

"Oh. Um, okay. Thank you for the apology," I replied.

"Are we cool?" he asked.

I nodded. "We're cool," I assured him with a smile.

He returned the smile. Then, he stepped aside to let me pass and make my way to Cash. Once I was close enough, my man reached his arm out, hooked it around the back of my neck, and curled me into his body.

"Did Roscoe apologize to you?" he asked.

"Yeah."

"Good."

For the next few minutes, everyone fell into their own separate conversations, or in the case of the guys, a bunch of bantering among them. I sat back and watched, loving that I was back here with Cash, experiencing it.

After all that had happened between us, after all that I'd learned happened between them and him, I was beyond grateful that it had all worked out and that nobody seemed to be holding any grudges.

When it was time for them to head out on stage, Cash was sure to give me a kiss that would easily last me until the show was over.

I didn't think anything could make me happier than having that.

But I was wrong.

Because no sooner had they stepped out on stage and finished their first two songs when Cash started talking to the crowd. At first, it seemed normal. Nothing was particularly different about it compared to any other time he talked to the crowd.

But then he did something he'd never done before.

He said, "I'm dedicating tonight's performance to a very special woman."

Surprisingly, the crowd went wild, cheering in response to his words.

"She's here tonight, and I want her to know how special she is," he went on. "I love you, Demi."

My eyes went wide as the crowd roared.

Cash's eyes slid to the side of the stage where he knew he'd find me. He winked at me, kissed his two fingers, and pointed them in my direction.

I couldn't wipe the smile off my face or the tears from my eyes.

I loved him with all my heart.

My broken, fragile heart that was now whole and healed.

EPILOGUE

Demi

TODAY WAS MY LAST DAY.

I was no longer going to be working at Granite.

It was the beginning of November, and I'd just recently gotten back to New Hampshire with Cash.

After I made the trip with him to Florida, I never came back home. He wanted me to stay on the tour with him, and it was where I wanted to be. So, I worked for Cal from the road and kept things going for him.

But as the My Violent Heart tour started to wind down, Cash started talking to me.

"I want to work on this new material I've written when the tour is over," he said one day a few weeks ago.

"Okay? Why can't you?" I asked.

"It's not that I can't. It's that I don't know where you stand," he responded.

"What do you mean?"

His eyes searched my face a long time. Then he answered, "I don't want to do the long-distance relationship with you, Demi. I want us together. I want you to move to Pennsylvania and live with me."

"Are you serious?" I shot back.

He nodded. "Yes. I love you, and I'm not going to be states away from you ever again," he declared.

"What about work?" I questioned him.

"Your job?" he asked before he shrugged. "It's up to you. You've been doing it on the road for a while now. If you want to continue to do it from my place, I'm fine with that."

"Cal probably needs someone who can be there on the nights that a band is playing, though," I explained.

"So, am I moving to New Hampshire with you then?"

He couldn't do that. He wanted to make more music. I wanted to hear his new music. So, there was absolutely no way I was going to put him in a position to be unable to make that music.

I shook my head.

"I'll talk to Cal now," I told him. "I'll let him know that I'm going to be leaving to move to Pennsylvania with you. I'll work with him until he finds someone to take over for me, and then I'll find something to do in my new hometown."

Cash grinned. "Okay, that's one thing down," he announced.

My brows pulled together. "Is there more?"

"I talked to everyone else in the band, and we've all agreed that we want you to be our new swag and merchandise manager," he said. As my eyes nearly popped out of my head, he added, "If you want to do it, of course. There's no pressure. But since your best friend is going to be in charge of designing all of our new apparel, I thought it would be a great way for you to continue to stay in touch with her on a regular basis."

Needless to say, I didn't turn him down.

And because I'd contacted Cal about it right away, he managed to find someone rather quickly. Of course, having had My Violent Heart play at Granite meant that when he put the word out that he was hiring for my position, there was no shortage of interest.

So, this was it.

I was here at Granite for the last time for the foreseeable future, and I was here with Cash, the band, Cal, and Sam.

I was in love and blissfully happy. And tomorrow morning, I'd be leaving my life in New Hampshire behind and starting a new one with Cash in Pennsylvania.

I couldn't wait.

It was a few minutes before the band was set to take the stage, and the place was packed. But as packed as it was, it didn't compare to the number of people at the venues I'd seen them play at.

So, for the band, this was an intimate setting, and they didn't seem to mind mingling with the crowd and their fans.

Cash was by my side and had said, "I think I should head back there."

"Okay," I answered. But then something caught my eye. "Hey, isn't that the woman from the hotel?"

Cash's body went solid. "What?"

I jerked my chin in the opposite direction. "Over there with Beck," I told him. "That's the woman whose husband cheated on her at the hotel I used to work at. It was the woman there the day you guys arrived the first time."

The tension left his body, and I belatedly realized he must

have thought I was talking about the woman from the hotel in Texas. That wasn't even a thought in my mind anymore.

Cash looked to where I had indicated and said, "I think it is."

"Do you think he's interested in her?" I asked. "A woman like that deserves a good man in her life."

Cash returned his attention to me and replied, "I can't say I disagree with you on that. As for Beck… I don't know. What I do know is that he's got a soft spot for single moms, so maybe there's something there for him."

"That would be amazing if they could work it out," I declared.

"Yeah," Cash agreed.

I smiled and said, "Okay. Go get yourself ready to take the stage."

He leaned down, kissed me, and said, "I love you."

With my lips still brushing up against his, I returned, "I love you, too."

A few minutes later, My Violent Heart took the stage. I sat back with my best friend, my cousin, and the rest of the crowd and enjoyed the show.

"I have something for you."

Demi looked up at me from where she was sitting on the couch.

We'd been living together at my house for several

months now, and life had never been better. It was my hope that things were about to improve, though.

"What is it?" she asked.

"Can you turn that down?" I asked, jerking my head in the direction of the television.

Demi didn't hesitate to not only turn the volume down but also pause whatever she was watching.

A moment later, the sound of Roscoe playing the bass guitar filled the room. Walker came in with the drums next, and Beck followed with the synthesizer. After the slower, seductive instrumental introduction, my voice entered the song. Killian came in on the guitar later as did Holland with some vocals.

I'd heard the song a million times already.

This was Demi's first time hearing it, so I kept my focus on her. She listened intently, and I could tell she was focused on the words.

She didn't react.

She didn't give me any indication of what she was thinking.

Or, at least, she didn't until it was over. That's when she allowed two tears to stream down her face.

She looked up at me and rasped, "I love it."

"It's yours," I told her. "That's the song I wrote for you. The first of many."

Her head moved back and forth as she bit her lip and fought back the emotions. Then, with her voice just a touch over a whisper, she asked, "What did I do to deserve you?"

I grinned and answered, "I am pretty spectacular, aren't I?"

Demi rolled her eyes. "Boy, do you know how to ruin the moment."

"You love it."

She laughed and leaned into me. "Yeah, I do."

"That's why you should probably make sure you hang on to me," I noted.

"I planned on it," she replied.

"Permanently."

"What?"

I reached behind me on the couch and closed my hand around the box before I lifted it between us.

"Marry me, Demi."

Her eyes darted back and forth between the ring and my face. There was no question she was in absolute shock.

But the shock quickly wore off.

The next thing I knew, she buried her face in her hands and burst into tears.

I wrapped my arms around her and teased, "That wasn't exactly the reaction I was hoping for."

"You've made me so happy, Cash," she cried. "I don't even know how to tell you."

"You could say you'll marry me," I suggested.

She looked up at me again through shining eyes and said, "I'll marry you."

With that, I didn't waste another second. I took the ring from the box, slipped it on her finger, and kissed her.

When she pulled her mouth from mine, she marveled at the ring. "It's beautiful," she said. "I never thought I'd have this."

"Well, it was custom made for you," I told her. "So it's the only one like it."

"Oh. Um, I... wow. I wasn't referring to the ring, but that's amazing."

"What were you talking about?"

She moved her hand between the two of us. "I was talking about this. Us. I never thought I'd have a romantic relationship at all. And now I'm sitting here on the couch in my man's house wearing the ring he just slipped on my finger. I'm getting married, Cash. I can't even tell you how happy you've made me."

"I feel the same, firecracker," I told her. "That's why I'm making it official. There's nobody else out there better than you."

Silence stretched between us a moment before she said, "I can't believe we're engaged."

"Believe it because it's real."

She looked at her ring one last time. Then she tucked her feet up underneath her ass and curled her body into mine. "Will you watch the movie with me?" she asked. "I just started it."

"What are we watching?"

"10 Things I Hate About You," she answered.

"Once a cynic..." I trailed off. She giggled. "Do you want any snacks before we start it again?"

"Snacks would be good," she said. "Surprise me."

"Okay."

At that, I kissed her once more and got up to get some snacks and drinks. Then I joined her on the couch to watch a movie that was going to make her happy. And as I sat there beside her, I realized that life had just gotten a little bit better.

Preview of

Rock Stars & Romance Book 2: Beck & Chasey

PROLOGUE

Beck

"I CAN'T DO THIS."

"What exactly do you mean by that, Bill?"

Something was wrong.

I didn't understand it; I just knew they were angry. They weren't shouting, though. My mom and dad never really shouted. But they did get angry. And when they were angry, I could always tell by the way their voices sounded.

And they always used each other's real names.

They didn't know I was watching. Listening.

I was supposed to be in bed. I had school tomorrow, and it was past my bedtime.

"I want a divorce, Sandy," my dad told my mom.

Divorce.

I didn't know what that was. It didn't sound like a good thing.

"A divorce?" my mom said. "Why?"

"This isn't what I want," he told her.

"What about the kids? Sadie is only two. And Beck? Beck is just six, but Bill, he adores you," she said.

That's when I knew a divorce was definitely a bad thing.

"He'll be alright," Dad said. "They both will. You wanted them; I know you'll give them everything."

My mom didn't say anything for a long time. Then she said something that proved I was right about divorce being bad. "Everything except a father."

Why wouldn't we have a father? Where was our dad going?

"I'm not cut out for this."

"What are we going to tell them?" she asked.

I heard him take in a breath and let it out. "You can tell them whatever you want. I've already packed a bag, and I'm leaving tonight."

"Bill."

Her voice sounded strange. She sounded scared. Sad.

"I'm sorry, Sandy."

"How am I going to do this on my own?" she asked him. "How do I teach Beck about being a man?"

Now I understood what divorce was. Dad was leaving.

And he was going to do it right now because I heard the chair move on the kitchen floor.

"Bill, wait." Mom was begging him. "We can work this out."

"We can't. I'm done."

I scooted back on the stairs to hide behind the wall because I didn't want them to see me. Then they were at the front door.

"Please don't leave us. We love you."

Say it back, I thought.

He didn't say it back. And he wasn't going to.

I knew that because I heard the front door open and close. Then I heard my mom crying.

I didn't know what to do.

Anytime I was upset, she always hugged me until I felt better. I thought I should do the same for her.

So, I got up off the stairs and walked to the front door. My mom was crying so hard she didn't even hear me. She was sitting on the floor with her knees up by her chest, her arms wrapped around her legs, and her face was resting against her knees.

I moved closer to her.

Then I sat down beside her, put my arms around her, and said, "*I* love you."

My mom hugged me back and cried harder.

I used to think my dad was the coolest guy in the world. Now I didn't think that at all.

In fact, I hated him for making my mom cry.

OTHER BOOKS BY
A.K. EVANS

The Everything Series

Everything I Need

Everything I Have

Everything I Want

Everything I Love

Everything I Give

The Cunningham Security Series

Obsessed

Overcome

Desperate

Solitude

Burned

Unworthy

Surrender

Betrayed

Revived

Hearts & Horsepower

Control the Burn

Behind the Wheel

Far Beyond Repair

How to Rebuild

Out of Alignment

Archer Tactical

Line of Fire

Collateral Damage

Silent Target

Rock Stars & Romance

Fragile

Wish

Closer

Underneath It All

Terrible Lie

Complication

Road Trip Romance

Tip the Scales

Play the Part

One Wrong Turn

Just a Fling

Meant to Be

Take the Plunge

Miss the Shot

In the Cards

Only in Dreams

Break the Ice

ABOUT
A.K. EVANS

A.K. Evans is a contemporary romance author of over twenty published novels. While she enjoys writing a good romantic suspense novel, Andrea's favorite books to write have been her extreme sports romances. That might have something to do with the fact that she, along with her husband and two sons, can't get enough of extreme sports.

Before becoming a writer, Andrea did a brief stint in the insurance and financial services industry and managed her husband's performance automotive business. That love of extreme sports? She used to drive race cars!

When Andrea isn't writing, she can be found homeschooling her two sons, doing yoga, snowboarding, reading, or traveling with her family. She and her husband are currently taking road trips throughout the country to visit all 50 states with their boys.

For new release updates, sign up for the A.K. Evans newsletter: http://eepurl.com/dmeo6z

Be sure to follow Andrea on all social media platforms, too.

Facebook
www.facebook.com/authorAKEvans

Facebook Reader Group
http://bit.ly/2ys50mU

Instagram
www.instagram.com/authorakevans

Goodreads Author Page
www.goodreads.com/user/show/64525877-a-k-evans

Bookbub
www.bookbub.com/authors/a-k-evans

Twitter
twitter.com/AuthorAKEvans